She took Elayna's arm and slowly pulled her closer. "Will I ever again make love to a woman without wishing it were you?" she whispered intensely. "Whatever the spell, Elayna, I demand that you release me."

Elayna looked up into Cydell's eyes. At that moment, she felt a true warmth and caring in her heart that threatened to rush to the surface. She had no defense against it. Even the power of the heartstone seemed to fail her and she was left to acknowledge that her intense hatred of this woman had somehow been replaced by a more tender feeling.

They stood that way for what seemed like an eternity before Elayna quietly said, "I cannot," and hung her head.

Gently, slowly, Cydell lifted Elayna's chin. Their lips were a breath apart.

"Then I shall have a taste of the reality," Cydell whispered, and kissed Elayna's lips with a soft, lingering kiss.

▶ ▶ ▶

HEARTSTONE & SABER

Jacqui Singleton

RISING
TIDE
PRESS

HUNTINGTON, NEW YORK

Rising Tide Press
5 Kivy Street
Huntington Station, NY 11746
(516) 427-1289

Printed in the United States on acid-free paper

Publisher's note:
All characters, places and situations in this book are fictitious and any
resemblance to persons (living or dead) is purely coincidental.

Publisher's Acknowledgments:
The publisher is grateful for all the support and expertise offered by the
members of its editorial board: Bobbi Bauer, Adriane Balaban, Beth Heyn,
Harriet Edwards, Marian Satriani and Pat G. And a special thanks to
Harriet and Adriane for their excellent proofing and criticism, to Edna G.
for believing in us, and to the feminist bookstores for being there.

First printing July 1994
10 9 8 7 6 5 4 3 2 1

Edited by Lee Boojamra and Alice Frier
Book cover art: Evelyn Rysdyk

Library of Congress Cataloging-in-Publication Data
Jacqui Singleton 1955—
    Heartstone and Saber/Jacqui Singleton
        p.cm
ISBN 1-883061-00-8   CIP 93-087608

Dedication

To Linda Lee Ebaugh, who was there from the beginning. Thanks for your love and encouragement, my eternal friend.

To all of my friends who encouraged me, paid for my dinners, loaned me money, and bought me stuff. I've been threatening to have a party. Now I think I really will. Really. I'm serious.

PROLOGUE

Gorson of Ornam descended the twisting spiral stairway that led down into the cellar of the deserted refectory. He paused briefly and held up his torch, slowly passing it before him. Yellow-blue flame danced in the darkness, catching in its glow the scurrying shadows of rats and spiders and the silver strands of cobwebs that hung from the low ceiling.

With a wary glance around, he continued down, at last stepping cautiously onto the packed dirt floor. There was a faint light emanating from the farthest corner of the vast room. His labored breathing filled the gloomy silence as he progressed slowly toward it. Gorson shivered in the chill of the place, thankful that this was the last meeting. After tonight, he would be free to leave Mauldar and its intrigues behind, his task complete. And forty lathium bars in his saddlebags.

He stopped a few feet away from the dark figure leaning against the dusty wall. Upon seeing him, the figure straightened. An overturned crate served as a table and held one candle, almost burned down to nothing. Still, in that fading glow, Gorson saw the face he had come to know and fear.

"Stand before me!" The woman's voice pulled him toward her like the powerful spell it was. Commander General Valkyra was a full head taller than Gorson. She obviously enjoyed the advantage and towered over him with a grimace on her full lips and an unflinching glare in her deep green eyes. A full, wild mane of bright red hair was almost afire, even in the shadows. Gorson could not keep his eyes off her voluptuous breasts, covered as they were by the Sentinel Commander General's uniform of black mail. Black woolen leggings and shiny, thigh-high black leather boots added a dramatic touch. Her chest was crossed by the red leather harness of the Sentinel Guard, and he did not miss the elaborately carved hilt of the saber at her hip.

The face was striking, but held no hint of humor or kindness or mercy. In his brief time in her employ, Gorson had learned that the woman before him, who was such a striking beauty, had a heart as cold as stone.

Her voice startled Gorson out of his musings.

"Do not desire that which you shall never touch, Gorson." Her lips almost turned up in a smile as she noticed the unmistakable bulge in his pants. "How do things progress in Avoreed?" she asked with a sneer.

"As planned. Even better," Gorson answered with a bravado in his voice that he did not really feel. "Those idiot villagers are so enraged that they are prepared to march on the palace and anoint *me* Hya!" he boasted.

Valkyra slowly nodded her approval, her eyes riveted on the man before her.

"Excellent. You have done well."

"Since you are so pleased, Valkyra," Gorson began, and hesitated a little as she raised an eyebrow.

"Yes?"

"I will take my payment now."

The sudden flash of movement startled him. Before he realized what had happened, he was on his back in the dirt, with a saber tip under his chin, staring into the flame of his own torch. Valkyra's face was a breath away from his.

"You shall receive payment when Avoreed is burned to the

ground and I have taken my share of the plunder!" she hissed. "Just be certain to wear the arm band you were given. So that my soldiers may spare you."

"There will be so much chaos. Perhaps they will not see..." Gorson's words tumbled out and over each other.

Valkyra snapped, "Do as you are told and you will be spared." She moved closer. Gorson's head would go back no further and the tip of her saber nicked him. She was so close now that he could smell the womanness of her. Her lips were a hair away from his as she whispered, "Do you not trust me?"

1

PILLAGE

Elayna started at the sudden, hard rapping on her door. Nudging a slumbering Caly awake, she quickly got up from the pallet to answer the urgent summons. Caly sat up, rubbing her eyes and smiling at the sight of Elayna's bare and beautiful backside as her lover hurriedly dressed.

Lacing her bodice, Elayna turned and frowned at Caly. The frown didn't last long and they smiled at each other.

"Will you hurry? I do not want whoever it is to find you here!" she urged in a hushed voice. Elayna brushed fingers through her silken blonde hair. It didn't do any good. She was annoyed that their sweet doze after lovemaking had been so abruptly disturbed, and irritated at the insistence of the knocking. Three more raps. Caly got to her feet and pulled on her tunic and leggings.

"So, the Fair Sorceress of Avoreed has a touch of modesty?" Caly teased. Elayna tossed Caly's satchel into her outstretched arms, turned her around and gently pushed her out through the back door of the little dwelling. Caly stopped long enough to give Elayna a quick peck on the lips before running off down the alleyway and disappearing around a corner.

Elayna adjusted her clothes and hurried to the door. When she opened it, she was amazed to see how quickly the sun had set. It was nearly dark and Orrat had not come home yet. She would have to check her annoyance until her caller left.

The stranger leaned casually against the splintered door frame with a frown that disappeared when he saw her. He stood to his full height and made a sweeping bow.

They had told him the sorceress was beautiful. He had dismissed it knowing that local people always proclaim the fairness of their own. But now, upon seeing her, his heart almost stopped. He couldn't help staring. She looked to be about twenty-five Passes, perhaps fewer. Her hair was the color of Nardian wheat, bleached by the sun. Full, sensual lips almost pouted under the upturned nose. Her eyes were deepest green with flecks of gray. The stranger imagined their color changed on a daily basis, depending on the fair one's mood. She was quite striking. His eyes followed her neckline down to the valley of her bosom. If he raised himself up on tiptoe just a bit, maybe he could catch a glimpse of...

"Is there something you wanted?" she asked briskly, as she folded her arms across her chest to block his view. His eyes traveled back up to her face and he smiled.

"I have come seeking the Fair Sorceress of Avoreed. I am in need of advice and I was hoping she could help me."

Elayna looked the stranger up and down. From the cut of his clothes, she knew he was no ordinary wayfarer. He was handsome in a rugged, road-worn way. His hair was a mass of black curls and he had strong features, just a hint of a cleft in his chin. But there was something about him Elayna didn't like.

"There is no sorceress here," she said calmly, and started to go back inside.

Suddenly, he caught her arm in a strong grip that lessened when she turned to face him again. Coldly, she looked at his hand on her arm and he removed it. Elayna silently cursed herself for not remembering to put on her heartstone before she answered the door. If she had been wearing it, it would have given her some idea of this man's intent.

The stranger chose his words carefully. "But I was told this is where I could find her. I have traveled far," he insisted. Elayna would have been convinced of his urgency but for the swirling darkness of his eyes, a seductive glint that almost drew her in.

"I am sorry. It seems your journey was for naught."

Disappointed, the stranger slowly picked up his satchel, and with a nod, turned and started slowly up the lane toward the center of the village.

Elayna stood looking after him. There were not many who would journey to Avoreed just to have a fortune read. And she was not certain why she had refused, except for the whispered warning she'd heard in her mind when she first saw him. She noted the saber at his side and that he moved with the ease and confidence and wariness of a fighter. Why had he sought her out?

It took a second for her to realize that Caly had reentered the dwelling and was now standing behind her in the doorway. She smelled of soap and hay. Caly followed Elayna's gaze, though the stranger had long since disappeared amid the throng of villagers milling about in the square. She wrapped her arms around Elayna's waist and pulled the golden beauty back against her. The fires of their lovemaking still smoldered within her, but Caly knew Elayna was distracted.

"Who is he?" she asked in Elayna's ear. Elayna shook her head. "Quite handsome, do you not think so?" Caly teased, hoping to draw Elayna out of her mood.

"You go to him, then, if you find him so!" In a mock pout she started to walk away, but Caly pulled her back and planted a kiss on her upturned nose.

"I have everything I want here," she whispered and held Elayna close.

Still, after two Passes, Caly wondered how she had come to be so fortunate as to have the most beautiful and desired woman for leagues in any direction from Avoreed. They were such a contrast to each other—Elayna with her womanly fairness and Caly with her field-tanned complexion and boyish manner. She ran a strong hand through her close-cropped hair, and the uneven length on top fell into her eyes. With her innocent face, no would guess she was older than Elayna by five Passes.

Elayna kissed Caly's lips and mussed her hair before extricating herself from her embrace.

"I must start evenmeal. You may stay if you wish," Elayna offered. Caly followed Elayna to the hearth and hopped up onto the table to watch her prepare the meal.

"I would, but for your brother. He is none too fond of me, as you know."

"It is only because you beat him at those silly games you two play. By Dornea, I wish you would let him win just once. He would find you much more appealing."

As she talked, Elayna took six small potatoes from the makeshift cupboard, washed them and put them in the large black iron pot hanging in the hearth. She then took a small sack from the table and drew from it a handful of herbs, which she sprinkled into the pot as well. Then, with a knowing wink at Caly, Elayna closed her eyes and whispered softly, tracing a fluid pattern in the air with her hands. The stew would be thick with succulent chunks of meat.

Caly watched with a smile on her lips. She never asked Elayna about her magical dabblings. Of course, she knew of the rumors. And she had to admit she'd seen some things that she didn't understand, especially when Elayna's mother was alive. Perhaps the mother had passed down those secrets to her daughter. Caly shrugged to herself. Elayna was very good at silence and Caly did not pry. Whatever Elayna was, she was hers. At this moment, anyway. For Caly never knew when the mysteries that seemed to beckon to her lover would some day enshroud Elayna and whisk her away forever.

◻ ◻ ◻ ◻ ◻

Micas Silenas angrily shouldered his way through the gathering crowd. He didn't know what was about to take place in Avoreed. All he knew was that he had failed in his mission. His master would not be pleased with empty results. The girl had been lying. The girl. She fit the description his master had given him. He had to admit the witch was a wonder in the flesh, and if he had not been on this mission for his master, he would have taken the girl for himself.

He had left his horse at the stables so as not to arouse suspicion, and he trudged there now to retrieve the mount. His horse also belonged to his master. As did he. Micas paused before reaching his destination. Perhaps he had time for a meal, a bit of wine. He needed time to think. Turning in the direction of the little inn he'd passed earlier, Micas adjusted his blade at his side and strode back into the throng at the center of town.

◻ ◻ ◻ ◻ ◻

Orrat knew he should have been on his way home. Elayna would be worried. And furious. But he was mesmerized by Gorson's speech. He tried to concentrate on Gorson's words as the growing crowd jostled him left and right. Some of the words he did not understand. What captivated him was the intensity with which the chosen leader spoke. Orrat had never heard anyone speak such things of the Hya, their ruler. But his neighbors all around him were rallying to the cause. They *would not* pay more taxes. If this led to an outright defiance of the Hya's orders, so be it. Everyone was prepared to accept the penalty. Orrat believed he, too, was prepared, but when he really thought about it, the possibility of working his life away in the penal mines was not very appealing.

That thought sobered him enough to start him on his way through the crowd and toward home. But first he would have to stop in the marketplace, just browse a little, maybe, and find something nice to take home to his sister—to appease her.

He walked briskly through the empty marketplace. Everyone, with the exception of a few merchants, was in the square getting ready for the bonfire, a nonviolent display of the village's displeasure with the Hya. This would make things more difficult, Orrat thought, as he scanned the rows of booths. Elayna had often told him he possessed the instincts of a predator and the soul of a thief...a leaning he would pay dearly for in his next visit to this world. Though he respected his sister's obvious powers, he did not in any way think any of her insights applied to him. He could do as he pleased. In fact, he thought he all but owned Avoreed. And he was an excellent thief. For all of his fifteen Passes, he considered himself every bit a man. The girls he knew seemed to think so, too. They followed him around and teased him and sometimes did silly things to get his attention. And when they stood close to him, so close he could feel the warmth of them through his clothes, he would break into a sweat and back away. He didn't have the height of the other boys his age, but his snow blond hair, green eyes and stern brow gave him an advantage over the local Avoreedans. He and Elayna and their parents were transplanted to Avoreed from the northern city of Lyfton. But Orrat couldn't remember much about his original home since they had settled in Avoreed when he was very young.

This was his home now and Elayna was all he had in the world, with the exception of their father's saber. He wore the weapon from a shoulder harness Elayna had contrived so that the blade would not drag on the ground. Some day he would grow into his father's belt, but in the meantime, the unusual style earned him the respect of his friends, who had no hopes of ever owning a weapon as fine. They were mostly farm boys, poor like himself. Orrat had had no formal training in its use, but his friends didn't know that and he had never been challenged. He looked strong and walked with a swagger, so the other boys left him alone. The saber was the only legacy his father had left him. It was only fair, he thought to himself; after all, Mother had given Elayna all of her mysteries.

A bright red length of silk lying a little off from the other bolts of fabric on the merchant's table caught his attention. It seemed to beckon to him. Calculatingly he thought, *Elayna loves red. This would be a perfect peace offering.*

Orrat sidled up to the merchant, who was a regular in the marketplace. He could not believe his good fortune, for the merchant had nodded off to sleep, probably not even aware that the marketplace was nearly empty. As he drew closer, he could hear the intermittent snorts. The merchant was fat, his body draped in a varied sampling of the silks he sold. Every now and then his body jerked and he would mumble in his slumber and become quiet again. Orrat waited in front of the stand, occasionally looking this way and that over each shoulder to see if anyone was close by. The marketplace had emptied of the few villagers he had seen before. The opportunity was perfect. Orrat felt the calm, the uncanny peace he always felt when he was about to apply his craft. The movement was barely noticeable. In a wink, the silk scarf was in his hand and just as quickly in his pocket. *Very easy.* Orrat was smug as he turned to walk away, but suddenly a hand hit his shoulder like a lead weight, stopping him in his tracks. He couldn't move.

The merchant stood above him, glaring down like a mighty hawk about to devour its prey. Orrat thought he would surely die— either from the stench of the obese, unbathed body, or the weight of the club-like hand pressing him by the shoulder down into the hard clay of the street. As insolent a gesture as it was, Orrat couldn't help fanning the air when the merchant finally opened his nearly toothless mouth to speak.

"Ah! I have had my eye out for you! You are almost as good a thief as the Hya herself. The difference is I have *you* here, in my grasp!" He grabbed Orrat by the hair. The boy was relieved of the shoulder pain only to have his head nearly yanked from his shoulders. The merchant roughly dragged him behind the stand and pulled the barrel he had been sitting on out into the open.

Desperately, Orrat babbled, "I have to get home! My family will come looking for me and you will be pleading to me for your life! My father is a huge man, bigger than you, if anyone can imagine there is someone bigger than you! You would not want to get him angry!"

Orrat frantically tried to save himself, but he knew he'd been caught. There was nothing he could say and the merchant didn't seem to be listening anyway. He was in for it now.

The merchant forced the boy to his knees beside the barrel, and grinning wickedly, drew Orrat's sword from his side.

"No!" Orrat yelled, almost over the din coming from the square. The merchant held the finely honed blade before him and nodded with approval. This was worth much, much more than the silk the boy had tried to steal. He shrugged. He'd have his merchandise back *and* a fine saber in the bargain. But first, there was only one way to cure a thief of his pilfering habits. Frowning, he looked down at the quivering boy. He would be a beauty if he had been a girl. There were those who would pay handsomely for such a prize. But that would take too much time and trouble. Best to teach the boy a lesson now and be done.

He raised the blade and held Orrat's arm, but the struggling boy was making it difficult to take aim. Fine. It didn't have to be a hand. Perhaps an ear. Orrat noted the change in focus and shook his head. He cringed at the chilling cold touch of steel near the top of his ear.

"Please," he pleaded. "You may have it back. I did not mean anything and I will never do it again. I promise!"

"Have you no courage, boy?!" the merchant bellowed. "I should do it solely because you are such a coward!"

There was a stinging sensation as the merchant slowly applied pressure to Orrat's ear. The boy could feel an ever-so-slight trickle of warm blood beginning to seep down the side of his face. His heart pounded so loudly in his ears that he barely heard the voice that made the merchant pause. Orrat seized the momentary distraction and jerked himself free of the merchant's grip, almost running head-on into his sister.

The merchant looked at the pair and roared with laughter as he stepped from behind his stand, still brandishing the saber. This was going to be easy...and quite enjoyable.

Elayna stood tall and regal some distance away. Her skirts blowing in the evening breeze, she was an imposing figure, though she carried no weapon. Orrat was relieved that she had found him and desperately wanted to go to home and forget the incident. But he also wanted his saber back.

"Is this the fierce father you spoke of, you miserable little dung pile?" The merchant was steadily closing the distance between them. Elayna didn't move a step, but focused her attention on the hulk. "Your father is prettier than my mother ever was. By Dornea, perhaps I shall take your father in payment for my goods."

"What did you take from him?" Elayna sternly asked her brother, not taking her eyes from the merchant, who was still advancing.

"Only a scarf, but he has it back. I owe him nothing and I want my saber!"

"Thieves should not go unpunished!" The merchant roared out at the smattering of villagers who had been drawn to the scene and now lingered to watch. "There is not a merchant in Avoreed who would not like to see this one sent to the mines!"

And then he lunged for them. The packed dirt under his feet suddenly turned into an oozing mire. His eyes wide with amazement, the merchant struggled to keep his balance while shouting obscenities at the pair. The more he struggled, the deeper he sank.

"What is this?!" he screamed as he tried again and again to move.

"Get your saber, Orrat," Elayna barked. For once the boy did exactly as he was told, and when he was at his sister's side, she grabbed him by the arm and shoved him homeward.

They left the bewildered and furious merchant up to his knees in the tar-like mess, swearing at the two figures hurriedly disappearing into the dusk.

As they hurried away, they did not see the shadow of Micas Silenas skulk back into the darkness behind the inn.

"But we must see the bonfire!" the boy protested. Orrat knew he was sorely vexing his sister. She was already so furious she couldn't speak to him. True, he was grateful that she had come along when she had, but she was not going to drag him home like a hound on a leash. He was a man, after all. "I shall stay if I like!" He stopped in his tracks, legs apart and his fists on his hips.

People brushed by him to get to the square, but he did not intend to move. Elayna stopped a few paces in front of him and looked back. He was the image of their father. Orrat had not grown into himself yet at fifteen Passes, but when he did, he would be a formidable young man. At this moment, however, he was acting like a spoiled child and Elayna had already lost what patience she'd had.

"I should have let him cut your ear off!" she said angrily. "And you will not see the bonfire if you do not come home and have your evenmeal first, which is more than likely cinders by now because I had to come looking for you!"

Orrat was about to retort when clamorous shouting from the convergence of villagers caught their attention. Elayna had been so intent on trying to get Orrat home that she had not noticed the crowd that had gathered. Now the crowd seemed to swarm around them, closing them in so that they could not move in either direction.

Elayna's frustration at Orrat faded as her attention focused on Gorson of Ornam, who had just stepped up onto the crude platform to speak. He was a relative newcomer to the small village and no one knew much about him. But his friendly, easygoing manner had won the villagers over almost instantly in the span of two turns.

During that fourteen-day period, Elayna had seen the young man around the village, speaking intensely to the elders and to small groups of farmers and merchants gathered in the marketplace. And he had noticed her watching him when he glanced up from his rapt audience, only to stare at her for a brief second before turning away again. Elayna had sensed something about the handsome stranger in that brief moment, but had never encountered him again. It was as though Gorson of Ornam took great pains to avoid the young woman known in the village as healer and sorceress.

She watched him now in puzzlement as he addressed the crowd. He was handsome. Fine, strong facial features, intense hazel eyes and a cleft in his chin. Abundant golden curls ringed his head like a halo. The young women of Avoreed found Gorson's tall, muscular body appealing, and many of them gathered at the foot of the platform just to be near him, to be swept up in his exciting presence.

Elayna had to admit to herself that the man was of spirit and fire. His words were put together so as to incite the agitated crowd. No matter what the outcome of this night, it would always be remembered as the night that a thousand Avoreedan voices were raised in unity. The air was thick with rebellion. These usually docile farmers and merchants were angry and ready to vent that anger at anything and anyone who tried to tell them they were wrong in their cause.

Elayna and Orrat were quickly caught up in the surge of emotion, the passion of belonging and fighting for what was good for all. It was a unity of spirit that was not often exhibited in Mauldar, for the Hya despised disloyalty in her subjects. And the Hya would surely hear of the uprising. She would be stunned that Avoreed had defied her, as the Avoreedans themselves were amazed that they had the unified strength to do so.

But Elayna's fervor faded as she listened to the guiding voice within her. *Something was wrong.* She felt the impending doom before seeing the horses thundering in from the surrounding hills. She looked on in horror as the attackers surrounded the village and the massive swarm of people. The villagers were like bees in a burning hive, only none could fly away. Their passionate enthusiasm quickly turned to panic as the clash of steel resounded amidst the screaming and crying and shouting. The smell of smoke wafted in on the breeze and settled thickly around them. Everyone seemed to be running in different directions at once. Who were these vicious raiders; where had they come from? And then someone screamed out above the tumult, "Sentinels!"

Orrat grabbed Elayna's hand as they pushed their way through the teeming mass of humanity. In her panic, she flailed her arms and fought and shoved and kicked a path for them toward the safety of their home. They ran, dodging the charging raiders, stopping only long enough to look over their shoulders at the devastating destruction that was taking place behind them and all around them. Fires raged. Everyone was running for their lives, cursing the Hya. Her name was on the lips of the dying as they whispered their last breath. Elayna tripped over bodies, pulling Orrat down with her, only to struggle to her feet again and keep running. Horses jostled into them, knocking them to one side and then the other.

And then they saw it. The dwelling they knew as home was ablaze. Flames licked out into the street from the doorway and the single window. Elayna's mind raced. She pulled Orrat almost off his feet and headed for the narrow alleyway behind the row of cottages. Smoke was so thick now that they could barely see where they were going. Destruction was the common nightmare and no one could escape.

When Elayna was taken with a fit of coughing from the smoke, Orrat got ahead of her. Now he led the way through the alley.

As her coughing subsided, she noticed that Orrat had stopped in the middle of the alley as noise and confusion erupted around him. He stood stock still, staring at the Sentinel who was in the midst of running someone through with one final saber thrust. He recognized the clothes, the mop of thick brown hair. Blood spilled from her mouth and her face was smudged with soot, but there was no mistaking Caly's form on the ground against the wall. A gasp beside him reminded him that Elayna was there. Instinctively, he stepped in front of her to block her view—the bloody sight of her lover dead in the alleyway.

Elayna pushed by him, oblivious to the horses now thundering up the alleyway toward them, and knelt beside Caly. Her clothes were shreds and tatters, leaving little doubt as to what she had gone through before they had mercifully killed her. Elayna was so stunned by the horrifying sight that she had no tears. She could not take her eyes off Caly, half expecting her to jump up suddenly and say it had all been a ruse.

Try as he might, Orrat could not stir her from her mournful vigil. Frantically pulling on her arm, he kept his eyes on the savage, bloody horsemen rapidly bearing down on them.

ᗡ ᗡ ᗡ ᗡ ᗡ

Isom Hawk lived in total seclusion high up in the Mauldaran Mountains. His position required that he be able to observe all doings in the daily lives of common folk; thus, his modest, elevated dwelling, tucked away from prying, curious intruders.

It had been a long, sleepless night, but then he never slept. Never. Isom did not require sleep. He did not give in to the weaknesses and needs of the mortal body. For him, night was the time for study. Daylight was the time for work.

Isom emerged from his dwelling and stepped out into a haze that had settled itself over the peaks of the mountains. Smoke. Absently lifting a water bucket from its nail by the door, he walked out into the field of grass. His feet became damp with dew, a dampness that would have chilled an ordinary man to his bones. Sensing disaster, he hurried to a vantage point just down the slope, where he could see down through a break in the trees. The village of Avoreed lay below him—smoldering ash. He stood for some time, rooted to the spot, and visualized what had taken place. It was as clear and detailed in his mind as though he had witnessed the pillage first hand. Sentinels dispatched by the Hya. Damn! A shimmer of icy rage swept through him. His plans would be delayed further.

□ □ □ □ □

Back from his trip to Avoreed, Micas Silenas watched the solitary black-cloaked figure of his master from a distance. The hooded priest's robes were misleading. Micas smiled grimly to himself. Everything about his master was misleading. Upon first encounter, the man Micas knew only as Master gave the appearance of an average monk, a servant of Dachas, the male counterpart of Dornea, the dominant female deity of their religion. Servants of Dachas were sworn to wander from place to place, city to city, to preach kindness and perform good deeds, sometimes even performing miracles. Priestesses of Dornea served in one of the many temples erected in her honor. These women were the most revered of personages, second only to the Hya herself. The priestesses were Dornea's chosen, untouchable on pain of death.

Micas thought bitterly, *Sometimes death can be a blessing. There is more than one way for a man to die. Worse than physical death, there is the long, slow, torturous death that comes with servitude. Especially for one as damned as I am.*

An eternity ago, he had gotten drunk and raped a priestess. Now he only remembered searing pain and then darkness. When he had finally awakened, he was lying on a cot inside the dwelling he now gazed upon from amidst the trees. And he was doomed to be servant to a master even the worst of demons would fear.

His master had the calm appearance of the blessed. His physical movements were calculated—never a wasted gesture. Sometimes he even appeared to move without effort across the space of the dwelling, as though his feet never touched the ground. The face was soft-featured like that of a kindly grandfather. But the illusion lasted only until you were close to him. Only when Micas was drawn in close had he glimpsed the darkness and begun to feel the hate that poisoned this strange and evil being.

He thought back to the folly of his drunken youth and how he had doomed himself forever to serve this...thing...for the rest of his existence. And now his master was after the girl. The witch. The fair and wondrous creature he had found in what used to be Avoreed.

"Come!" The mental shout of his master echoed through Micas' mind like an internal thunder clap. His mount moved forward without being coaxed. Micas was not looking forward to the reprimand he knew awaited him. The horse stopped. Micas dismounted and knelt, his hands folded as though in prayer. Head bowed.

"Speak!"

"I have seen the girl, Master," Micas began. His voice was strong and steady. In his youth, before his fate was sealed, he had feared neither man nor beast, and as far as he could tell, he still had a brave heart. His fate had not yet destroyed his courage. But Micas had learned to respect the powers he did not understand and to act humbly. Only a mortal fool would attempt to defy such evil. Isom still gazed out over the mountains.

"And the heartstone?" he asked.

"There was no stone, Master." As his master turned to face him, there was a sudden gust of wind that nearly blew Micas off his knees. But no trees stirred.

"I feel the power of that stone even as you deny its existence!" Isom bellowed. "You have failed me!"

"No, Master!" Micas had earned his master's disfavor before. He was not eager to pay the consequences. "If not for the coming of the Sentinels, I would have put another plan into action. But as you see, there is nothing left of the village or the girl. She is dead...."

Eyes blazing, the black-cloaked figure intoned, "The power comes from Mauldar. The girl has been taken there. And there you shall go." For the first time Isom looked at his servant. Micas flinched from the darkness of those eyes. In those eyes, he saw his own soul which was no longer his.

"Do not fail me again, mortal wretch," Isom warned ominously.

"I will not, Master." Micas's own words reverberated around him as he jumped to his feet. With a panicked sob, he extended his hands out from his sides to touch the cold hardness of glass which now encased him.

Slowly, deliberately, Isom picked up the jar, took up the reins of the horse, and started back to his hut to plan his servant's next move.

2

ENCOUNTER

Cydell Ra Sadiin stood at the window of her study and gazed out, transfixed, at the two, full, silver-blue moons of Mauldar. It had been a long day and still it was not over. She awaited word from her commanders regarding Avoreed.

Some days earlier she had been informed that the people of the small farming village were going to stage a protest against the new taxes imposed by the tax master of the province. Before she was able to dispatch her scribes to the village to conduct an inquiry of the tax master's already questionable practices, the people had taken matters into their own hands. At duskfall, she had dispatched a small company of Sentinels to oversee the protest and make sure there would be some semblance of order. They were not to harm any of the citizens of Avoreed, simply keep the furor down and prevent any looting. She would have the tax master brought to the palace as soon as possible.

Cydell swore a warrior's oath that would have brought her old nurse to her knees. This was something that should have been handled when first she had gotten wind of the tax master's avarice. But she had gotten sidetracked, called away to Saven for two turns, to settle a dispute among two of the more volatile hill tribes.

A dispute that, left unresolved, would have resulted in a bloody plains war. And now she had returned to this unpleasant business in Avoreed.

With a sigh, she walked over to her desk. There were a dozen candles around the study, all burning down in varying degrees and adding a warm, soft glow to the massive room. Her ornate wooden desk was cluttered with sealed parchments yet to be opened. There were quills strewn over the desk and on the floor, testaments to her frustrations. So much work to be done; grain orders from the eastern seaports, produce orders and transport schedules from the seaports to the mountain cities, herb vendors requesting permission to extend their trade boundaries throughout Mauldar and to all of the surrounding provinces. It never ended. Cydell had promised herself a respite as soon as she returned from Saven. It was not to be.

She closed her eyes and rolled her shoulders. Her body was surrendering to the stress of ruling. It was beginning to betray the careless youth and overwork of forty-two Passes. But to look at her, one only saw the tall, handsome woman who was Hya. Dark, smooth skin glowed in the candlelight. Aristocratic breeding was evident in her perfect nose, full lips and arched brows over large hazel eyes framed by long dark lashes. There was only a trace of character lines at the corners of those eyes. The high cheek bones and thick salt-and-pepper curls were traits of her line, in both the men and the women. Cydell had inherited all of her father's features, including his sturdy build, which was sleekness in her because of her height. Her muscles were firm from constant riding and Sentinel training. She was the only Master Sentinel for leagues, and the only woman in the region to ever earn that distinction.

Thoughts of her father invariably made her think of the Sentinels, the elite saber unit developed by him during the days when he was Hya and the outlying tribes were a constant threat to the provinces of Mauldar and the city of Mauldar itself. Soldiers were rigorously trained in specialized combat skills, ethics and techniques. Only a chosen few could endure and eventually master the gruelling discipline.

Those warring tribes had been tamed long ago by the Sentinels of her father's time, and Cydell had continued the training and increased the number of Sentinels until her special forces numbered in the thousands. Word of the prowess of the Sentinels had spread throughout Mauldar, and no one, unless they were of foreign blood, had dared challenge the city since that time.

Cydell knew that the peace would not last forever. But in the meantime, there were other matters to attend to. Already there were reports of random attacks on the smaller villages to the east of Mauldar. Conflicting reports of renegade Sentinels. Looting. Burning. Villagers taken as slaves. Her Sentinels could not be responsible. She kept her personal guard tight and disciplined, and she was always wary of a breach in their loyalty. She had learned her lessons well. Her father had taught her how to rule, as it was her destiny since she was born of the Ra Sadiin line. Her mother, it seemed, was only there to comfort the child who would some day rule Mauldar. The girl had learned from her father that to falter, even briefly, was the greatest weakness. So when she surpassed the skills of the teachers in the palace and outrode the equestrian trainers, her father was pleased and proud. Her mother simply watched. She saw her daughter's tears less and less as the little girl became a strong woman who could fight and ride and rule. Sometimes, infrequently, when she and her daughter were alone, she would try to teach her about the beauty of softer things, such as love and compassion. Cydell would listen, but the things her mother spoke of were foreign to her, things she could not touch. So she had made these feelings her foes and was ever on guard against them.

With a start, she returned to the present and looked wistfully at the disarray of the study. She and her father had spent many hours going over ledgers together, making sure that everything was as it should be. There had been very little time to play for the crown princess, nor were there many other children around the palace, with the exception of her cousin, Kovi. Her mother never ventured into the study. She loved the garden and sometimes, on rare occasions, Cydell would wander into the garden and find both her parents there, holding hands or in an embrace. She rarely saw that softness in her father when he dealt with her. And one day she understood. Her father treated her like the son he had always wanted.

Resigned, Cydell went to the desk. Before sitting down again, she pulled the wrinkled linen blouse out of her riding pants so that it hung loose, and then rolled up her sleeves. Her marin, a beverage of ground and steeped suka beans, had gotten cold again and she thought about summoning Josn to bring her more. But the old woman was probably in bed for the night and she hadn't the heart to wake her. Instead, she picked up a quill, and running her fingers through her black and silver curls, settled into the work once again.

Gorson struggled in vain between two Sentinel guards as they led him through the palace, through a maze of passageways to the great study where the Hya waited. His body hurt and his mind swirled with confusion and rage. Valkyra's mercenaries had rained a storm of destruction down on the village of Avoreed and he had been caught in the middle of it. None of the raiders had heeded his pleas. None had noticed the red arm band that was to secure his immunity and signal his alliance with the raiders. It had happened so quickly that he barely remembered the untimely arrival of the Sentinel regiment. Gorson found himself just as confused as the panicked villagers. As he'd fled the platform, he'd caught glimpses through the smoke of Sentinels fighting Sentinels. Even he could not tell the true Sentinel Guard from the impostors. Valkyra had done her job extremely well. Except where he was concerned.

The guards' boots tapped a macabre rhythm on the hard wood floors, echoing around and around in Gorson's head until he thought he would have to beg them to be still. At last they stopped before a huge wooden door and knocked.

They forced him to his knees before the door of the inner chamber. One of the guards knocked twice in succession and then again.

"Come!"

Gorson felt his stomach muscles tighten at the sound of that voice. The guard opened the doors and made a sweeping bow.

"We have captured the leader, Hya. Gorson of Ornam." The Hya waved a hand and the Sentinel straightened.

"I am more concerned with the tax master. Bring Hadeeb Saan to me," she said without looking up. The stillness in the chamber caught her attention and the Hya looked up at the Sentinel Guard lieutenant. It was then she noticed the cuts and smudges on her face and the bloodstains on her tattered mail. The lieutenant's boots were nearly singed through; her hands were cut and bleeding.

The Hya slowly rose to her feet and she muttered in amazement, "What in the name of Dornea...?" Her gaze then traveled from the lieutenant to the other two guards, who were in the same condition. The prisoner between them could barely stand, nor could he look into her eyes.

"Report, Lieutenant," she ordered. The weary guard bowed her head.

"Permission to speak freely, Hya."

"Speak, dammit!" she bellowed, already agitated by the dread news she knew she was about to hear. But her lieutenant did not falter. She related a detailed account of the raid. The chaos her Sentinel regiment had found upon arriving in Avoreed. She told her of the death and destruction and the pillage. Cydell walked away from her as the impact of the lieutenant's words hit her. *False Sentinels. This time as close as Avoreed. Avoreed. There was nothing left of Avoreed.*

The lieutenant finished her report and watched as the Hya turned from her place by the hearth to study the prisoner. Rage flashed in the hazel eyes. Her fists clenched and unclenched as she strode across the chamber. Four calculated steps closed the distance between her and Gorson of Ornam.

Gorson tried not to flinch as he looked into those eyes. Something told him that he would be detained in Mauldar indefinitely.

"What do you know of this?!" The Hya's voice was controlled. Too controlled. "Who is behind these raids? Speak!"

"I know nothing, Hya! The people of Avoreed sought only a speaker to voice their displeasure with the high taxes, and they chose me!"

"Lies!" The Hya slammed her fist on her desk so hard that even the guards jumped, startled. "This massacre was not merely about taxes! I knew of that matter and was in the midst of resolving it!" She turned suddenly to her lieutenant. "Were the taxes recovered from the tax house?"

"We found nothing, Hya. Only the body of Hadeeb Saan," she answered. Cydell looked again at Gorson.

"Why did my people suddenly need *you* to speak for them?! Who would destroy a village to get barely a Pass's worth of taxes?! Who would do this?!"

Gorson's voice was a whisper in the lingering echoes of the Hya's rage.

"I do not know, Hya. You must believe me!" He would have gladly given up forty bars of lathium to be free of the Hya's steady gaze. She stepped away from him then, almost as if to see him better. To study him.

"I do not believe you, Gorson of Ornam. I do not trust you. But I feel I owe something to those of my people of Avoreed who did." She went to stand behind her desk where she paused a moment and then looked again at the prisoner.

"When is the next prison convoy due to depart for the mines?" she asked coolly. Gorson's head shot up as he looked wildly from his Hya to the Sentinel guards.

"Dawn, Hya," the lieutenant answered.

"See that he is on it!" she ordered.

"No!" Gorson struggled in his panic. "Hya, I beg your mercy!"

"Take him away. Lieutenant, a word."

Gorson was dragged screaming from the chamber. The lieutenant stood at attention before her Hya. Waiting.

"No one leaves the palace grounds. None of the guard. None of the watch. And pass this word. Anyone dealing in Avoreedan plunder, slaves included, will be put to death as a traitor. You are dismissed."

"Yes, Hya." The lieutenant made a curt bow and left the chamber. Cydell closed her eyes, her head in her hands as her elbows rested on the desk. She would get to the bottom of this, she swore. She would get answers. And soon.

Minutes later there was a knock on the study door. "Come!"

To Cydell's surprise, Valkyra, the Commander General of her Sentinel Guard, stormed in, her mane of red hair flying in all directions in her haste. The Hya was unmoved by the Commander's obvious anger. "I did not summon you, and I am very busy."

Valkyra ignored the dismissal and stood directly in front of the desk, blocking the candlelight from the parchments Cydell was working on. Only then did the Hya look up.

"Is something amiss?" she asked irritably.

"Why have you restricted my Guard?!" Valkyra demanded. She had to remind herself that she could push Cydell only so far. Her Hya could be as volatile as she herself. Worse.

"I find that there are traitors among the army. Perhaps even among the Sentinels, though I hope not. I will not tolerate it."

"Then tell me, how am I to carry out the watch?" Valkyra fired back and crossed her arms over her chest. Cydell put down her quill and leaned back heavily in her chair.

"That, Commander, is your problem. Treason is mine." Cydell did not flinch when Valkyra leaned in to her.

"Do you even know who is responsible, Cydell, or are you going to execute the entire army to make your point?"

Cydell raised an eyebrow. It was a silent signal for Valkyra to back down and adhere to the proper protocol. The Commander General stood at attention and tried to maintain an air of respect.

"I *will* have names before the sun rises. And there will be no more traitors in your guard by dusk on the morrow. Until then, the restrictions stand. I want none of my Sentinels leaving Mauldar until this matter is settled."

Valkyra knew that was the final word and it was precisely what she had expected. She would simply have to circumvent the restrictions. Thus far, Gorson was the only liability in her plans. But that was nothing to concern herself with. She had gotten word of his capture and subsequent sentencing. Anything could happen to a prisoner on the way to the mines. And there was the small matter of forty bars of lathium that she could now keep. Valkyra pretended annoyance as Cydell watched her.

"Is there something more?" Cydell asked impatiently as she picked up her quill.

"I will work with what I have," Valkyra conceded at last.

"That, Commander, is no more than I expect," Cydell said by way of another dismissal.

Valkyra started for the door but turned to look back at her Hya for a moment. The Commander General was glad she was able to separate business from pleasure. Her ambitions to create her own personal army of mercenaries had nothing at all to do with her feelings for Cydell. She realized, however, that perhaps some day it would come down to the two of them, facing each other on the field of battle with all of Mauldar as the prize. And if her plans continued to go as smoothly as they had gone of late, that time might arrive much sooner than anticipated.

Still, Cydell Ra Sadiin was the only woman who had ever bested Valkyra in battle. And in bed. Her passion for the Hya's touch was seconded only by her passion for combat. And Valkyra's only submission was to Cydell during their nights together—a surrender of the sweetest sort. It continued to amaze her that although Cydell was cold and exacting as a ruler, she burned with so much fire and passion as a lover. It took Valkyra's breath away.

Valkyra remained lost in thought as she stood at the door remembering. She would never forget the cloudy morning when she had dueled with the Hya herself for the honor of becoming Commander General. Hundreds of Sentinels had lined the walls surrounding the practice yard which encompassed the Sentinel quarters. Everyone had turned out to see if Valkyra would indeed become Commander General by besting the Hya in a saber contest.

It was the first time Valkyra had come face to face with the Hya and she had had to struggle mightily to concentrate, for she had felt the attraction in that first moment of eye contact. If Cydell felt anything, she did not show it then. But that was not unusual. Sometimes, even now after five Passes, Valkyra wondered if their mutual attraction was simply the melding of two cold hearts.

They had battled for the better part of the morning, and by mid-sun, both women could barely raise their sabers to continue. Both were drenched with sweat and deeply fatigued. Valkyra still remembered the aching in her legs and arms. There were several flesh wounds inflicted by the Hya's quick passes, but the Hya had incurred a few wounds as well. Oddly, perhaps fortunately, the match had come down to a draw, and Valkyra had received the new saber in honor of her new post as Commander General of the Sentinel Army. Cydell had left the yard without a word. Valkyra had collapsed.

Later, that evenfall, Valkyra had been summoned to the palace by the Hya. Alone with this formidable and striking woman, she had felt weak and defenseless, yet aching with desire to be held by her Hya, and loved and caressed.

There were no preambles with Cydell. She took what she wanted without apology. They had made wild and furious love for the first time almost in the very spot where Valkyra now stood. And every time since then had been like the first. No less desire. No less passion. Valkyra never wanted it to end. Even though she knew of Cydell's insatiable appetites, for there had been other women...many other women, Valkyra had never been permanently ousted. The Hya always came back to her.

Now she waited by the door, hoping that Cydell would give her some indication that they could share a bed this evenfall, but there was none. It was as though she had left the study already. And finally, without another word to her Hya, Valkyra silently saluted, turned, and left the chamber, closing the door quietly behind her.

Free again. Micas Silenas rode slowly down the mountain to the road which would lead him into Mauldar. He savored the sweet air as it filled his lungs, even relishing its chill. The birds' songs delighted his senses and he allowed nature to bathe him in sound, as sunlight warmed him to his depths.

He had waited in his glass prison for three long suns as his master devised another plan. This time, with several options. The dwelling had been dark those three suns. Micas knew, as he'd sat in his transparent prison, tucked away on a shelf, that his master was plotting a way to capture the girl. Nothing was ever explained to Micas. He simply followed orders. He didn't understand the significance of the jewel the girl carried. All he knew was that his master was obsessed with retrieving it. Micas dreaded to think what would happen to the poor girl should his master ever possess her. He would probably torture her mercilessly since she had something his master desired. On the other hand, perhaps that fact would save her. But it was none of his affair. He had only to do as he was told. He had no choice.

Isom knelt by the pond not far from his dwelling and gazed into its depths. His own gaunt face, hollow cheeks and steel blue lashless eyes should have peered back at him. He should have seen his own bald head reflected in the pond's surface. But he had no reflection. He had not expected to see one. Instead, he saw a blonde beauty sobbing in darkness, holding a young boy close to her. There were others there in the darkness, but the girl was his only concern. And although he couldn't see the jewel, he could feel its power transcend the distance. He felt it pulsing through the very fiber of the girl and back out to him. Isom wondered if the girl even knew just how much power was hers. Could she imagine that she held the secret of his existence?

An eternity ago, Isom Hawk had known what it was to be alive. He had known the fire of passion, the comfort of another human's touch. Before that fateful day when he had escaped into the valley of Lyfton, he had known the freedom of the soul. He had known what it was to laugh and to love, to feel pride and victory in combat. His saber had earned him a reputation. It had earned him the respect of Machiin Ra Sadiin, who was the most powerful man of the time and great-grandfather of the Hya who now ruled. Machiin's regard for the swordsman was so great that he appointed Isom master trainer of his elite guard. Though the memory was painful, Isom relished it. He relished the glory of being unbeatable, indestructible, and invincible...until that day in the Lyfton Valley.

Under Isom's tutelage, the Hya's guard had become a fierce, indomitable force. They were artful with their blades, swift of movement, almost elegant in combat. Machiin Sadiin's constant praise and the glorious victories of the guard had swelled Isom's head. No doors were closed to him. No woman refused him, mated or not, because no man could challenge him and win.

But his vanity was to be his undoing. Isom became enamored of the wife of the guard captain, a striking woman with raven hair and eyes that hypnotized him. He took the woman against her will and killed the captain when he challenged Isom to reclaim the honor of his ravaged mate.

The Hya Machiin was so angered at the murder of his guard captain that he exiled Isom, instead of executing him for his destructive arrogance. Angered and embarrassed by his dismissal, Isom swore to avenge himself on Machiin. The night before his departure from the palace of Mauldar, Isom stole into the chamber of the sleeping Hya. He would have killed him with one fatal blow of his saber had Machiin not been warned of Isom's treachery and prepared for it. The two men fought. The Saber Master was too skilled for the Hya and dealt him a fatal blow, but not before the Hya wounded his assailant.

With grim determination, Isom escaped from the palace through the same window from which he had entered. Clumsily, he had pulled himself up onto his waiting mount and galloped off into the night, leaving a trail of blood behind him.

To this day he did not know how he had managed to stay mounted, given the severity of his wound. He didn't know when he had lost consciousness. And then, out of the blackness that embraced him, he had awakened to the delicious aroma of broth. He was amazed to find that he was still alive and glad he had triumphed over the Hya's near-fatal stroke.

For a long time he had drifted in and out of consciousness, and when his fever finally broke, he thought he had indeed died and gone beyond. His attendant was a fair beauty, not so young, perhaps forty Passes. But her skin was smooth and tan, and from what Isom could tell through his partial delirium, she was firm of body. She spoke to him in soft, soothing tones and he grew to love the timbre of her voice. Her eyes were the greenest green, and when she did smile at him, he thought his heart would melt.

The woman mystified him. She rarely spoke, yet she tended his wounds and fed him with a tenderness he had never experienced before.

His wound healed quickly, miraculously. But he had no desire to move on. He only wanted to remain and be cared for, maybe even loved by this woman. Some days he would sit and watch her after his chores were done. She was always busy. There was always something simmering in the large black pot hanging in the hearth. There were jars containing peculiar concoctions; satchels of herbs lined the shelves. Around her neck, hanging from a black thong of leather, hung the most wondrous stone Isom had ever seen. It was as large as his thumbnail. A beautiful, rich-colored amber that was dark around its edges, yet seemed to contain a fire in its center. The stone mesmerized him, but he did not desire it.

Isom harbored but one desire. He wanted the woman. But she remained a mystery to him. She spoke only when he spoke to her. She did not ask him about himself and did not seem curious about how he had received such a wound. Often, within her hearing, he would wonder why he had not died. The woman would look at him and smile, and in answer, tell him that perhaps it was not the will of the goddess.

However, she remained impervious to his charms and thanked him graciously when he did things for her. But she moved awkwardly away from him when he would sit close to her.

Isom was bewildered by her disinterest. His charms had never failed him before. With hope and love filling his heart, he decided to give her more time to know him and perhaps love him.

What he had not foreseen was the morning she politely asked him to leave. It happened just as she was going out to gather herbs, as she did every morning. In spite of the shock of her request, he smiled at her and told her he would be gone when she returned. She had smiled in return, and left him. But Isom had no intention of leaving. Not yet. Not until his desires had been satisfied.

On an impulse he decided to follow her. He stayed behind her and out of sight as he followed along a well worn path through the woods.

When she stopped in a clearing, Isom hid himself behind a tree and waited. He had not waited long when to his surprise, the woman was joined by a cloaked stranger who walked into her arms. They kissed and embraced. *So, she did warm to the touch of a man after all,* Isom thought. But his satisfaction at discovering her secret was short-lived. In her ardor, the woman had thrown back the hood of the robe the stranger was wearing. In that moment, to his disbelief, Isom saw that the stranger who had stolen his lady's heart was a woman. A striking, dark-haired beauty who looked to be many Passes older.

Appalled at what he had witnessed, Isom could watch no longer. He stealthily made his way back to the cottage to await the woman's return. He posted himself by the window and finally saw her emerge from the woods at mid-sun.

Upon entering the cottage, she had been surprised to find that he had not left as promised. Isom lunged at her, telling her as he cornered her exactly what he was going to do. Then he relayed what he had seen in the woods. Suddenly, she was angry. But Isom did not let that anger deter him. He was too close to his prize now to stop and think of the consequences. His longing for her grew even as he drew closer to her. In a small corner of his mind he wondered why there was no panic in her eyes. There was, instead, a defiance, a cool rage that he noted but ignored.

She had struggled, but she was no match for his strength. Mumbling under her breath, she uttered words he did not hear, much less understand. And when he was done, he stood above her, smiling at how he had left her: her skirts ripped and soiled; her blouse in tatters, breasts and neck bruised. She made no sound. Not a sob. Not a whimper. She only looked at him, unblinking. Suddenly, he could not look into her eyes. There was a brief moment when he felt remorse about the way he had repaid her kindness, but he shook it off, eyeing the magnificent stone around her neck. She was quite still when he reached for it, and he wondered if she was conscious. And then, when his hand closed around the stone, he roared in pain as it seared with intense heat through the flesh of his palm. Isom jerked his hand away, trembling in a sweat of agony. He heard her voice through the fog of pain that engulfed him. Although her voice was barely a whisper, he heard and understood the meaning of the words plainly.

"I curse you, Isom Hawk, in the name of the dark goddess, walker of the night. As your life was given to you again, so shall your soul ever be captive of the darkness it has brought upon itself. Only the bearer of this stone may free you."

Her words had echoed through Isom's mind as he quickly left the cottage and the wood. He rode out into a night darker than any he had ever known.

For the next twenty Passes, Isom spent his exile studying the black arts. He learned to draw power to him, to rule the winds and the tide. And with every spell he cast, Isom lost more and more of his mortal soul. He became a cold and empty shell. So much of what used to be a whole man was destroyed by his obsession with the elusive heartstone. He found, in all those Passes hence, that there were no spells, no gods to return his soul to him or erase the pain that he felt to this day—the burning pain from the wound that never healed; the seared hole in the flesh of the palm of his hand; the torment of a soul no longer his own.

□ □ □ □ □

Elayna opened her eyes to escape the visions of Caly that played over and over again in her mind. There was still the darkness, the stench, the weeping and whimpering of her neighbors and friends. Everyone despaired, dreading their own fate. Orrat sat close to his sister, his head on his knees. Elayna felt for his hand and on finding it, held it. He did not try to pull away this time, in this darkness. He needed to know that he still had her. Elayna thought sadly of all the losses Orrat had known in his young life. She sensed that of late he had begun to trust again, to think the sad times were finally over. He needed reassurance now that although they were only a small family of two, he was loved. With a sigh, she thought about the simple but good life they once had, and had lost so suddenly.

The space they were in was cramped. Orrat kept his knees bent because there was no room to stretch his legs. Elayna sat with her legs folded beneath her, her skirt tucked under. The place was damp and smelled of moldy hay and urine. Elayna felt insects crawling in her scalp, her hair now limp and stringy with filth. There were other bodies oppressively close, but there was no way to see what condition they were in or who they were. Small children were crying from fear and hunger. Elayna thought oddly of the pot she'd left simmering on the hearth. She thought of Caly sitting on the table watching as she prepared evenmeal. Caly's laughter rang bright and clear through her memories. Elayna wiped the tears away with the back of her hand.

She felt Orrat watching her in the dark and took his hand again, giving it a reassuring squeeze. They had each other...for this moment at least. Elayna's heart constricted as she thought of the likelihood that they could be separated; she held her brother's hand tighter.

There was no way to tell the time of day in the darkness. The Sentinels had taken anything they thought might be valuable. Their father's saber was gone. Lost. She felt for the leather thong and traced it until her fingers found the heartstone. She grasped it softly, thanking the goddess that she still had it. Then, in a moment of inspiration, she closed her eyes and began to recite the words her mother had taught her.

A glow started to spread around her and Orrat, and then gradually found its way to the center of their space. The sobbing lessened as others began to realize what was happening. When the glow brightened, they were able to see who had brought the light. Even this small glimmer was like sunlight in such complete and unrelenting darkness. Elayna could make out a few familiar faces now. They smiled their gratitude in the shadows. Here was someone of their own. Someone of the goddess to let them know all was not lost. The soft glow seemed to say there was always hope. How they loved their Elayna.

While Orrat was tolerated as a mischievous petty thief and a prankster, his sister was the healer. She was the soft and gentle beauty who helped to ease their pain, heal their sickness. She warned them of storms and drought, told them the best times to plant. As soon as they could walk after giving birth, the mothers of every new little Avoreedan took their children to Elayna to be blessed and to have her place her hands on the baby. From the power of the touch, Elayna could discern the child's disposition, its strengths and weaknesses. She had earned her village's respect and love, and they saw to it that she and Orrat always had fresh vegetables and skins and other staples. Now, she wished there was more she could do to help, but her position was just as precarious as theirs. All they could do was wait.

◻ ◻ ◻ ◻ ◻

Cydell rode her black stallion toward the training yard. There was a crispness in the air, a mild breeze that caught in the billows of her flowing black cloak. She wore a tailored linen shirt under the red Sentinel weapons harness across her chest, her short blade and saber clearly visible. The black riding leggings felt smooth against the sides of her saddle and sunlight glinted off of the impeccable shine of her high black boots. She barely acknowledged her attendants, or others who hailed her as she lost herself in the steady creaking of leather and the jingle of the stallion's bridle.

The gruesome business of the past two suns had put her in a very bad mood. She did not enjoy executing the disloyal. Fortunately, her investigation had revealed that there had been no true Sentinels involved in the slaughter. The leader of the uprising, Gorson, had been mysteriously killed en route to the mining colony before he could reveal any significant information.

Her own informants had reported back to her of the illegal slave auction the mercenaries had scheduled. This auction was to be the first stop for the unfortunate Avoreedans before being sold to the plains tribes, probably at much higher prices than the original owners would pay.

Cydell was furious at this news and had ordered the executions of several mercenaries captured by her own Sentinels during the raid. As the executions were carried out, a dark pall hung over the palace, and the usual lines of people waiting to see Cydell during her morning rides evaporated. Everyone feared for his head and wisely stayed out of her way. *It is just as well,* she thought darkly. *I am not in a very sunny frame of mind.*

She turned the precocious stallion into the training yard. Her Sentinels were going through their paces and she watched for a moment before calling out.

"Lysis! Bateez! Holett!" Her voice rang across the training yard. The young Sentinels she had summoned immediately stopped in their practice and jogged over to her. They were winded from the exertion of the exercises, but found the energy to bow their respect, so pleased to be singled out from their comrades. "Mount and fall in," she ordered in a strong voice, with a trace of a smile on her lips. They were so eager to please. She hoped they would never fall prey to greed. "We have business to attend to," she said briskly, then turned and rode out at a fast trot, not waiting for the young Sentinels to join her.

Orrat stood beside Elayna on the wooden platform, squinting into the harsh, mid-morning sun with fifteen others of his fellow Avoreedans. He was scared. He wanted to run. But he saw how his sister carried herself, with all of the pride their parents had instilled in them. So he also stood with his head high.

Elayna looked out into the crowd. Predictably, the wealthy from the surrounding countryside had turned out in force to purchase

Avoreedan slaves. Her anger at the Hya mounted, as she blamed her for their plight. Here she was, she and the few miserable survivors of Avoreed, lined up across the platform, exposed to the light rain that was falling. They were cold and hungry and terrified. Elayna, too, was dispirited. She looked at Orrat and noted the arrogant lift of his chin. He caught her eye and she read his fears. If only they would not be separated.

The auctioneer was a stooped old man whose clothes were no cleaner than those of his captives. He organized the proceedings with a sense of his own importance, briskly shouting out orders and positioning his captives just so on the platform, so as to best please his potential customers. The crowd was steadily growing. Everyone was anxious for the sale to begin.

Elayna sensed the heat of someone's stare out in the crowd. As she scanned the many wagons and mounts, her eyes met the familiar face of the young stranger who had come to her cottage asking for her. Their eyes locked. She knew his intention was to buy her. She also sensed his desperation, sensed that he *had* to buy her. He gazed at her steadily, but it was as though he were watching her through someone else's eyes. The heartstone which hung between her breasts was growing warm, almost hot, but she did not raise a hand to hold it away from her skin. She couldn't move. She couldn't look away from those hypnotic eyes.

The bidding had begun and Elayna realized suddenly that they were bidding on her. There was an old woman dressed in silk robes bidding from her seat in her elaborately decorated coach. Elayna knew what she had in mind for her, for there was a group of three girls surrounding the old woman. They looked tired and worn. Their clothes were nice, in a cheap way, and they sauntered through the crowd, boldly eyeing the men, not interested in the auction at all. Clearly, they were drumming up business for later.

Several men of varying ages began actively bidding for her as well. And of course, the young stranger with the dark eyes was in the running. He had never taken his eyes off her. As the price rose, some of the bidders conceded to those who obviously had enough onas to continue bidding. The dark stranger never faltered. He met every price and raised it.

Elayna's heart began to thump in her chest. She sensed Orrat's anxiety and knew that he was on the verge of crying out. They were going to be separated. They would never see each other again. The bidding continued. Orrat was becoming more agitated. It had to stop before the boy did something that would probably get both of them beaten to death.

"Sold!" the auctioneer shouted, grinning with satisfaction. Never in his wildest dreams had he thought the fair beauty would bring so much. With authority, he pointed to the young man in black, and the stranger stepped forward.

Orrat could not contain himself any longer. He grabbed Elayna in an embrace and held her tight. This brought uproarious laughter from the crowd. Some even threw half-eaten fruit and horse dung onto the platform to express their displeasure at such a show of weakness. But Elayna held him and let her tears fall. It seemed even Dornea had deserted them.

Suddenly a hush fell over the crowd. The only sounds were those of horses' hooves on the packed dirt of the road. All looked up in wonder as four riders made their way to the front of the platform. Immediately, Elayna knew who the leader was. Although she had never in her life seen the Hya, Cydell Ra Sadiin, she had heard about her. Finally—here was the woman who was the cause of all of their present misery, the one responsible for Caly's death. Her heart burned with hatred as she held Orrat's hand.

He watched, wide-eyed and awed at finally meeting the Hya, too awestruck to share the anger and hate his sister felt. He had never seen a figure so grand, so commanding. He knew the two men and the one woman who accompanied her must be Sentinels, though they were not in uniform. There was no mistaking their intent, for their sabers were drawn and at the ready. Elayna looked at the auctioneer. He could only stare, mortified, knowing he had no defense. He also knew these were the last seconds of his life.

As though acknowledging some silent command, the assemblage fell to their knees, heads bowed. The Hya rode her horse into the midst of the silent crowd and directly up to the auctioneer. She did not dismount. Her voice blasted the quiet like an explosion.

"Who is in charge of this auction!?" she thundered, gazing into the auctioneer's paling face.

"I only follow orders, Hya," he mumbled, almost stumbling over his own feet. Her gaze remained stony.

"Whose orders? I ordered no auction. I was not aware that there were slaves being held here. From whence did these slaves come?" The Hya did not give him a chance to answer. "Are these by chance Avoreedan slaves? How can that be?" she shrugged in mock bewilderment. "I did not declare war on Avoreed. I have no quarrel with Avoreed. Why have we suddenly all of these Avoreedan slaves?" Her gesture encompassed Elayna and all of the prisoners on the block. Elayna could almost hear the auctioneer's sweat drip onto the platform in the silence. But she was confused by what the Hya was saying. Had she, or had she not, ordered the raid on Avoreed?

The Hya dismounted impatiently and handed the reins to one of her Sentinels. Her thigh-high boots thumped as she ascended the platform. Elayna was spellbound. Never in her life had she thought she would be in such close proximity to their sovereign. The Hya was not a monster as she had imagined. In fact, she was a striking woman of impressive stature. The face was the color of lightly creamed marin, the eyebrows scrutinizingly arched over large hazel eyes and long thick lashes. Her mouth was set with the irritation of the moment. The snug riding pants hugged her well-muscled buttocks and thighs.

She paused directly in front of Elayna and Orrat and lightly touched Elayna's shoulder. It was the signal to rise and Elayna stood up tall. Now they were almost eye to eye. Elayna was determined not to show her own uncertainty by looking away. She would face Caly's killer squarely and not be afraid.

"Are you of Avoreed?" she asked Elayna while at the same time marveling at the fairness of the young woman.

"Yes." Elayna's answer was surprisingly audible.

"And the others?" she asked. With that question, a chorus of strong affirmatives rang from the platform, weak though the people were. The Hya signaled to one of the Sentinels, who immediately dismounted. "Unshackle these people. Take them to the temple for medical care and then to the refectory and the stores for clothes and food."

The Sentinels took the key from the auctioneer and began to undo the leg shackles. A murmur went through the crowd. Some had sought to sneak away, but a mounted Sentinel blocked their escape in all directions.

The Hya remained in front of Elayna as the Sentinels unlocked the last of the shackles. They commandeered one of the wagons and began to move the villagers toward the refectory. She turned a dark eye on the auctioneer.

"Are there more?" she demanded. The old man pointed a shaky finger toward three rows of sheds just behind the platform.

"Release them!" she ordered.

The old man started away and the Hya indicated that one of the Sentinels accompany him. She turned to the crowd and addressed them.

"Return to your homes. Save your onas for another time. No one in Mauldar will own Avoreedan slaves. Ever."

Those gathered wasted no time mounting, returning to their wagons and leaving the scene. They realized how fortunate they were to have escaped without being arrested. Only the dark young stranger lingered behind, and after some time, with one last glare at Elayna, he, too, rode away.

Finally, the auctioneer was arrested, becoming in his turn, a prisoner, a captive. At this point, Elayna and Orrat were the last two villagers left on the platform. For a moment, the Hya seemed to be leagues away from what was taking place around her and they wondered if they should go with the others or wait to be dismissed.

At last she looked again at the young woman and saw the strength in her eyes. Such beautiful eyes. She then looked at the boy. He seemed sturdy enough, with the same defiance as the young woman. Abruptly, the Hya turned and left the platform.

"Bring the boy!" she tossed over her shoulder.

The Hya mounted her prancing stallion, and with one last look at Elayna, alone on the platform, added, "Bring her as well," and she rode away toward the palace.

◻ ◻ ◻ ◻ ◻

"Shit!" Valkyra swore as she paced back and forth, kicking up dust in front of the mouth of the cave that served as her private camp outside the oppressive walls of Mauldar. It was here that her steadily growing band of mercenaries made their camp, well hidden in the caves at the foothills of the Mauldaran Mountains.

Pak Alesis stood patiently, his massive arms crossed on his barrel chest, waiting for his captain to finish her tirade. In some ways, he enjoyed just watching the tall, shapely woman marching back and forth before him. Dressed only in a mail shirt and tight black leggings and boots, she was surely a sight to set a lonely mercenary's desires aflame.

"How did she know about the auction?!" Valkyra got command of her temper and shot an accusatory glare at her second-in-command. Pak scratched the stiff, scraggly overgrowth of beard and shrugged.

"No one looks forward to a lifetime of hard labor in the lathium mines. I know not of one man who does not favor freedom to a death there." He looked warily at his captain before he continued, "You were warned beforehand that Avoreed was too close. That there would not be enough time before the Sentinels..."

Valkyra backhanded Pak across the face. The big man reeled back a step, his visage darkening as he eyed the seething woman. The men milling around the camp looked up and then quickly away. Pak would not dare retaliate against Valkyra. The renegade Sentinel Commander General was a ferocious fighter, with or without her saber, and would not hesitate to kill any one of them. Besides, he thought calculatingly, the raids had been very profitable for everyone, until now, and there were still plenty of villages in the region yet untapped. The mercenary army was growing with every sun, and the men held dreams of being a part of the mighty army that would finally vanquish the Hya. Pak and the rest of the men would take their punishment in exchange for all the lathium bars yet to be theirs.

"When I want your advice, I will beat it out of you!" she spat at Pak in her frustration. To the rest of the men she shouted, "Meet here again in four suns. We shall plan our next campaign then. In the meantime, return to Mauldar. If you see or hear of anyone talking too much about the raid, kill them. This includes your own dear comrades." She eyed each man intensely as she continued, "The Hya has spies everywhere. Everywhere. Watch your backs."

Her gaze encompassed the camp and she noted an imitation Sentinel mask that had been tossed into a stand of trees.

"Get rid of that thing!"

Valkyra walked briskly to her mount and swung up into the saddle with one last look at Pak, who stood holding the reins for her.

"If I am needed, you know where to contact me," she snapped. Roughly, she snatched the reins away from Pak, spun the horse around, and galloped off in the direction of Mauldar.

"Yes," Pak mumbled under his breath, "in the Hya's bed."

◻ ◻ ◻ ◻ ◻

Later that evenfall, Cydell stood in front of the fireplace staring into the flames. The lygen she was sipping tasted good, but what she really needed was sleep. Not yet, however. There was still one more matter to be resolved before she could retire. She had asked that the young Avoreedan woman be brought to her. The boy had been warded to the Sentinels. He was of age, and when she had asked him what he thought about the possibility of becoming a Sentinel, he had jumped at the chance. Cydell admired the boy's boldness in speaking to her. It was refreshing not to be cowered to, especially by one so young. But before agreeing, he had secured Cydell's assurance that his sister would be safe. Touched at his obvious love for his sister, she had given him her promise.

Cydell was not looking forward to this audience. It was plain from the look in the young woman's eyes that she held Cydell personally responsible for the destruction of Avoreed. Cydell wondered if the woman had lost anyone in the raid. If so, who? A mate perhaps?

She finished the last drop of lygen just as there was a knock on the study door.

"Come," she answered.

Cydell's personal attendant, Josn, entered and went through the motions of a bow. Josn was so old, no one really knew the exact number of Passes she had been alive, and when asked, she only smiled her toothless smile and went on her way. Cydell marveled at how Josn moved so quickly all about the palace as she performed her duties. It was hard to keep track of her, but she was always there when Cydell needed her. Josn had attended Cydell since the Hya's first breath, as she had attended Cydell's father and his father before him. The lines and creases in the old nurse's face were deeply etched. Her brows were sparse, as was her silver white hair, but the eyes were still bright and the mind was alert, even if the short body was round and stooped. But what most amazed Cydell about Josn were her hands. The hands she remembered holding her, comforting her when she was a child, were the same. Exactly the same. Young hands. No age marks. No lines. Josn's hands looked younger than Cydell's. She had always wondered about this strange phenomenon, but somehow never asked.

Now Josn stood before Cydell in her thick skirts, worn slippers and clean white apron. The woman should have been asleep long ago.

"I have brought the girl," she announced matter-of-factly. She rarely, if ever, addressed Cydell as Hya. Cydell had to remind Josn, when dignitaries were expected, to please use the proper form of address. Otherwise, the old nurse usually forgot, but Cydell didn't really mind. She and Josn were as the moon and the tide. One always affected the other. Always had. And it would always be so.

"Send her in." Cydell sat at her desk and waited.

Josn neared the door but did not go out to get Elayna. Instead, she looked at Cydell and Cydell cocked an eyebrow in a silent question. "Be mindful," Josn whispered loudly.

"Mindful of what?" Cydell was already tired and irritated and did not have time for guessing games.

"This girl is not of the ordinary vein."

"Oh? Why not?"

"She is one with the goddess. There is a power about her."

Cydell noted the reverence in the nurse's voice. Apparently, Josn truly believed the girl was connected with the goddess of the old religion, the old faith. There were still those who remembered and practiced their faith freely. Personally, Cydell did not put much store in it. She only knew that fear of the gods kept her people humble, most of them, and out of trouble.

"I care not about her beliefs," Cydell said. "As long as she does not disrupt my household with them. Send her in if you would, and enough prattle." Cydell tried to sound stern, but she smiled when Josn waved a hand at her and left to bring the young woman. In the brief moment before she entered, Cydell lit an herbstick and inhaled deeply. Almost instantly, she could feel her muscles begin unbinding. Now that she thought of it, she should have asked Josn to bring more lygen. She needed to relax.

Elayna stood in silence and looked about the room. Its size threatened to engulf her, but she liked the smell of freshly polished woods. Her eyes roved to a wall shelf filled with bound ledgers and parchments. Beside it she noticed a glass casing that was almost as tall as she was. It exhibited delicate glass figurines of all shapes and sizes. She wanted to examine the glass pieces further, but remembered she was before the Hya.

Cydell studied the young woman in silence. She was not of Avoreedan decent. Lyftonese, most likely, for they were the fairest people in the region. She had to admit that the young woman was breathtaking.

Elayna had been given good clean clothes to wear. Her hair had been washed and brushed until it shone in the candlelight of the study. It fell around her shoulders like a golden cloud. Cydell knew the girl was exhausted so she shook off her own imminent fatigue and began the interview.

"What is your name?" Cydell asked brusquely, sounding much harsher than she had intended.

"Elayna Ahn-Audaan, Hya," Elayna answered. The name and the voice which spoke it rolled around and around in Cydell's mind. To shake off the distraction of the beauty of the woman, Cydell rose and walked slowly to the front of the desk and sat one-hipped on the edge. Elayna did not back away from the Hya's closeness. *That defiance again.*

"You hate me, do you not?" Cydell asked softly, feeling the soothing effects of the lygen. Given another time and more pleasant circumstance...

"I do not know you, Hya." Elayna answered softly. Cydell nodded. *A wise response.*

"I did not order the raid on Avoreed. But have no worries. Those responsible have been dealt with." Cydell sounded almost apologetic.

"That is reassuring, Hya. But..." Elayna started but stopped herself. She had to remember to whom it was she was speaking. The Hya looked at her.

"Continue," she ordered.

"But such reassurance cannot restore my village or the lives of my...friends." Elayna thought of Caly and felt her sorrow and anger mounting.

"Yes. That is unfortunate. But you are alive. Which brings us to the matter of what to do with you."

"You are Hya. You may do as you wish." The two women's eyes met.

"I realize that is my option, Elayna Ahn-Audaan. I would like to give you a choice, as I did with your brother."

Elayna tensed. "What have you done with Orrat?"

"He is safe, as he wished you to be. I promised to be mindful of your care, and I shall be. Young Orrat is quite brave. He will make an excellent Sentinel." Cydell went back around the desk and sat. "Have you decided yet what you would like your fate to be?"

"It matters not as long as I can be near my brother."

Elayna tried to mask the anger she felt for the woman before her. It was obvious she was trying to make amends for her misdeeds by offering the homeless Avoreedans a choice. But in fact, they had no choice. Elayna knew that she was as much a prisoner in the palace as she had been on the auction block.

Cydell watched Elayna and thought about what Josn had told her. *If she has so much power,* Cydell thought, *why does she not fly out of the window?* A smile played on her lips.

"Why do you look at me that way?" Elayna asked during the quiet pause, and brought Cydell back to the present. *Damn the herbstick!*

"I am told you have some sort of...sorcery."

"It is not sorcery. My parents were of the old beliefs, as am I."

Cydell nodded. "I see. You believe strongly in your goddess?" she asked mockingly.

"Yes, Hya."

"And I assume you would give your life in service to this goddess?" Elayna knew that the Hya was leading around to something simply by the tone of her questions. She put herself on guard.

"I would, Hya," she answered. Cydell leaned forward and propped her elbows on the desk.

"Then why would this goddess allow you to be captured, your fate decided by the whims of mere mortals?"

Elayna looked the Hya in the eye. Her dislike of this woman was apparently justified.

"Was it Dornea who willed you to attack Avoreed?" she asked simply. "To kill all of those innocent people?" *And my Caly,* she thought.

"I have told you that was not my doing! Will you not believe that?" The Hya was on her feet again, angry.

"Is it so important that I believe it?" Elayna fired back.

Cydell thought a moment before she spoke. "No. In fact, it is not. And mind your tongue," she warned, almost as an afterthought.

"You goad me to anger and then expect me not to show it. Does the Hya treat all of her prisoners this way? With so little regard?"

Cydell was not used to being questioned, to being asked to explain herself. She was used to unconditional obedience.

"I could have you disciplined for your insolence," she said ominously. "Would your goddess save you from that?" She walked over to the mantle, placing one booted foot on the stones of the fireplace.

"Does the Hya believe in anything besides her own authority?" Elayna asked sweetly. Cydell held up a warning finger.

"Mind yourself. My patience is wearing very thin this evenfall. I have half a mind to arrange for you to meet your goddess face to face." Elayna swallowed and tried to restrain a retort.

"I believe," Cydell continued, "that Dornea guides the hand of the ruler to lead and provide for the people. Dornea gives the ruler wisdom. The wisdom of a god. Not perfect. Just as the gods, unfortunately, are not perfect." She looked into the very green eyes. "What is it your goddess gives to you?" she asked.

"The courage not to be intimidated by those who would rule me," Elayna answered.

"Yes. One would need much courage to stand before the executioner," Cydell watched Elayna closely, "or to work one's life away in the darkness of the mines."

"If that is your will for me," Elayna agreed softly.

"My will is to turn you over to Josn. She will instruct you as to the running of the palace. Teach you a skill, perhaps."

"Then I am indeed a prisoner," Elayna sighed, finally speaking her thoughts.

"Your options are limited. I cannot very well turn you out into the streets of Mauldar. You have not an ona to your name. There are elements in the city who would devour you before you'd gone a league from the palace. But...I suppose your goddess would protect you from such treachery."

"As she will protect me from you," Elayna replied stubbornly.

"Be that as it may, I am not willing to trust the goddess to undo the damage done to Avoreed. I shall rebuild Avoreed, though it will not be done in a turn, not even in a Pass. But it will be done."

So saying, Cydell pulled the long gold rope that hung beside the wall shelves. Josn entered immediately. Cydell smiled, knowing the old nurse had been listening outside the doors.

"Find quarters for our...guest. She shall be in your charge," Cydell looked at Elayna again. "I hope this pleases your goddess."

"It is her will," Elayna answered quietly. Josn indicated the door and Elayna turned to follow her. She stopped in the doorway and turned back to face the Hya. The dark woman was watching her with a strange expression in her eyes.

"Hya?"

"Yes?"

"Thank you for the care of my brother." Elayna meant it. However, the Hya's kindness toward Orrat did not lessen her own dislike of the woman. Cydell did not answer but waved a hand in dismissal, looking up only after the doors closed.

Rosewater. The scent lulled Cydell as she slowly closed the door of her inner bedchamber. The many candles gave the chamber a warmth and a glow that Cydell looked forward to at the end of a long sun. There were no windows in the chamber, although there were two in the outer suite.

This room was Cydell's haven. There was a small desk heaped with parchments in the far right corner. Not grain orders or dock schedules, but the writings of a moonwatcher she had chanced to meet in CoDach some Passes ago. Cydell found that she liked the woman's words and had pleaded with the moonwatcher to send her work to Cydell at the palace. Wrapped in Cydell's arms after making love, the moonwatcher had promised that she would.

Josn always placed fresh roses in Cydell's chamber, for she knew how much the Hya loved those particular flowers. The nurse had somehow found an endless supply. There had been fresh roses every night for as long as Cydell could remember.

Her eyes traveled to the immense wall hanging. Two nymphs in a wood. Teasing each other by a pond. Gold thread outlined the bodies, the trees, the birds and insects in the trees. Shades of green, deep blues, whites and rusts soothed the tension away as the Hya undressed and slipped naked between the bedclothes of white satin. The dim light from the fireplace bathed her consciousness and she felt herself drifting. In the light slumber, Cydell saw herself as a child running through the gardens of the palace, her mother in close pursuit. She saw her mother's face, so radiant in the sunlight; her mother's arms enfolded her, holding her close. And then there was the tall, strapping girl walking through the yard with her father and listening attentively as he instructed her, pointing out certain tactics of the Sentinels at practice. At that point, the dreams faded and she shifted, ready for a deeper sleep.

After a while, she heard the click of the lock being turned. The small door that led down to the kitchens opened and the intruder entered, treading softly. She smiled drowsily in anticipation. She had been taught to sleep lightly, and as weary as she was, the whisper of clothing being removed and the light creaking of the wood floors woke desires that had gone unanswered for almost three turns. The shadow climbed in beside her and gently blew warm breath into her ear. That tingling sensation thrilled the Hya all over and she turned and moved above the red haired Commander General. The two women kissed playfully. Sleep would yet again be delayed.

"You make the noise of a thousand soldiers, Commander," Cydell teased, whispering softly, biting the woman's earlobe and moving down to nudge her face in the valley of Valkyra's breasts. Valkyra laughed, a sound that came up from her depths, as Cydell tickled her navel with her tongue and traced a line back up to her lips. "My Commander is losing her touch."

Valkyra shifted and the two women wrestled playfully, rolling around on the wide bed. Cydell admired the suppleness of Valkyra's long body. The woman beneath her was her best fighting Sentinel. She had seen her battle five enemies at once and emerge without so much as a scratch. Valkyra only allowed herself a lover's surrender. And that only to Cydell.

"Just be certain you do not lose *your* touch!" the redheaded fighting machine whispered breathlessly as Cydell pinned the Commander with her body, then raised both arms above her head. Cydell captured one of Valkyra's thighs between her knees. The Commander raised her pelvis in a halfhearted effort to free herself. The movement against Cydell's thigh brought a sigh to Valkyra's lips and she moved more deliberately. Slowly, to match Cydell. Cydell gently caught a taut nipple in her teeth, encircling it with her tongue, first one and then the other. Soon the chamber was filled with the sounds of passion as both women became lost in the glory of fulfillment long overdue. Their rhythm set the candle flames to dance, such sweet fire.

Valkyra palmed lazy circles on Cydell's flat belly and entwined one slim finger in the delicate gold chain that encircled her waist. They lay nestled against each other, fires of passion cooling to embers. After such wonderful exertion, Cydell was beyond conversation. But she knew Valkyra was a talker. Ever the chatterhen even after lovemaking. So she closed her eyes and waited for Valkyra to begin.

Valkyra's thoughts drifted to the events of the past few suns. That day, throughout the city, the talk had been about the illegal auction and the Avoreedan refugees. One refugee in particular was on Valkyra's mind. One they called the Fair Witch. Rumor had reached the Commander about the green-eyed beauty who was among the Avoreedans. Valkyra knew her lover, her Hya. She was told the woman had been brought to Cydell for a private audience and wondered if the witch's first audience with the Hya had ended like her own.

"Cydell?" she whispered in the Hya's ear.

"Yes?" From the tone of Valkyra's voice Cydell knew what was coming. The palace had many ears and eyes and Valkyra had her own loyal following; those who reported everything and everyone that captured the Hya's interest.

"You had an audience this evenfall?"

"I have had many audiences this evenfall."

Cydell turned over onto her side, feigning sleepiness. Valkyra was immediately at her back, leaning over her. Long red tendrils fell over Cydell's face. Cydell brushed them away.

"An audience with a woman. An Avoreedan woman," Valkyra prodded. "Elayna. Yes?" There was silence. Cydell did not like jealousy. The Commander General was careful to pose her questions gently, but her curiosity had to be satisfied.

"They say she is very beautiful."

"Yes." Another silence.

A different tactic was needed. "Will you send her to the mines? I cannot think what she would do here in the palace."

Valkyra was sitting up now, staring blankly into the candle flames. Already she felt as though Cydell had pushed her away to make room for the Avoreedan witch. However, Valkyra's sudden curiosity and jealousy did not disturb Cydell. She could no longer stop herself from surrendering to the groggy weariness that was finally claiming her.

"Please, Valkyra," Cydell mumbled, wanting to sleep. Whatever the Commander's worries, they would keep until the morn. The Commander leaned over Cydell again.

"One more question?" Cydell moaned and shifted irritably. Her next lover, she promised herself, would be a mute.

"Do you find her desirable?"

"Yes. That is why *you* are here asking silly questions, instead of *her*. No more!" Cydell determinedly settled herself into sleep. Valkyra sat up for some time in the shadows of the flickering flames. This Fair Sorceress of Avoreed would not be the one to take the Hya away from her. She would make sure of that.

3

MAULDAR

Sylvan was on the Sydonian continent, which covered eighty-five percent of the planet surface of Brevyk IV. It was the largest of three continents on the planet, the other two being Croxas, across the seas to the west, and DiMeer, the vast ice country to the north. The three continents were remote unto themselves, with their own individual issues to attend to. Brevyk IV, being of no strategic military importance to any of the more technically advanced planets in the remote Pralynian system, was, for the most part, left alone to develop and advance, generation by plodding generation, into the technical age of warp drives and hyperspace. It seemed that the inhabitants of Sylvan, on the planet Brevyk IV, were in no particular hurry to begin exploring the wonders of their own galaxy. Their heavens were ruled by the gods; their lives were ruled by the Hya; and they were quite pleased with their world as it was.

Though now prosperous under the current Hya, the region and the city of Mauldar had been ravaged during the Tribal Wars of twenty Passes ago. Barbaric tribes from the north had joined forces with the plains tribes to conquer the great city and the surrounding provinces. The war had seemed interminable and many hundreds of thousands of lives had been lost before a peace treaty had been signed. But finally, a lasting peace had been achieved, and now goods flowed freely from Mauldar to all of the tribes, while craftspeople journeyed from province to province. It was during the time of reconstruction, after the war, that the great city walls were built around Mauldar's perimeter—the High Provincial Council's hope of thwarting any future devastating attacks.

It had been many Passes since a chieftain looked down from the mountains or across the plains and desired to conquer the vastness and prosperity that was Mauldar. Peace treaties and the highly trained Sentinel Guard, in addition to the Mauldaran regular army, were great deterrents to war.

The hard-won peace lasted in spite of the fact that each province was unique unto itself in language, culture, and in the products that each produced. Eastward, beyond the mountain ranges, was Rabelle, a seaport province which exported fish and oils, and in turn received fruit and vegetables from CoDach, woolens and silks from Saven, and poultry, beef and pork from Tyroda.

The capital city of Mauldar in the province of Mauldarach was the hub of regional activity. It was the center of social and cultural achievement, and the place where judicial and political decisions of great import were made. The surrounding provinces of Saven, CoDach, Rabelle and Tyroda were as satellites to Mauldar.

The city teemed with life from sunup to sunset. And the Mauldaran roadway leading into the city gates was always crowded with caravans, merchant wagons and grand coaches. There was a steady influx of newcomers, from thieves to wanderers to aristocrats; from old warriors to young men and women just starting out to seek their fortunes. Craftspeople flocked into the already overcrowded city to apprentice at the many guild houses. Artists, dancers, poets and singers honed their talents in the busy marketplace in hopes of being discovered by a wealthy patron. The numerous taverns hosted weary travelers—adventurers and warriors who sat at ale-stained tables in the great hearthrooms, spinning tales of heroic deeds, bloody battles and wild sorcery.

The palace of Mauldar rose in the center of the city like one tall, lone blossom in the plains. Five crystal spires reached skyward and marked for leagues the center of the capital. The palace compound itself was gargantuan—a city within the city. There were separate barracks which housed the Mauldaran army, numbering over fifteen thousand men and women. They were posted equally among the provinces. Finally, there was the Sentinel Guard of a thousand specially trained women and men, who were the Hya's personal guard, also stationed throughout the provinces. These two fighting forces did not include the intricate network of two thousand archer scouts, who were discreetly dispersed throughout the territory.

The palace stables boasted over a thousand of the finest horses. The immense gardens were maintained by the most highly skilled gardeners, and when the wind blew just right, the strong, sweet scent of rose and lilac wafted into the marketplace. Only certain vendors were granted permission to come within the palace walls to hawk their wares to the cooks and seamstresses and ironsmiths and leatherworkers who saw to the needs of the Hya and her staff.

The training field was adjacent to the soldiers' quarters and the two refectories, where the soldiers ate. At all hours of the day one could hear the apprentices and Sentinels shouting in mock combat and crying in pain from the wound unintentionally inflicted by an overzealous opponent. The training field was surrounded by hundreds of feet of railing. Practice dummies made of grain bags stuffed with cloth hung on roughly made wooden stands. They were like a permanent army within the confines of the fence—always ready but never defeated.

On this particular day, the sun made a spectacular appearance after the cloudy misery of the past few days. Merchants lined the walkways and hawked their goods with enthusiasm. The streets were alive with activity, with the sounds of laughter, gossip, children yowling, merchants swearing. The jostle of horses and wagons and carriages in the crowded thoroughfare made it almost impossible to pass anyone or to get to the booth of your choice. Small children ran carefree through the winding lanes and darted in and out and around the slow-moving human traffic.

It was Cydell's habit, frequently, to ride through the marketplace in the morning, and see for herself how her people were faring. Mauldarans were comforted by the sight of their ruler out among them. She was approachable as no other Hya had been. Even children were not afraid of her, and often she would toss onas and sweets to them as she passed. Old women ventured forward on those mornings and placed flowers in the mane of the young black stallion she rode. They gave her loaves of freshly baked breads and sweet rolls, for they knew of the Hya's infamous sweet tooth.

By the same token, fathers would shoo their lovely daughters inside and away from the Hya's discerning eye. As much as they loved their Hya, they preferred their daughters married to a young nobleman, rather than bedded for a turn or a Pass by the Hya, and then turned out, changed and spoiled, spurning all men who wanted their attentions. Although there were more wealthy women than men, the men held the titles. And a good title was worth more than a mating with a wealthy matron. Of course, if one could have both, all the better.

The sexual mores of the time were liberal. Women and men could mate with whomever of whatever gender they pleased, as long as households which demanded strong heirs to continue their lines had them. There were more and more matriarchal households, since women could sire, as well as conceive children. This oftentimes left the irate father of an unclaimed and pregnant daughter railing after a womanizing stableboy or a wandering swordswoman.

Cydell never had a guard accompany her in the mornings. There was no one, unless they were new to the city or a foreigner, who would dare challenge the Hya, even as she rode alone. As for her own people, they would think very carefully before committing a crime, for the punishment would be swift and terrible—a lifetime of servitude in the lathium mines. And so, even though the High Provincial Council chided her endlessly for her apparent carelessness, she scoffed at their fears, and continued her solitary morning rides. She was not going to give up her time to herself, her time to be with her people.

This particular morning rose fair and bright. It would be a good sun. Especially after all the morbid business of the past several suns. She felt rested and sated, thanks to Valkyra, her passionate Sentinel Commander General. It felt good to be out in the sunlight, riding at her leisure. The warm sun reflected off her simple white shirt that was opened at the neck, with the sleeves rolled up her forearms. Her black riding pants were embroidered along the sides with a pattern of tiny flowers. And her fine leather boots gleamed, for the stable attendants always made sure her boots shone and her tack was polished as though they were new. Her saber was strapped to her left side, blade newly sharpened.

Cydell felt wonderfully alive and vibrant. She teased the merchants she knew and sampled their goods as they brought them to her side, holding the cloth or fruit or bottled wine up for her inspection. If she had bought all they offered, there would have been no way to carry it all back with her to the palace. Her habit was to send a courier from the palace back to the merchants to pick up her purchases.

Finally, several hours later, she turned the sleek stallion in the direction of the training yard. There was something she had to deliver, as promised.

❏ ❏ ❏ ❏ ❏

Orrat stood at attention, or he would have been at full attention if not for the horsefly buzzing around his face. He tried to blow it away because he knew he should not move his arms to swat it away. But the blast of air he blew upward only lifted his bangs. His first morning as a Sentinel ward and he had already learned about protocol. Fourth in the line of twenty wards, the fair-haired Avoreedan stood out from the crowd of darker, taller boys his age. But none of them had his stocky, well-muscled build. And none of them had his sense of mischief. The boy to the left of Orrat was trying not to giggle as he watched his new friend out of the corner of his eye. Orrat's blond bangs would go up and down at intervals. It looked funny, but this was not the time to laugh. Not when they were in the middle of their first inspection.

The Commander General walked slowly along the line of young boys, inspecting each one. Those who did not meet with her approval were assigned some unpleasant task in the refectory and ordered to polish the boots of an entire barrack. There were girls in the line, as well, and their penalties were no less severe.

Valkyra strolled down the line. She wore training leggings that fit the contours of her body snugly, and thigh-high boots which were polished to perfection. The sleeveless cotton tunic was crossed with a leather harness and a wide belt at the waist, from which hung a short knife. Her saber hung at her left side, in the scabbard worn only by a Commander General of the Sentinels. It was every ward's dream to one day own the ornate belt and the saber that went with it.

When Orrat's bangs shot up again, his friend Rii could not contain himself any longer. The giggle was just loud enough for Valkyra to hear, and she took her time as she made her way down the line, finally stopping in front of the two boys. Orrat tensed. Perhaps it was best to let the fly land where it would. Unfortunately, he had come to this conclusion too late.

Valkyra looked from Orrat to Rii and back to Orrat. Sentinels perched on the fence were snickering and nudging each other in the tense quiet. Orrat knew he was doomed.

"Do you not know what attention means, young Orrat?" Valkyra asked between clenched teeth. Orrat was amazed she knew his name. The Commander made it her business to know the names of all wards, especially those from Avoreed. Particularly those who reportedly had beautiful sisters. She eyed the boy intensely. If this was the family resemblance, the sister must be a beauty indeed.

"Yes, sir...um...Commander!" Orrat managed to blurt out after an eternity.

"Perhaps you and young Rii here will know the meaning better after fifty chin touches."

"But..." Orrat began. The Commander General moved in so close to him that he could see the yellow flecks in her eyes, feel the warmth of her breath. Rii was already on his palms and toes, body prone, touching his chin to the dirt.

"Something more, ward?" The words stabbed at him in a harsh staccato.

"No, Commander!" Orrat hit the ground so fast he almost hit his chin. Valkyra knelt in front of him and grabbed a handful of blond hair. He could not help but look into her unsmiling face.

"If this lack of discipline occurs once more, ward, I will personally feed you a meal of horseflies. Is that understood?"

Orrat was trembling with the strain of holding his body weight on his toes and hands.

"Yes, Commander!" he shouted.

Valkyra rose, satisfied. "Fine. Proceed."

Orrat was going down for the tenth time when a familiar voice called his name. He ignored the summons. Seventeen. Eighteen. Nineteen. The Commander's feet paused before him again. Now what?

"Cease!" she barked. Orrat fell flat in the dust, his elbows bent, looking like a blond grasshopper. Rii quickened his own pace so as not to lose control and laugh at his friend again.

"Always answer a summons from your Hya, ward." Valkyra brought Orrat to his feet by his hair. The young boy did not flinch. *The Hya? What could the Hya want with me?*

Cydell, who had been standing by, watching, stifled her own urge to laugh at Orrat's antics. At least, she thought, the boy had a sense of humor. Unlike his sister. But Valkyra's handling of the boy bothered her. Though she was Hya, she never questioned the training techniques used in the training yard, for they achieved the desired results. Better not to favor the boy any more than she was going to already.

It had taken some doing, but the Watch Captain, after many inquiries and dead-ends, had found the boy's saber. A reward had been offered and the word had spread through the marketplace. Finally, a merchant had come forward with the prize.

Orrat bowed and looked up at Cydell. His face was covered with dust and his clothes were twice as filthy. But he sensed that what mattered was that he gave her the proper respect.

"Yes, Hya?"

"The other part of our bargain," Cydell said as she ceremoniously presented him with his father's saber. Orrat was speechless as he reverently accepted it from her. He looked up at the Hya as a single tear streaked his cheek. "By the time you leave this training yard," Cydell was saying, "you will have learned how to keep hold of your weapon."

"Yes, Hya."

"You may go and join the others, now." Cydell turned the stallion and rode for the palace stable. It was only when Orrat started to strap the weapon around his waist that he noticed the new leather of the belt.

Elayna fared no better in the kitchens than Orrat had on his first day in the yard. Josn had gotten her up before sunlight and hurried her down to the kitchens to begin the day. She had barely had time to splash water on her face and don the new skirts the old nurse brought to her. Her chamber, if it could be called such, was tiny. Plain gray walls and room only for a washstand, a small table and a cot. The only thing that kept the little place from being a cell was the window which looked down into the courtyard of the stables.

The kitchen was already bustling with activity. Large iron pots hung above the fires that were constantly burning. Two of the three wooden tables in the center of the massive room were loaded to overflowing with a mouth-watering assortment of roasted meats and breads and fruit. A rail-thin woman was shouting orders to the rest of the serving girls and Elayna had to step aside several times to avoid being bumped. Two old women sat on stools in front of an open window shelling peas and cackling to themselves. They stole glances at Elayna and nudged each other, keeping their secrets between them.

Josn took Elayna gently by the arm and sat her down at the third table while she looked around in the midst of the confusion for something to give the girl for morning meal. Cheese, bread and fruit miraculously appeared before Elayna. She ate with relish, not realizing until that moment how famished she was. She had just finished the last bit of cheese when Josn took her by the arm and hurried her down a corridor away from the kitchen. At the end of it, she lifted the wooden bar from its cradle and swung the little door open wide.

"Be mindful of the steps," she warned and was down them before Elayna could ask any questions.

The only light in the dimness of the cellar was coming in through the row of small windows high up in the walls. Sunlight streamed in to reveal bins of vegetables, vast shelves of wines and sacks of the fine Soluman beans used to make marin. Josn knotted her apron and began to fill it with fresh vegetables and a few select fruits. When she looked pointedly at Elayna, Elayna did the same.

The old nurse had been the only person to show her any sort of kindness, and Elayna desperately wanted to ask her questions about the running of the palace. But Josn started talking before she could work up the courage to speak.

"You are all the talk this morn," she announced, not once taking her eyes off her bin.

"Am I?" Elayna really hadn't heard a thing, but then, no one was speaking to her anyway. "What have I done to deserve such an honor?" Josn moved to another bin. Elayna was trying to figure out how the old woman selected her fruit so quickly. Her apron was almost full and Elayna had just begun.

"The Fair Witch of Avoreed, here in the palace. We are the ones honored."

Elayna looked at Josn in the haze of sunlight, searching the old woman's face for some sign of sarcasm or humor, but there was none. She was sincere in her respect. Quietly, she went to Elayna and looked into her eyes.

"Perhaps one day you shall tell me of your lineage. I have heard the stories. You are not one to be taken lightly."

Tears welled in Elayna's eyes. Everything, all the disastrous events of the past suns, seemed to flood her memory at once and she could not stop the sobs. The fruit she had managed to gather in her apron tumbled to the cellar floor and she went to her knees weeping. Josn knelt in front of her, close to her, and with one hand pressed Elayna's head to her breast.

"So long overdue, these tears. But they must be shed," she said gently. Elayna pulled away, and on her knees reached across the floor to gather the goods she had spilled.

"My life is gone," she said simply, trying to wipe her tears away.

"Just beginning. Not gone," Josn reassured her softly.

"I am a prisoner. My brother is a prisoner. And Caly is dead. Because of her!" She put the last of the fruit in her apron and rose to her feet to stand defiantly before Josn. Josn rose as well, without the difficulty one would expect from someone her age.

"You blame the Hya? But my dear, the raid was not her doing."

Elayna rushed to the bins and gathered fruit in her anger. She didn't care what she picked up. She only knew she did not want to hear a defense of the Hya.

"Tell that to those who are dead," she snapped bitterly. "I shall never forgive her! Never!"

Josn watched her and finally said, "Come. We have plenty now. We must not be late with the Hya's morning meal."

She led the way up the stairs and back into the corridor where she emptied her goods in a basket there and turned to bolt the cellar door once again. Before she picked up the basket, she turned to Elayna and lifted her chin so Elayna had no choice but to look into the clouded eyes.

"Some day you will understand. Trust in your goddess, who has spared you. The gods have no idle days." She gently touched Elayna's cheek, picked up the basket and started back to the kitchen.

Later, in the Hya's dining chamber, Elayna was initiated into the ritual of serving the Hya's meal. Reluctantly, she had helped Josn prepare the meal and followed the serving girls who brought the food up through the winding palace halls to the chamber. Now, Josn called out instructions, to ensure that everything would be perfect for her beloved Hya, as it was with every sun.

Now the serving girls stood at the ready. Marin steamed from the silver carafe on the serving table. *So much fuss for one meal,* Elayna thought. *For one person.*

Josn hurried from the window.

"She comes!"

The room was suddenly quiet. Josn pulled Elayna in line close beside her to await the Hya's entry. Footfalls from out in the corridor drew nearer. The Hya had a distinctive stride. They all knew it, recognized it. Elayna watched the other serving girls and realized that they did not feel the anxiety she felt. Their tension was from something else. The honor of serving. Her heart leapt to her throat as, seconds before the chamber door swung open, Josn whispered, "You will serve her."

There was no time for Elayna to protest. She knew nothing about serving anyone except Orrat, and that did not demand a great deal of skill. There was no protocol to serving a growing boy. He required no presentation with his meals. Just the food itself, and plenty of it.

The Hya swung breezily into the dining chamber. Her cloak fell from her shoulders. A serving girl scooped it up before it hit the floor and whisked it away. Cydell crossed the room to splash water on her face from a basin sitting on a little wooden table. Another serving girl was at her side in an instant with a drying cloth. Still another brought rolled parchments to the table and placed them beside a vase of roses.

The Hya didn't speak until she was seated.

"My marin, please!"

Josn shoved Elayna forward as she handed her the carafe of steaming marin. Elayna took it and walked slowly toward the table. She hesitated. Cydell waited. Finally, the Hya looked at her.

"It is not my habit to drink from the carafe. Pour, please."

Elayna could not stop her hands from shaking. She had poured marin before. It was not so difficult. *Just remember how much you hate her*, she told herself. *Remember Caly*. In that moment, she was in the alley again. Holding Caly once again. Before the soldiers attacked.

Josn's scream brought her back to the dining chamber. The Hya was on her feet, swearing. Josn hurried over with a drying cloth to soak up the marin that had overflowed onto the table and into the Hya's lap. Flustered, Elayna set the carafe on the table with a crash, and not knowing what else to do, ran from the chamber.

She waited in agony the rest of the day for the reprimand she was certain would come. But none did, and no one came for her until it was time to prepare noonmeal. Surprisingly, Josn said nothing about the morning incident. She just chattered away as she explained the other duties Elayna would be expected to perform. Elayna followed in silence, nodding now and again to let Josn know she was listening and that she understood.

When at last her duties were done, Elayna sat down under a shade tree not far from the training yard. She was waiting for Orrat to join her before they retired for the night. As she remembered the events of the day, she felt stupid and embarrassed and berated herself endlessly for her clumsiness. She did not want to serve the Hya. She hated the Hya. Word of the incident had probably spread all over Mauldar by now, and it was difficult enough in the kitchens without this.

She looked up and waved to Orrat as he climbed over the fence and jogged over to settle himself in the dust beside her. His face was red from practicing in the sun all day, but his clothes were clean and he looked well. He hugged his sister and then drew away from her so he could see her face.

"Tears?" he asked with a concerned frown.

To Elayna this did not seem to be the same boy who had clung to her in the darkness of the auction sheds. This was not the brother who had stood by her to face their fate as one. Clearly, Orrat had quickly become acclimated to his new existence, as though Avoreed had never existed.

"It has not been an easy day, then? Nor has mine," he chattered on as though nothing were amiss. As though this alien city was where they belonged. Elayna was getting angrier by the second. "I heard about the marin this morning. The wards are convinced you were trying to assassinate the Hya." He was smiling, hoping to draw his sister out of her dark mood.

"And would you then have killed me?" Elayna pouted angrily.

Orrat frowned. "Why do you say that?"

"You are so quickly loyal to her. Do you forget what she has done? How you came to be in this place?" Orrat put a calming hand on her arm, but she shook it off.

"You of all should know about fate, Elayna," he reasoned earnestly. "You taught me to follow the will of the goddess. I will try to survive in the life I am given." Orrat rose then, and seemed to Elayna so much taller than only a few suns before. "What did I lose in Avoreed? A tiny box of a cottage? A life as a thief?" He held out his arms to encompass the yard. "I mourn for those who were lost in Avoreed. But here, here is where the gods have cast me. I have the chance to be something more than a thief. The Hya has given me this chance, and I want to make her proud."

"You are too young to understand," Elayna countered forlornly, shaking her head.

Orrat knelt down to her and looked into her eyes. "I did not lose a love in Avoreed. I know that is what makes it so difficult for you. I am sorry about Caly. I truly am. But we go on, Elayna. As mother and father would want us to."

"They would *not* want us to honor our captors. They would *not* want us to honor a woman who hides behind the emblem of Mauldar while her soldiers carry out her sinister orders."

Orrat rose and looked down into his sister's face. "Why do you hate her so? As she promised, those who raided Avoreed have been executed. She cannot bring back those who are dead. Not Caly. Not the others. She has agreed to rebuild the village. It may even be better than before." Then, almost as an afterthought, he added, "And she even found father's saber...."

"I tire of hearing of her great deeds!" Elayna was on her feet in anger. "Since you love her so much, perhaps you should serve her table!" She stalked off toward the kitchen entrance of the palace and left Orrat sadly looking after her.

◻◻◻◻◻

It was late. The crowd in the inn was thinning, much to Micas' pleasure. Though he had onas enough to stay in the best inn Mauldar had to offer, he had chosen this one. The atmosphere was rustic. There was a long room with small oak tables. A blazing hearth at the end of the room. The serving maids were pretty and the food looked good. But Micas, like his master, did not require food. It was ale that gave him pleasure and a sense of belonging, a sense of almost being human. Almost.

The owner, a heavyset, jovial sort, nodded in greeting to the dark stranger as he mopped the floors. There was one serving maid now. The others had somehow managed to disappear during the course of the evening. Micas watched this girl as she ran a cloth up and down the well-worn surface of the bar in slow, lazy strokes.

There was a lone figure seated at the table directly in front of the hearth, studying the flames in silence. Micas ignored him. He was more interested in the young maiden. She had moved closer now to clean the table beside his, smiling when she caught his eye. Micas only looked at her, not knowing how to answer her seduction.

She was a pretty girl, though her hair was damp, uncombed and plastered to her head with perspiration. Seductively, she tucked the loose skirts between her thighs and at her waist, to keep them out of her way. When she walked, she made sure Micas noticed her buttocks against the fabric.

Turning from Micas for a moment, she sought the attention of the lone figure by the hearth. The person wore a full hooded cloak and did not indicate whether he or she was even aware of the barmaid's proximity.

Micas knew he should retire to his room so the innkeeper could close the bar. He knew he should not even think about the pretty barmaid who had all but offered herself to him. The ale was good. Very good. But it did not ease his fear.

He could not shake the cloud of dread that threatened to engulf him, for he had failed once more to secure the Avoreedan sorceress for his master. For the past few suns he had heard his master's summons; a summons to return to the mountain. So, there must be another plan. Perhaps one that did not include him. Had he become dispensable, more doomed now than ever?

He was afraid to sleep. Afraid to be alone, especially in the night. In the darkness. He could not risk the dreams, those dreams that became his worst reality. The master could do that. The master could make Micas part of that other world. Micas had been there before. It was much worse than the small glass prison. Much worse than feeling his master's will exploding in his mind, or the menacing whisper he now fought to ignore.

Pain would come if the summons went unanswered. The pain, unbearable pain, would come. And then the madness. Bending to his master's will, doing things he would feel no shame for. Maybe that was good. He would not feel, would not care whom he hurt. Women. Children. Animals. His fiendish master might let him go physically, but mentally, he would never relinquish his hold on his servant.

So Micas sat watching the barmaid. The lone figure by the hearth was still silent, unmoving. For one last night, he wanted to be as free as his soul, what was left of it, would allow.

But the master's summons bellowed in his mind and he cringed from the shot of pain. It had begun.

◻ ◻ ◻ ◻ ◻

Two suns after the marin incident and still Josn kept Elayna away from the Hya. Elayna began to feel she had been demoted somehow. She did not dare question Josn about the Hya's reaction to having had steaming marin spilled in her lap. So she had been kept busy in other parts of the palace, and of course, her presence was always requested in the kitchens. Though the cook had warmed to her somewhat, others of the kitchen staff still tried to make her mere existence as difficult as possible.

Elayna decided during those days that she should thank the Hya for recovering her father's saber and returning it to Orrat. She knew that on this particular day, the Hya, who had been away at a council gathering, was due to return. A likely place to catch her, Elayna thought, would be the study, since she always reviewed parchments which had been delivered during her absence.

As soon as her kitchen duties had been completed, Elayna stole quietly up to the study. It amazed her still how the palace could be teeming and busy with people during the course of the day, and so quiet, almost hauntingly empty, in the evening. There was no answer when she knocked. So, looking down the corridor, one way and then the other, she turned the latch and quickly slipped inside.

She did not light the candles in the sconces by the door, for Josn had started a roaring fire in anticipation of the Hya's return. Moonlight bathed the furnishings in a white, shadowy glow. As she slowly entered the inner chamber, her attention was drawn to the case containing the glass figurines she had seen that first night in the palace.

Bending to get a closer look, her own reflection smiled back at her through the glass as the figurines breathed a rainbow of moonlight. Horses and swans posed and sparkled only for her in that moment. Elayna felt comfort and the most singular sense of peace she had felt since arriving in Mauldar. If these animals were alive, they'd be my friends, she thought.

On a childish impulse, she opened the door of the case and gently lifted the crystal horse out. A sigh escaped her lips as she marveled at the perfect detail of the little figure, the artistry of creating something so tiny and so intricate. As she held it high to let the moonlight shine through its glass body, she closed her eyes and softly whispered words of power. She opened her eyes when she felt movement, and then her eyes widened in amusement as the tiny hooves tickled her palm. She became lost in the magical moment she had created and marveled at the beauty of the little creature, touched by magic and filled with moonlight.

"I shall call you Caly," she whispered. The horse nodded as though he understood.

"Who is Caly?"

Startled, Elayna dropped the little horse and watched it shatter into a million glistening pieces. Horrified at what she had done, she knelt and hurriedly tried to pick up the fragments.

"Leave it," the cold voice instructed. Cydell strode into the study and tossed her riding gloves on the desk. Elayna rose slowly, trembling.

"I am sorry. So sorry. I shall pay for it, somehow."

"Let me guess. The crystal horse?" Elayna nodded. "There is no price on it. It was a gift from my father."

In the unforgiving silence that followed, Cydell took off her cloak and folded it neatly on the back of a chair. Elayna wanted to run. But not before she had done what she had come to do. At the moment, though, she was too stunned at being discovered and breaking the little horse to speak.

The Hya walked to the window.

"Why are you here? In this room?" she asked ominously. "There are numerous other rooms for you to wander in."

"I was awaiting your return." Elayna met the Hya's gaze and held it.

"Well?" Cydell held out her hands with a shrug, a silent invitation for Elayna to continue.

"I wanted to thank you for finding my father's saber. It means so much to Orrat."

Cydell went to her desk, lit the candle there, and finding an herbstick, lit it in the candle's flame.

"When I make promises, I try to keep them. Sometimes it is not so easy," she explained, not taking her eyes off the comely sorceress.

"But you make them still?" Elayna asked. Cydell shrugged.

"Most times, it is a matter of diplomacy. However, this time it is different. There is something about young Orrat. I like him."

"Yes. You have won him as well." Elayna walked past Cydell to the door, but the Hya's voice stopped her from leaving.

"But I have not won you?"

Elayna turned so she could see the Hya's face. It was lost in the dim shadows of the candle and the moonlight.

"You shall never win me!" she blurted. Cydell absorbed Elayna's anger with a raised eyebrow.

"And I hope to Dornea you never serve me marin again," she quipped with a slight smile.

"I did not mean to...." Elayna was disarmed by the Hya's reaction to her outburst.

"I know. As you did not mean to break my horse?"

Elayna did not defend her actions. She should not have come to the study.

"You did not answer my question," Cydell persisted.

"Which question, Hya?"

"Who is Caly?" It was a moment, an eternity before Elayna spoke.

"It is just a name," she said quietly and started again for the door.

"You are not dismissed until I dismiss you!" Cydell bellowed. Elayna turned on her,

"What is it you want from me? To hold you in regard as Orrat does? It will not happen. To forgive you, somehow, for destroying what precious little I had of this world? That, also, Hya, will never happen!"

Cydell walked toward her, " 'Never' is a favored word of yours. You are very young, for only the very young use that word so often. And you will find that 'never' is not so long a time.

"What do I want from you? For now, I would like you to make my horse as you found it. I could have your head for destroying my possessions. However, I did make a promise."

The two women studied each other silently. In that moment, looking into the Hya's eyes, Elayna saw and felt something that confused and excited her. She knew what the Hya was thinking. As much as she wanted to shut the thoughts out, she couldn't. She, too, was intrigued. Drawn in. But she fought her feelings because she did not want them to be true.

"Now you are dismissed." The Hya's voice was barely a whisper. Elayna quickly left the study and ran down the corridor and up the stairway to her tiny chamber.

As Valkyra strode down the corridor, she saw the figure of a woman, blonde hair pulled back, running out of the study. She entered the inner chamber just as Cydell flicked the butt of the herbstick into the fire. Cydell looked up. The Commander General sauntered over to within a breath of the Hya and stood with her legs apart, arms hanging loosely at her sides, one hip seductively swaying to a silent rhythm. Cydell's blood was feverishly hot. As hot as the flames in the fireplace.

"What did you do to frighten the witch away?" Valkyra's voice was teasing. Sultry. Smoky with seduction. Cydell stepped close to her. The Commander General shrugged the linen tunic she was wearing from her shoulders and let it fall. Cydell cupped a breast in each hand and gently kissed them. She looked into Valkyra's eyes and pulled her in closer. Pelvis to pelvis. Her voice was hoarse with desire.

"She is not my concern at this moment." They stood melded to each other, swaying to their own rhythm.

□ □ □ □ □

Later, Valkyra languished on the thick pile of pillows, enjoying the last heated tremors of lovemaking. She lay ravaged and open, basking in the warmth of the fire.

"Cydell?" she whispered. There was no response. She sat up and saw Cydell standing before the case which held her collection of glass figures. Valkyra rose and went to her, leaving her clothes where they had fallen. She wrapped her arms around Cydell's waist and rested her chin on her shoulder, trying to see what she was staring at. Cydell did not seem to be aware that Valkyra had joined her.

"You took my breath away tonight," she whispered in Cydell's ear.

"I am glad you were pleased," Cydell did not look up from the case. It was as though she were entranced.

"I am always pleased. But tonight you were much more ...passionate...than usual."

"Perhaps it was the herbstick." Cydell responded in the same monotone. It was not the right answer. Valkyra wanted to hear how Cydell's love for her had made her want her more. The vision of the blonde witch leaving the study flashed in her mind. She moved away from Cydell and dressed quickly, anger burning in her heart. Cydell didn't notice when she strode to the door.

"Perhaps, Hya," she spat, "you felt the witch beneath you! Not me!" Valkyra raged on for several minutes. Cydell looked at her then, but said nothing. Finally, the Commander General stormed out of the study.

Cydell turned her attention back to the figurines. Slowly, she opened the case and lifted out the wondrous glass horse. Incredibly, it was intact! Perfect. As though it had never been disturbed. She stared at the glowing figure in her hand in disbelief.

4

ILL WINDS

Windsom Keep was a stone fortress built as a monument to the strength of all Northern tribes. A unification point for all serious intertribal disagreements. And each tribe had contributed something—labor, materials, skills—to the Keep's construction. As a result, every tribe felt the Keep to be the center of its existence.

It was nestled high in the Mauldaran Mountains on the western range. The moat and smooth stone outer wall kept would-be invaders at bay. The very structure was intimidating. Designed to be a stronghold, it was equipped and stocked with enough weaponry and foodstuff to sustain thousands for an indeterminate length of time. It had been the command post during the Tribal Wars. Chieftains from all of the warring tribes had brought their people to the Keep for protection when the Sentinels invaded the mountains. The tribes that did not reach the haven of the Keep in time were wiped away from the mountainside, lost to the fury of the Sentinel army.

It had been many Passes since the Tribal Wars. Now, Windsom Keep was maintained by a permanent staff selected by each tribe to be caretakers until the next Gathering, which took place every two Passes. Its massive hallways and chambers were kept free of dust and cobwebs. The great kitchens were constantly maintained, hearth fires always burning, for the household never knew when one of their own would come upon the Keep in the dark of night needing food and shelter.

Madras Nii Sadiin, distant cousin of the Ra Sadiin line, head of the Sadiin tribe which had decided not to leave the mountains for the life of the city, stood on the study balcony of Windsom Keep and looked out into the crisp autumn morning. He closed his eyes and breathed in the fresh air, the scents of pine and wild, sweet lilies. Fall had come early and would leave quickly, a prelude to the hard mountain winter.

There was much activity at the Keep, as the staff prepared for the arrival of those more indigent tribes who would sojourn north to take winter refuge there. Livestock were bought from valley farmers and herded into the massive indoor pens. The cellars were being stocked with vegetables and fruits, various grains, and wines.

It was Madras' task, his tribal duty and honor, to attend the Keep in the Pass of the Gathering, to make certain all was in readiness. The Gathering would take place in the Spring and would last for four turns. All tribes came to Windsom to trade, honor marriage contracts, have contests, eat, drink and generally have a large-scale family reunion. It was a great responsibility to arrange all this after wintering in the Keep, but one that Madras looked forward to.

He had earned the honor of Keep Master for the Pass of the Gathering. Prowess and wisdom as a warrior, honor and mercy as a man, had won him the respect of his people. It was often said that Sadiin blood yielded leaders, no matter what their station in life. If a Sadiin was a thief, he was the best thief. If a soldier, the best soldier.

Madras thought of his cousin, the reigning Hya. He had met Cydell only once when they were very young, before the Tribal Wars, before the distrust and dishonor. From all he had heard, his cousin was a wise ruler. Her people loved her and she had won the trust and respect of the tribes with the various treaties and trade agreements. Through shrewd negotiations and brilliant diplomacy, Cydell had managed to maintain the peace established between her father and the tribal chieftains so many Passes ago. In the late spring, after the Gathering, Madras thought he might journey to Mauldar and visit his estimable cousin. He wondered how much she had changed after so many Passes.

Madras himself had certainly aged. Battle scars left him aching. His dark curls were streaked with gray, particularly the sides, and his skin was weathered from too many nights of sleeping out in the elements and riding under blistering suns.

He left the balcony, feeling a bit of a chill through the white linen tunic he wore, though the calfskin leggings and boots kept his lower half warm. Perhaps age was responsible for the frequent headaches of late, the odd nightmares, the voice in his head. He had not the time to be taken with sickness. There was much too much to be done, he thought impatiently.

The dreams had not disturbed him at first. At first, he had attributed them to too many wild onions in his stew, and had spoken to the cook. But wild onions or not, the dreams still continued. He would wake in a sweat these nights, sitting straight up in his bed, trembling in the darkness like a frightened child. He saw that face everywhere. Heard the menacing voice, beckoning, commanding. At first, Madras thought they were old spirits of the Keep, long dead. But it was too real, too threatening, seductive and complete in its evil. He had suffered with the headaches for two turns now, and it seemed that each day they increased in intensity. Each day he felt himself losing control, losing more of the memories that made him who he was. It frightened him, for he felt it was age taking his mind. Madness was not in the Sadiin line, that he knew of. Perhaps it was in his mother's blood and she had never told him. Perhaps it was simply starting with him.

Madras forced himself to think of more pleasant things, like the rich colors of the mountain trees, the slight chill in the morning air and the festivities of the impending spring Gathering. With a sigh of relief, he opened his eyes. Thank Dornea the headache had subsided. For now.

The loss of one servant did not deter Isom from finding another. A good plan was like a prolific vine. It started with one single
intent and blossomed and grew and expanded, rooting itself deeply
in the soil of the mind. Now that it was clear that Micas was a failure, a disobedient failure, Isom decided to take matters into his own
hands, but not before devising an apt punishment for his devoted, but
inept, servant.

For Isom, pwer had become as seductive as a drug—more
alluring and desirable than a beautiful woman. And he had been drawing power for Passes beyond Passes. He could now destroy with the
blink of an eye, the snap of a finger. He could invade minds. Ignite
them. Singe them until they were smoldering embers. He could turn a
grown man, a warrior, into a sniveling child. The dark force that was
Isom could walk through dreams. Construct them. Demolish them.
Bend others to his will from leagues away. And now he had a plan,
the best plan. This plan would be the one to give him life and breath
and substance once again. This plan would give him his soul again.
And when it was all over, he would be master of his own fate. He
would have the girl, the stone, and Mauldar.

◻ ◻ ◻ ◻ ◻

Orrat thrust his saber through the practice dummy as though
the stuffed bag were his mortal enemy. He withdrew it without stepping back. The dummy swung forward, hit him full in the chest and
knocked him to the dirt. Rii, who was practicing beside him, embraced his own dummy and doubled over with laughter. Then he held
out a hand and pulled his friend to his feet.

The boys were the same age, only Rii was more muscular,
more defined than Orrat. Orrat silently compared his body with Rii's
as they often practiced without tunics. Out in the heat of a midday
sun, Rii's dark, thick upper body glistened with sweat, his chest heaving from his exercises. The wards had become fast friends.

Rii was darker than the Hya and the dark-complexioned na-
tives of Mauldar. His people were the savage Barrach tribe, who
inhabited the southernmost region of Mauldar. After the brutal mur-

der of his parents by a rival tribe, young Rii had learned to survive on his own, living outside the community and protection of his village. The Barrach believed that without family or roots of some kind, one was an outcast, a lost soul among them. So, after acquiring the skills he would need in the world—to fight, to hunt—Rii set out on his journey to Mauldar for the sole purpose of becoming a great Sentinel warrior. And he had not once looked back.

Upon reaching the great city, he had lived in the streets until one fateful day when he had confronted the Hya on her morning ride. He had told her of his desire to become a Sentinel and she had pulled him up behind her on the black stallion and taken him to the palace. He thought his heart would burst that day as he had ridden through the streets with the Hya, for all to see. From that day, he had worked hard and earned the favor of the trainers and the respect of the older Sentinels, as well as his fellow wards. Now he had a new goal. To become a Master Sentinel like his champion, the Hya.

He smiled at Orrat, his face a dusty mask on his black skin. His hair was straight and jet black, pulled back and tied behind with a thong of leather. It had grown to midway down his back since he had arrived in Mauldar, and it was never to be cut. A man's hair length was the measure of his prowess as a warrior. Thus were the teachings of the Barrach.

"Quite the Sentinel you are." He beamed even white teeth at his friend. "A practice dummy can knock you on your fair ass!"

Orrat wiped the sweat from his brow with the back of his hand, which made his face dirtier. He'd decided since meeting Rii that he'd let his hair grow out as well, especially since his sister was occupied in the palace and did not have the time or the means to butcher it now as she had done in Avoreed. She had teased him about his hair, which always fell in his eyes, as it was not yet long enough to pull back. So he kept it out of his eyes with a leather thong, the other half of the strip of leather Rii had made his thong from. Both boys agreed that this in some way bonded them, an external symbol of the closeness they felt for each other in their hearts.

"What matters, my dear Prince of the Barrach, is that *you* cannot knock me on my fair ass!" Orrat emphasized his point by

jabbing a finger in Rii's chest. Rii swatted Orrat's finger away. They
grinned at each other. A silent challenge. Smiling, wary, they slowly
began to circle each other in a prelude to a mock battle. Other wards
began to gather when they noticed Orrat and Rii squaring off.

Rii teased as he assumed a defensive posture, "It is a custom
of my people to display the scalp of an enemy on their belt. When I
return to the Barrach, they will hail me as their chief. For none will
have a blond scalp to rival the one I will now take!"

Orrat smiled wickedly and said, "You will return to Barrach,
for certain. Swathed and ready for the funeral pyre, for they will
need to bury their would-be chief! He will return without his head!"

"Shall we put it to the test?" Rii asked, grinning.

"My dear friend," Orrat replied with a flourish, testing his
saber in the air, "I had no idea you had chosen this day to die!"

Rii struck first. Orrat defended himself and jumped nimbly
over the sweep of the saber. The other wards backed away and widened the circle around the fighters, cheering their favorite. Both boys
were popular among their peers as they were natural leaders and always available to help a ward who was having difficulty with a tech-
nique. They were boastful only to each other, and the others enjoyed
their antics. The balance of his father's saber felt good to Orrat. He
fought as he had been taught. They teased each other, dodging blows
and rolling to their feet until it was plain to all who were watching
that they were evenly matched.

Valkyra rode into the practice yard after making her rounds
and frowned when she saw so many practice dummies hanging still.
She dismounted quickly and strode toward the commotion. Her older
Sentinels had gone to the center of the yard to watch the two wards
go at it. So, Valkyra thought, her most worrisome, and, she had to
admit, her best wards were at it again. The pups would never learn
discipline if they continued to disregard orders. She favored Rii, so
young and fierce, and in spite of herself, she found Orrat charming as
well. But the young Avoreedan was a constant reminder to Valkyra
that his sister tempted the Hya's lusty appetites.

The crowd of wards and Sentinels parted at the Commander
General's approach. Trainers, too, had been watching to judge the

fruits of their labors, even if it were just for sport. They were impressed with the young wards' abilities and grumbled in dismay when they saw the Commander General approaching. She would put a stop to the sport for certain, and very likely punish the boys, particularly young Orrat. All were beginning to note, lately, how the Commander General made an example of the boy at every opportunity. She never seemed to miss a chance to belittle him before his peers. But no matter how hard she rode the boy, Orrat always rose to the challenge and it pleased the trainers immensely. He was never disrespectful and took everything the Commander General handed to him, no matter how unfair. As a result, the young Avoreedan had earned the trainers' respect, while the Commander General garnered their scorn.

The young wards were too involved in their mock battle to notice the Commander General's arrival. With a lightning saber stroke, she sent their sabers flying through the air. Rii and Orrat were too stunned and out of breath to react.

"This does not look like practice to me," she boomed evenly. "If you are so eager to fight," she pointed her saber at Rii and then touched the tip to Orrat's chest—it hurt but he did not wince— "then fight. Without your sabers," she ordered. The boys looked at each other. Valkyra looked at them and tossed her saber aside. "No. Not each other. Fight me."

A trainer stepped forward to object, for the boys had not yet been fully trained in weaponless combat, but Valkyra's raised hand stopped him. The trainers knew Valkyra's skill and temperament in battle. Even though the wards were inexperienced, she would show them no mercy. They feared greatly for Orrat in particular. Valkyra now had the perfect excuse to hurt the boy.

"Well?" she challenged, eyeing them each in turn. She took the stance. Orrat and Rii shrugged at each other and took their stance as well, smiling. This seemed to them to be only a continuation of their previous play. It would be fun.

Suddenly, the crowd fell silent. There was no cheering now. The Commander General's arrival had turned the lightness of the sport into a dangerous game. Both boys held their own at the onset, doing well against Valkyra's greater skill. Deliberately, she paced them, first going through easy maneuvers, building their confidence.

Orrat got in a lucky kick and the Commander General fell to the dust when his foot caught her off-balance. She was on her feet quickly, and when Orrat looked into those eyes, the smile vanished from his lips. Rii stood waiting to be challenged, but Valkyra's attention was focused only on Orrat. She did not like to be bested, especially by a green ward. Rii looked on, fearing for his friend. He realized now that it was no longer sport. Someone, probably Orrat, was going to get hurt.

Orrat felt himself beginning to tire. The muscles in his legs burned and it was becoming more and more difficult to evade the Commander General, for she came at him now with a vengeance. Then, executing an advanced move, Valkyra tripped Orrat, pulling his feet from under him. He landed hard and did not have the strength to rise. Valkyra, blinded by jealousy, ignored the hand Orrat held up as the sign of surrender and instead, grabbed it and twisted his wrist so that she straddled him, applying more pressure as she bent his thumb back. Orrat winced as he tried to turn onto his side to lessen the pain. As far as he was concerned, the game was over. If she did not let go soon, she would break his arm. He was confused by her action, for as wards, they had been taught fairness and mercy in battle. The crowd of Sentinels began to murmur their disapproval.

Finally, Valkyra let Orrat's arm drop, smirking down at him as she stepped away from him. The yard was quiet as everyone stared. Looking around, coming out of her victory, she noted the displeasure on the faces of those watching and in a belated attempt to rectify her mistake, offered Orrat a hand.

"Forgive my fervor, ward. I was too late reminded of your lack of skill. However, you fought well." She finally turned to Rii. "You as well. Since you defended yourselves admirably, there is no punishment. This time."

She waited for Orrat to accept her hand. Scowling, he rose slowly, holding his arm and backing away from her, not taking his eyes off her. Rii went to him, but Orrat shook his head. He would stand on his own for as long as he could.

Valkyra looked around the yard full of Sentinels and realized, in that moment, how much of their respect she had lost.

"Resume practice!" she commanded coldly. She then turned back to address Orrat, but the two boys were already walking toward the refectory. She did not call them back.

Elayna burst into Cydell's private chambers. The Hya and the Commander General separated at the intrusion, and before either woman could question her, Elayna had crossed the room and proceeded to slap Valkyra full across the face. Hard. It surprised and impressed Cydell, but Valkyra was so outraged, she was speechless. She grabbed Elayna's wrist and would probably have twisted it from her arm if not for Cydell's intervention.

"Let her go," Cydell ordered calmly.

The Commander General swore venomously, rage flashing in her eyes. Elayna had the same look of fury in hers, and though the Commander had her wrist in a viselike grip, Elayna was showing no indications of pain.

"Valkyra!" Cydell shouted harshly, "I said let her go!" Valkyra pushed Elayna away and her hand went to rest on the hilt of her saber. She pointed a warning finger in Elayna's face.

"Touch me again, Avoreedan bitch, and your brother will truly be orphaned!" she seethed.

"I have no fear of you!" Elayna matched the Commander General's fury. "That was for nearly breaking Orrat's arm! I do not have to hide behind a saber's blade to defend myself! As does the mighty Commander General!"

"You feel you may challenge a Sentinel?! Then do so! But do it at a time when your precious Hya cannot protect you!" Valkyra was about to draw her saber.

"Stay your hand!" Cydell ordered.

"I shall teach her to respect her betters!" Valkyra growled.

"Yes. Let me see for myself the glory of the Sentinels, as I

have seen before," Elayna mocked. "Have you stooped now to bru-
talizing innocent wards?"

Valkyra moved threateningly toward Elayna. Cydell blocked
her path.

"Let her come!" Elayna said evenly, standing her ground.
"Since you insist on behaving like a hound from the abyss, perhaps I
shall turn you into one!" she hissed defiantly.

"Grand talk from a whore!" Valkyra raged.

"I share no one's bed. Can you say the same?" Elayna shot
back.

Cydell did not have to call for Josn. The old nurse stood in
the chamber doorway watching the scene, with two wide-eyed serving girls peering over her shoulder.

"Have you no duties to occupy you?!" Cydell bellowed. The
serving girls scurried away. "Josn, see to Elayna. We shall discuss
this matter at another time. Without threat of sabers."

Josn hurried Elayna out of the chamber. Valkyra paced in
her anger and frustration, while Cydell watched and waited for the
Commander General to calm herself. She could not get Elayna's fury
out of her mind.

No one had ever caught Valkyra off guard, but the witch had
managed to do just that. Valkyra's words of some nights before rang
in the back of Cydell's memories. She could not explain why she had
felt such a need that night in the study. Elayna had stirred that need,
that fire. Cydell had to admit that to herself. And just now, Elayna's
rage had touched off that spark again. Let it die, she told herself. Just
let it die.

"What of the boy?" she asked. Valkyra shrugged.

"I was overzealous in an exercise. That is all." Their eyes
met and Cydell knew instinctively that she was not hearing the whole
truth.

"I will not have the boy broken as you have broken others
who did not earn your favor."

"So, you *do* favor him," Valkyra sneered.

"If I do, it is not your concern. Mind your treatment of him.
He will make a fine Sentinel."

"And the witch will make a fine bedmate."

Cydell absorbed Valkyra's accusations as she poured herself a steaming cup of marin from the carafe on her table.

"You do not have to worry in that respect. The girl hates me almost as much as she hates you."

Valkyra neared the door. A white hot anger marked her words.

"I will teach her the proper respect for a Sentinel."

"You will go out of your way to leave her to herself," Cydell warned darkly. "I believe she could turn you into a hound if she was of a mind. And I have no need for animals in my Sentinel Guard. Besides horses." She looked pointedly at Valkyra. "But she does have a way of sneaking up on one. Does she not?"

Valkyra gave a derisive snort and quickly left the chamber.

"You hit her?!" Orrat almost squealed. "I do not believe that!"

"I believe it," Rii sat on the ground polishing his saber. Elayna sat beside him while Orrat paced heavily back and forth in front of them, stirring up dust.

"I will not have her mistreat you," Elayna explained.

"I can take care of myself! Now they will think I am a babe who must have his sister fight his battles for him!"

"I wish I had a sister," Rii mused to himself, but loud enough for Orrat to hear. Orrat shot his friend a warning glare and knelt down to appeal to his sister.

"Please, I beg you, stay out of the matter. Valkyra is not a good one to have as an enemy."

"He is right in that, Elayna," Rii nodded, and held his saber up to the sun, admiring the shine. "She will not rest now until she has run you through and posted your head on a pole in the training yard."

Orrat punched Rii's shoulder, saying, "We do not need that manner of assurance." Then he frowned at his friend.

"I shall hold my tongue then."

"That would be best," Orrat agreed.

Suddenly, Rii was scrambling to his feet.

"Attention!"

They had not seen the Hya approach. Hurriedly, Rii and Orrat tried to brush themselves off. Elayna was about to rise when the Hya extended a hand. She hesitated only briefly before accepting it and the Hya gently pulled her to her feet. Awkwardly, Elayna removed her hand and chided herself for not being able to stop the flush of color that rose to her cheeks. Orrat noticed his sister's reaction and was surprised and pleased, and smiled to himself.

"At your ease, wards." Both boys slumped in relief. Cydell tried not to smile. "Elayna, a word." She indicated a private spot away from the noise of the training yard. They walked.

The Hya wore leather leggings and a white waist-length tunic. Her saber swung jauntily from the belt at her side. Elayna knew she had been riding by the faint smell of horses about her.

"Will I lose my head?" Elayna asked. This time Cydell did smile. She also found herself enjoying the way the sunlight played in the highlights of Elayna's silky hair. Elayna felt the Hya's light humor and allowed herself a smile as well. When she thought about it, she didn't know how she had summoned the courage to slap the Commander General. There were many other things she could have done, spells she could have used. It was just that it made her blood boil to know that Valkyra had taken unfair advantage of Orrat. She had acted purely on instinct. And she was not sorry.

Surprisingly, it felt good to walk with the Hya. Elayna clenched and opened the hand the Hya had held only a second ago. It was still warm. Her touch lingered. It was not unpleasant.

"I would not recommend making a habit of assaulting my Commander General. Your life could be shortened considerably. It still might be."

They stopped beside a fruit vendor's wagon that, when Cydell thought about it, had no business being there. Absentmindedly, she took two apples from the pile and left onas in their place. Elayna took the one that was offered her.

"If there are further difficulties," the Hya continued, "and I anticipate that there will be, see me at once. Understood?" Elayna nodded. The Hya looked at her and cocked her head to one side. "I do get the feeling you can handle yourself with spells and such. However, one must never be without defenses. I shall teach you the saber personally, if you like."

The offer caught Elayna off guard.

"Is this a device to bring me to your bed?" she asked suspiciously.

Cydell smiled charmingly, "My lovely sorceress, if, by the grace of Dornea, you *do* come to my bed, it will not be in payment of lessons," she countered.

Embarrassed and confused, Elayna turned to walk away, but Cydell held her with a gentle hand on her arm and looked into her eyes.

"Where is the Elayna who smiled at me only a heartbeat ago? I wish not your love and devotion. Only your civility."

"You have my gratitude for your kindness to Orrat. That is all I can give, Hya."

The Hya's features clouded as she let Elayna go.

"As you wish, Fair Witch. I see that in your heart, you have condemned me as a murderess. Would you have dominion over the tides and not be responsible for floods? I do not rule the hearts of my people. I can only dictate their behavior and make them pay for their crimes if they go against me. I have done that with those who destroyed Avoreed. I can do no more."

The Hya looked past Elayna and suddenly pushed her aside so hard that Elayna fell. She heard the Hya's saber against its scabbard and cowered, thinking the stroke was meant for her.

The stranger in black had missed his mark. He turned now on the dark woman who challenged him. Elayna pulled herself out of the midst of the clash of sabers and gasped when she saw her attacker.

It was the man who had come to her door the day Avoreed was burned. The man who had also intended to buy her at the auction. He had been fairly handsome then, but now the handsomeness was gone. She recognized him by the clothes he wore, though they were now stained and dusty. The aura of evil about him was stronger than it had been that day, even now in his obvious madness. His eyes were glazed, as though with fever. The face was a grimaced mask that revealed an eternal agony. Dark circles ringed his eyes, and his growth of beard was patchy and unkempt. His only strength seemed to be in his fighting, and that he did with a vengeance.

Cydell held the advantage in her calm. Her strokes were clean, calculated. She met him stroke for stroke as she took measure of his skill, and though he might have been skilled at one time, he was too hungry now for the kill. The clash of steel drew Orrat, Rii and some of the other Sentinels from the training yard. Two Sentinels stepped forward to help defend their Hya, but she waved them away. The boys watched with their mouths open. They did not know the defenses Cydell was using, for they had never seen a Master fight. She paced the battle, seemingly with ease, while the stranger fought wildly, making mistakes a ward would not make.

He rushed for her, raising his saber high to land a crushing, final blow. But Cydell ducked and rolled into a kneeling position so that her saber slashed upward, ripping through his torso. The move caught the stranger off guard, but it was too late for a defensive move. His saber clattered to the dust. Standing, in shock, his maddened gaze met Elayna's and he stumbled toward her, reaching one hand out to her. Orrat and Rii quickly stepped forward in her defense, their sabers drawn. The stranger faltered and fell to his knees.

Elayna watched him all the while, reading the crushing sadness in his eyes now. He was imploring her to come closer, to listen to what he had to tell her. When he finally fell to the ground, Cydell was kneeling at his side. She turned him over to get a better look at his face and rested his head on her thigh. The stranger's eyes still searched. He mouthed words no one could understand.

Elayna stepped between Orrat and Rii and knelt at the stranger's side. He recognized her and caught hold of her sleeve, pulling her closer, down to him, with an urgency so intense that it almost frightened her.

"Be warned, Fair Witch. Be warned of one who seeks to destroy you." The words were barely a whisper, "He seeks to reclaim his soul."

And now, at last, an incredible peace surrounded Micas. His attack had been one last effort to please his master. One moment of obedience to ease the pain that had consumed him so. He felt himself smile. It was finally over. He could not venture a guess about where his soul's journey would end. All he knew was that he would no longer walk this world. He would no longer be a servant. And in the end, he hoped he had redeemed himself, saved some part of himself, some good part that remained, by trying to save the witch.

5

WAR

An unnatural wind stirred the trees surrounding Windsom Keep. Trappers complained of the sudden lack of game where once an overabundance existed. And though the hearthfires of the Keep were always roaring, there was a bone-numbing chill within the stone walls. Servants wondered at the eeriness that had settled around the once warm and welcoming structure. Older folk, wise people, knew the portents of evil. Young people scoffed at the gloomy tidings and buckled down for what, to them, merely forecast an early and bitter winter.

The master, Madras, kept to himself these days. If he noticed the gloom, he did not speak of it. He did not speak at all these days. His time was spent on the balcony of the study. Hours on end. Muttering to himself. Serving trays, untouched, piled up at his chamber door. The servants took them away worriedly and questioned among themselves their master's wellness. But the important thing was the running of the Keep, and they could do that to perfection on their own.

Out on the study balcony, Madras mumbled to himself as he stared out into the darkened sky. The power that surged through him gave him a feeling of incredible physical and mental strength. It seemed that the very forces of nature could not resist his will, and the soul of every man was but a puff of smoke in the wake of his might. His eyes were wide, sunken and unblinking. His hair, untrimmed, had grown into a curly mane around his head and was completely white. The beginnings of a beard gave him an unkempt appearance. But none of that mattered. This was no time for mortal primping.

Suddenly, the work of the Keep was no longer his concern. There were more important matters to attend to. He had developed dark and ambitious desires of late and they required the harvesting of much power. Thus it was that every weak mind Madras tapped into, was bent to his desperate demands, for his urgent orders were disguised as hope and easy victories. Soon, battle cries rose up and echoed throughout the forest and mountain ranges, carried on the winds to the villages nestled in the foothills and valleys. Finally, rumblings of war reached the pinnacle of power that was Windsom Keep. Within a fortnight, the tribes had absorbed that power and worked themselves into a blood frenzy. The lines of war were drawn.

□ □ □ □ □

Something was gnawing at Cydell. She wore only a light blue silk robe as she sat, legs extended and crossed, in the cushioned armchair in her outer chamber, nursing a shimmering, long-stemmed crystal glass of lygen. The thick, blue liqueur was smooth and fiery as it coursed down her throat, but it did nothing to ease her troubled musings. She was still lost in the strange events of the previous sun.

After extensive questioning, it became clear that no one in the palace had ever seen the stranger in black before the day he died. She had dispatched scouts into the city to question civilians. Their reports were disturbing. The stranger had been in the city for a little more than two turns now. He had frequented several inns during his stay and only after the disappearances of three barmaids had anyone looked upon him with suspicion. Mauldar was usually a quiet city, for a city its size. Murder was punishable by death, and such a law did not encourage criminals to bide their time there, for it was known that the Hya rarely, if ever, granted pardons.

Try as she might, she could not get the stranger's face out of
her mind. The way he had looked for Elayna, sought her out. The
words he had spoken to her. In the end, Elayna had held the man as
though she knew him. Cydell could not shake the sense of foreboding
she felt now. She did not know fear, but she disliked the anticipation,
the anxiety of waiting for something terrible to happen. Somehow,
she also had the feeling that Elayna was at the heart of it.

*The Fair Witch has created quite a stir since her arrival in
Mauldar,* Cydell thought. Her spies throughout the city reported that
there were Avoreedans who now refused the Mauldaran healers and
would only let Elayna tend them, no matter how minor the injury.
And there was still that mystery of the glass horse. It had shattered.
Cydell had seen the pieces of glass on the floor. Yet now it was whole
again.

As Cydell slowly brought the cup to her lips again, she
glanced up to see Valkyra emerging from the inner chamber wearing
only a white silk robe. Open. The vision was an abrupt, but not unwelcome, distraction. *Valkyra doesn't have the goodness of soul to
be a goddess,* Cydell thought, as her energies began to stir; *but she
certainly has a body sculpted by some very gifted deity.* She watched
Valkyra walk toward her, slowly, temptingly. The soft glow of the
candlelight bathed her body in a velvety smoothness. She was golden
red, moving as softly and effortlessly as a shadow. Her full auburn
tresses framed her face, hiding one side until she brushed the unruly
tendrils away. Valkyra smiled seductively, desire glinting in the deep
greenness of her eyes as she traced with one finger an invisible trail
from the valley between her breasts down to her navel.

That movement took Cydell's attention from her long legs
and flat, well-muscled torso to her breasts. Perfect mounds, pert and
full. Pink areolas centered with taut brown nipples. Valkyra could
always arouse. She could tease Cydell to madness. *But when the pleasures of the flesh were satisfied, what emotions lingered?*

As she watched Valkyra move to straddle her in the chair, a
vision of Elayna flashed across Cydell's mind. She closed her eyes to
force it away. Valkyra pressed her body into Cydell's. Lips to lips.
Breasts to breasts. Cydell saw the haunting eyes of the witch as

Valkyra settled on her and began to move. Slowly. Enticingly. Elayna's flashing eyes would not go away.

Cydell leaned her head against the back of the chair as Valkyra gently massaged her temples with her fingertips. The hands that wielded a saber and broadsword to rival any man's skill were quite tender as they kneaded Cydell's breasts. And Valkyra's body undulated. Slowly. The lygen glass fell from Cydell's hands and spilled out onto the woolen Sudeeshan rug. Her arms hung limply at the sides of the chair as she surrendered.

Valkyra smiled, knowing the fire she was building in Cydell. Cydell simply sat, enjoying the firm fingers that seemed to be everywhere.

"Why do you not touch me?" Valkyra asked in a husky whisper.

"You began the game," Cydell answered hoarsely, "it is yours to play out as you will."

Valkyra chuckled deeply, wickedly, and placed hot kisses along Cydell's throat, down into the valley of her breasts, gently teasing her nipples with her tongue and teeth.

Cydell sighed with pleasure. It was becoming more and more difficult to remain passive. She yearned to respond, but was not certain who she would find herself making love to, as Elayna's presence in her mind refused to leave. So she let it stay and gave herself to Valkyra's ministrations. Cydell chided her body, knowing it was Valkyra's touch that excited her so, and yet wanting the body now slithering down to the rug in front of her to be Elayna's. She lifted her leg so that it rested over the arm of the chair. Valkyra cupped her mound and held it to feel the moisture and the heat. Cydell's face contorted in ecstasy as Valkyra's tongue found the center of her joy and lingered there to suckle and torment her. Cydell's fingers twined through Valkyra's hair to pull her sweet tormentor closer. But in Cydell's mind her fingers clutched the blondness of the witch. She felt the agony and pleasure of her betrayal even as she moaned in release, the waves of fire soaring through her body so savagely that she thought surely her heart would stop.

☐ ☐ ☐ ☐ ☐

Elayna sat up in her cot with a start, her heart pounding in her chest. The throbbing pleasure between her thighs reminded her of the realness of her dream. Too real. It reminded her of the strength of her power, the part her mother had warned her about so often, the power of desire. The ability to impose it on anyone, so that they, too, would feel it, nurture it.

"No!"

She jumped up, weak-kneed, and stumbled to her window, sobbing as she looked out into the night. There had to be an escape from this place. The passions she felt had to be a lie. She could not want so much, such pleasure from someone she hated so. But she *had* dreamed that fiery dream, and she believed, as she had been taught, that dreams seldom lied.

☐ ☐ ☐ ☐ ☐

The dining chamber was quiet. Josn and even the serving girls felt the Hya's dark mood as they brought her food and marin and set it before her. Valkyra sat across the table from the Hya with a questioning look on her face. She was confused, for after the past evenfall, she would have thought Cydell would feel as blissful as she did. They had made love until sunrise. Valkyra was sated, and judging from Cydell's responses, the Hya should have been as well. Yet, she sensed there was something deeper Cydell was hiding. Valkyra had never been privy to the Hya's innermost feelings, for Cydell did not choose to share anything with her except her physical pleasures. She would just have to wait out the mood. As usual.

Her glum thoughts were interrupted by the unwelcome appearance of Elayna, who swung into the dining chamber in a flurry, flustered at being so late. Elayna turned pleading eyes to Josn, who smiled and nodded that she join them. It was clear she was not angry at the girl for having slept later than she ought. Gratefully, Elayna took her place beside the old nurse and ignored the irritated look on the Commander General's face.

The Hya did not acknowledge her presence and Elayna was glad. She could not face the woman knowing how real her dream had been, how much she had wanted it to be real. But that was last night. That had only been a dream. Something to be buried and forgotten. She would will herself not to do it again. This woman was a murderess, a manipulator. Those around her were blinded by her strength and occasional charm. Secretly, Elayna was afraid that she, too, would succumb to that seduction. She decided that she would merely serve out her time until Avoreed was rebuilt, and then she would leave this place and this woman behind to make a new life for herself and Orrat. In view of the troubling encounter with the stranger, there were more important things to consider than a dream of passion.

The stranger's words haunted her. Since seeing him, the heartstone she wore seemed to have come to life, and she could no longer wear it close to her skin as before. It had become as a fire inside, burning within itself. So now she wore it over her tunic and tried not to think about the meaning of its strange vibrations.

Cydell could only stare at the bowl of honeyed grain, chilled zada fruits and the golden slices of freshly baked bread she had been served. The only thing of interest to her was the marin, which she had had too much of already, on top of the lygen and furious lovemaking of the past night. She was sullen, trying to figure out how the witch had invaded her dreams so, imposed on her desires to the point where she had to stop herself from calling Elayna's name out loud. Thank Dornea she had retained some of her wits about her in the throes of passion. Otherwise, Valkyra, no doubt, would have slit her throat.

She stole a glance at Elayna, who stood as still as a statue beside Josn, and would not meet her gaze. It had to be some magick. Some sorcery. But if Elayna were trying to seduce her, why then would she not look at her? Cydell knew Valkyra was waiting for some acknowledgment of last night, but she could give none, none that her body had not already betrayed. That, she could not have hidden if she had desired to. But the tender words of love would not come.

So they all attended her in silence. No one spoke. No one dared breathe too loudly. Valkyra helped herself to the food, chewing vigorously and casting suspicious glares at Cydell.

They all jumped at the sudden commotion outside the chamber door. A guard burst in, and before he could speak, was shoved aside by a dark little man dressed in royal finery and carrying a staff much taller than he was.

"Forgive me, Hya. But...." Cydell waved the guard away. With a parting growl at the short intruder, the Sentinel left the chamber and closed the door behind her.

"Cousin!" Kovi Bak Sadiin hopped nimbly into the chair to Cydell's right and began helping himself to everything on the table. He was as dark as the Hya, with the same curly hair, though there was no hint of gray in his. He had a broad nose, where Cydell's was narrow, and full lips, with just the shadow of a moustache above his upper lip. He smiled the smile of someone who has no worries and expects everyone else to be as free as he is.

"If you insist on abusing my guards, Kovi, I may not be of a mind to stop them should they decide to feed you to their horses," Cydell admonished him with a smile. It was a smile of relief that something had happened to break the oppressive silence in the chamber. Kovi sucked loudly on a piece of fruit, licking his fingers to the great annoyance of the Commander General.

"Bah! Do you think your fierce Sentinels frighten me?" He paused in his eating suddenly and looked around the chamber. "Are we in mourning here, Cousin? I have had better times at executions." One of the serving girls giggled. Cydell shot her a glare and the girl cowered behind Josn.

Elayna had not been able to stop staring at the little man since he had entered the chamber. The Hya's cousin's exploits throughout Mauldar were infamous. Oftentimes amusing, his entanglements with young men were even more entertaining. Somehow, with all the trouble he seemed to cause wherever he turned up, Elayna had expected him to be much taller, more imposing. It wasn't until he winked at her that Elayna realized how rude she was being.

Kovi hit Cydell's shoulder to get her attention and pointed at Elayna. Cydell did not look up.

"How much for her?" he asked, leering at Elayna.

"Josn is not for sale."

"Not Josn! Sometimes I wonder how you ever became Hya!" he scolded. "I mean the pretty fair one. She is one of yours, is she not?" Before Cydell could answer, Valkyra was on her feet, with a snarl of disgust, and out of the chamber. Cydell cut her eyes at her cousin, who was hiding his laughter behind his pudgy hand.

"Forgive me, Cousin. I was not mindful of your Commander General's sensitive nature." He laughed outright, then, and reached for another slice of bread.

"Well," Cydell could not help a smile, "be mindful hence-forth, or I shall pick you up and toss you out into the courtyard myself!"

"Such ill humor," Kovi clicked his tongue. He could always draw his cousin out of a sulk.

"And your presence here has not helped!" Cydell sipped her marin. It had cooled and she snapped her fingers for the cup to be warmed. Elayna took the carafe and went to the Hya's side. Cydell tensed as she recalled the last time Elayna tried to pour marin for her, but this time the witch filled the cup without mishap. Kovi caught the brief look that passed between his cousin and the serving girl. Now he understood the Commander General's sudden departure. Elayna bowed and went back to her place beside Josn.

"Did you invade Lyfton to acquire such a treasure?" he tried to whisper. It didn't work. Elayna felt herself blush.

"Avoreed," Cydell answered absently.

"You invaded Avoreed?" Kovi prodded.

"No!" Her eyes narrowed as she addressed Kovi. The little man's eyes widened. He could only push Cydell so far.

"WHAT DO YOU WANT HERE?!" she finally bellowed in irritation.

"My, we are in quite a nasty humor this sun, are we not?" Kovi recovered from the threat in his sweetest guise. "I want nothing but to visit my cousin, whom I have not seen in several turns. And I am greeted by such hostility!"

"Be grateful I do not have you drawn and quartered! And stop drinking my marin!"

"You never were one to share your possessions, were you?" Kovi sipped from her marin cup anyway and set it down out of her reach. "In truth, I do have news."

"What kind of news?" Cydell was immediately interested. Rarely did Kovi ever leave his lavish estate for a mere pleasure ride to the palace.

"I am told by my trappers that there has been much activity in the mountains of late. It seems the tribes are stirring." All humor left Kovi's features as he delivered his tidings. Stories of the bloody Tribal Wars had been passed down for generations. Personally, he did not want to live through another war of any kind.

"That is not possible. All treaties have been signed and secured for ten Passes to come. If the chieftains were displeased, I am sure I would have been notified." Cydell reasoned, but in her heart she worried. Her nameless anxieties at last had their source. Now this, in addition to raiders masquerading as Sentinels, then stealing taxes from the villages and murdering her people.

"It is my feeling they are notifying you now."

Disturbed, Cydell rose and went to the window, her brow creased with worry. "How can this be?" she mused aloud.

"My suggestion," Kovi began as he stuffed more fruit in his mouth and beckoned for Elayna to refill the marin cup, "is to seek out our distant warrior cousin, Madras. You do remember him?"

"Yes. It has been many Passes. He is a respected tribesman, from all I have heard."

"Then you should summon him here and confer with him. I feel sure you will then discover what is brewing amongst his people!" Before Cydell could respond, Valkyra burst into the chamber followed by another woman dressed in skin leggings and a sleeveless wrap. She was tall and tanned from the sun. Her hair was short and pale blonde. There was an intricate silver ornament, as delicate as a spider's web, that wrapped around the outer edge of the woman's left ear. Over her shoulder hung a long bow and a quiver filled with arrows.

The woman seemed to take command of the chamber simply by stepping into it. She regarded those assembled with discerning, azure blue eyes. Valkyra stepped back, but not out of earshot, and let the woman present herself to the Hya. Elayna watched the proceedings with interest and mounting dread. Her stone was vibrating against her chest as though the jewel would explode into itself. She tried to ignore it.

"Who is she?" Elayna whispered to Josn.

"Zavia Wyere. Captain of the Hya's scouts."

Elayna frowned. "I have not heard of these scouts."

"Not many know of their existence. They have been trained by the Hya. Hand-selected. They are everywhere, throughout the region. Throughout the city. Posted in every village. Altogether, they are perhaps the only beings who may match a Sentinel in combat. They number in the hundreds," Josn smiled and looked proudly on Zavia, "and there is not a male among them."

Zavia stepped forward to meet the Hya and they gripped each other's forearms in greeting. Kovi watched the scene with interest. Even he did not know the ravishing warrior woman with the large blue eyes. He quickly understood from watching how she carried herself that he did not want to know her as an enemy.

"You bring ill tidings," Cydell predicted with some foreboding.

"That is true, Hya." Zavia's eyes sought out everyone in the chamber and rested for a moment on Elayna before she turned her attention back to the Hya and continued.

"The northern tribes are agitated. We were not worried at first, for they tend to flair every Pass or so. It is usually nothing serious; simply making us aware of their presence. This time, however, they are not only blowing smoke." She took a breath and looked at Cydell.

"Go on." Cydell was poised for anything. In a way, she was glad to have her suspicions confirmed.

"They have moved on Rogelle. Stole into the village in the night and sacked it. There were no survivors."

The silence after this announcement was deafening. Zavia let her words settle into the quiet. "A third of my company is still in Rogelle. I dispatched a scouting unit to follow the tribal raiders. Perhaps we may determine their next move."

"So you think they will continue in this fashion?" Cydell asked.

"It appears to be the onset of war, Hya."

"Damn!" Cydell paced in anger and agitation. "Clear this clutter!" she commanded. The serving girls, Josn and Elayna hopped to attention. The table was cleared in a heartbeat and the kitchen staff hurriedly left the chamber.

Cydell brought in a thick parchment from her study and laid it out on the table. Kovi was silently watching his cousin. Valkyra and Zavia moved closer to the table and stood in silence as Cydell studied the map.

"For the present, Zavia, I want small units of your scouts sentried throughout the tribal regions. Bring me the names of the chieftains leading this assault, and do not be long in returning."

"Yes, Hya," Zavia nodded gravely.

"Valkyra, dispatch riders to alert all Sentinel outposts in the villages south, east and west of Rogelle. No doubt they have already heard news of the attack, but I want them on full standby," Cydell ordered. Valkyra snapped a salute.

"Yes, Hya."

"Also, double the watch at the city's perimeters. I do not feel the tribes would be foolish enough to attempt an attack on Mauldar, but I would prefer not to take chances." The Hya turned to Zavia. "If there is another attack, I want prisoners. We *will* get to the bottom of this!"

Zavia and Valkyra bowed and quickly left the chamber to carry out their orders. Cydell paced like a caged tiger.

"Why would they do this? Without the slightest provocation?!" She turned to Kovi as though he had the answers. "This is what I do not understand."

"Nor do I. They were defeated before. Soundly. The Mauldaran forces and your Sentinels will defeat them again," Kovi stated matter-of-factly.

"You are so certain of this?"

"I am. Remember, you have a history of not wishing to share your possessions. Neither your food nor your holdings. They know you will not let this get out of hand. A trouncing by the Sentinel Guard is not something one quickly forgets. I am certain."

Another knock.

"Dornea! What is it now?!"

"You must calm yourself, Cousin. You are making yourself an old woman before forty Passes!"

"I have already seen forty Passes, you little...!"

"Temper, temper."

"And I will not be calm until I have some answers! Come!" she bellowed.

The guard entered and bowed. Cydell impatiently dismissed the courtesy with a wave of her hand.

"What is it?!"

"A priestess to see you, Hya," he announced.

"A priestess? I have no time for blessings."

Unheeding, the priestess brushed by the guard and hurried into the chamber. The guard rolled his eyes and shook his head. Apparently, no one was going to allow him to do his job this sun. Dornea's servant wore white silks beneath her woolen cloak. She was on her knees before the Hya only a beat before Cydell indicated that she should stand. Cydell did not frequent the temples and was often scolded by the High Provincial Council for her lack of piety.

All priestesses looked the same to her—dark-featured, beautiful women who always seemed to have an aura of peace about them. All the same, it was difficult for her not to be irritated at this untimely intrusion.

"Forgive me, Hya, for I know you are in the midst of important matters of state."

"Yes. How may I be of service to you?"

"I think, Hya, that I may be of service to you."

Cydell frowned, "How so?"

"We have had visions of a great evil that has manifested it-self within the region of Mauldar."

"We have just learned of that same evil, Priestess. It is called raving tribesmen. Speak of something we do not know," Kovi inter-rupted. Cydell held up a hand to silence him. The priestess contin-ued, undaunted.

"Yes. We know of the activity of the northern tribes. They are driven by this wickedness..."

"Let me understand you," Cydell paced. "The tribes are at-tacking, not because of a sudden disregard for the treaties, but by reason of this...evil?"

"Yes, Hya." The priestess watched the Hya's face for some sign that her sovereign really understood the seriousness of the mes-sage and was not feigning concern to placate her. "We know the might of the Sentinel Guard, Hya. But they will not be enough to stop the encroaching darkness. The power which compels the tribes will not be turned back by sabers and arrows." She paused to be sure she still had the Hya's attention. The Hya's cousin was smirking, hiding a giggle, but the Hya seemed to hang on every word.

"The evil must be destroyed at the source," she said.

"Which is?" Kovi asked as though waiting for the punch line of a tremendous joke. The priestess ignored him and turned so that she addressed the Hya directly.

"Windsom Keep."

Cydell regarded the priestess for a moment. "The tribal for-tress?" she asked incredulously.

"Yes, Hya."

Kovi made a disgusted sound and hopped down from what Cydell had begun to think was going to be his permanent place at her table.

"I have heard enough for one sun. I must return to attend my own affairs." He stopped when he reached the door. "Evil indeed," he shook his head, began whistling and left the two women alone.

"Forgive my cousin, Lady."

"There is no need. One believes what one believes. But with all proper respect, Hya, rarely are the oracles misguided. I beg of you, go to Windsom Keep..."

"I?" Cydell cocked an eyebrow. "I will not journey from the palace with threat of war so near the city gates. My Sentinel Guard..."

"*You* must go, Hya. *You* must make the journey," the priestess implored her.

Cydell paced the chamber. "Suppose I were to believe your oracle. You have said that sabers and arrows will not conquer this evil. The only skills I possess are those of a warrior. How then may it be defeated? What can I do alone, that my entire army cannot?"

The priestess paused before answering. In her silence, she slowly walked across the room and stood before Cydell's great-grandfather's saber where it hung on the wall.

"The fiend should have died by this blade. But for some reason, he was spared. Healed by the mercy of the goddess," the priestess whispered softly, as though entranced. "That mercy was betrayed with violence against the very one who had restored his life. The goddess ransomed his soul, and now he has harnessed the power of darkness, in hopes of reclaiming it." She turned to the Hya again.

"It is *this* blade, in your hands, that must deliver the final blow before this evil mage captures the heartstone and all of Mauldar."

There was a long silence before Cydell spoke.

"What is the heartstone?" she asked.

"There is someone here, in the palace, who knows of it. We have felt her power and have pleaded with her to come to the temple so we may learn more of her powers. But she will not abide."

"I will consider your counsel," Cydell stated quietly.

"You must not only consider, Hya. You must act. The evil one's power is strengthened with each new sun. Hundreds of thousands will be slaughtered, for the tribes no longer reason as men. There is no mercy in their hearts. And if there are survivors in this world after the destruction and devastation, they will be doomed to a life of darkness and slavery."

When the Hya did not respond, the priestess sighed and went to the chamber door in a whisper of silken robes. She looked back at the Hya once again before leaving.

Lost in thought, Cydell took her great-grandfather's saber from its place on the wall. She was not one to believe in such nonsense as good and evil. These were intangibles, only words used to frighten the irreverent into kneeling before a god or goddess who might or might not bless them at all in the end. Skill was power. Wisdom was power over any enemy. *But how could one fight what one could not see?* And yet, as her mother had often told her, one must believe in something.

She slowly shook her head. War in her forty-second Pass? In this moment, she felt every sun of those Passes. She had earned her own command as a young Sentinel during the final three Passes of the Tribal Wars. How boastful and proud her father had been of his warrior daughter's skill as a fighter. Cydell absentmindedly fingered a scar from those battles. It was time again to defend her city and her people, and now her rule. Her physical strength would be tested. Now. At forty-two Passes. True, she had been trained to kill in many ways, but could she still? Daily exercise had kept her physically strong and her skills honed, but did she still have the heart of a warrior? Had she grown soft during the many Passes of peace?

Her greatest fear was becoming old and fat, surrounded by healers who could do nothing to give her health again. Loss of wit. Sour of humor. An old shell of a woman who could barely move to relieve herself, much less rule.

But the priestess had said she had to go. Cydell swung her grandfather's saber over her head, and with a skillful two-handed sweep, conquered a mass of imaginary enemies. She smiled to herself in the silence of the chamber and brought the ancient blade before her face in a Sentinel salute. At forty-two Passes, her position as Hya demanded that she do all within her power to protect her people. At forty-two Passes her body was firm and muscled, sleek and lean. Cydell knew how she did not want to die. But she did not know what awaited at Windsom Keep, for she had no concept of the face of evil. Sorcery was beyond her. She knew only that if this evil had a physical presence, she could fight it. And even at forty-two Passes, strike at least one fatal blow.

The first thing Cydell did that evenfall was to handpick fifty of her best Sentinels to accompany her on the journey. Valkyra was among them, and had her orders to prepare to leave Mauldar at dawn the next sun.

Cydell was in her chamber seeing to her own provisions. As always, she traveled light. The stewards had instructions to prepare Shadow, her young stallion. If she knew the horse, and she did, having broken him to the saddle herself, he was already prancing in his stall in anticipation.

There were two more tasks to attend to before Cydell could rest that evening. As if she had read her intentions, Josn burst into Cydell's chamber just as she completed her packing.

The old nurse stood in the doorway, eyes fixed on the saddle roll and pack Cydell held in her hands.

"You cannot do this!" she cried. "The High Provincial Council will not allow it!" Cydell had rarely seen Josn so upset. This would be most difficult.

"The High Provincial Council has nothing to do with this. If going to Windsom Keep will protect my people, then it must be done." She looked at the old woman before her and softened.

"You know my duty better even than I, do you not?" Cydell smiled warmly. Josn went to her and placed both her hands in Cydell's. Cydell gently rubbed the back of Josn's hands with her thumbs.

"Have no worries. I have every intention of returning," she tried to soothe her.

"Those are only your intentions. They may not be Dornea's," Josn's eyes misted. After all their Passes together, it would be unbearable to lose her charge now.

Again, Cydell spoke soothingly but firmly. "I have trained all my life to rule and to defend Mauldar. Perhaps this is the true test." Cydell kissed the old woman's tear-stained cheek. "I expect my chamber to be warm and fragrant upon my return."

Josn gathered herself and gave her charge her most respect-
ful bow. Cydell caught her by an elbow before she could get down
very far.

"How often have I told you, old one, I am *your* servant. Do
not bow to me."

Josn pulled Cydell to her and embraced her as she used to do
when a very young Hya Regent would fall and scrape her knees.

"You had best mind yourself," she whispered in Cydell's ear.
"The young sorceress will help you, if you allow it." They released
each other and Josn started for the door.

"Speaking of Elayna, send her to me. Please."

"Gladly, my dear Hya."

It was not long before there was a tentative tapping on her
chamber door.

"Come!"

Elayna poked her head around the door.

When Cydell looked up and saw her, she smiled. "The Commander General is not lurking in the shadows here. She is much too
busy preparing for our journey, as you will be. Josn will see that you
have all you require."

"Where am I going?" Elayna asked as she stepped into the
chamber. When their eyes met, both women were speechless for the
briefest moment. Cydell regained her composure first. This was not
the time for remembering passionate dreams.

"I was visited this sun by one of the priestesses. In short, she
strongly urged me to make a journey to Windsom Keep. Apparently,
the Keep is at the heart of the current uprisings amongst the tribes.
Thus, these preparations." Cydell indicated her pack. "It seems you
are involved in the matter somehow, and shall accompany me."

The news did not come as a surprise to Elayna. She trusted
in her goddess and would follow whatever path was chosen for her.
But somewhere in the recesses of her mind, Elayna knew the trouble
at Windsom Keep was what the dark stranger had told her of with his
dying breath. And if his initial intention had been to kill her, why had
he tried to warn her? If this journey was her fate, then so be it.

Sensing Elayna's hesitation, Cydell said, "If you have concerns for Orrat's safety, put them to rest. He will be well protected here in the palace. However, your personal protection does concern me."

"Oh?" Elayna's eyebrows rose. "My goddess protects me. There is no need for concern."

"Yes. Well. These tribes, I am sure, have scouts throughout the woods we will travel. I could be mistaken, but I doubt they will wait for you to say a prayer before they slice off your head."

Elayna folded her arms across her chest and stood her ground. "Do not concern yourself, Hya. Your name would be the last I would call should I have need of protection."

"I will make certain that it is. I shall teach you the saber as we journey. I know not what lies in store at the Keep, but it is a fair journey. You should be quite adept by the time we arrive there."

Stubbornly, Elayna persisted, "I have my own defenses. Do you think I am so helpless merely because I do not know the saber?!"

This was not turning out as Cydell had anticipated. She had thought the witch would be glad of the lessons. Obviously, she was not.

"Why must you fight me at every turn?!" Cydell argued in exasperation. "Granted, if you had a saber as sharp as your tongue, you would do very well indeed at protecting yourself!"

"I do not require knowledge of the saber!" Elayna countered.

"Fine! I dare say you will have a change of heart very quickly when the Commander General decides to have a bit of sport with you! You are dismissed. Josn will supply you with clothing more suited for travel, as well as other supplies."

With that, Cydell angrily turned back to her packing. Elayna started to reply, thought better of it, and briskly left the chamber.

◻ ◻ ◻ ◻ ◻

Orrat slipped quietly from the ward quarters and ran crouched to the back of the refectory. The familiar form of his sister was huddled in the moonlight against the stonework of the refectory walls. Elayna hugged him tight. She was glad for the darkness so he could not see her tears. They sat in the shadows cast by the moonlight, leaning back against the cold stone. Orrat rested his arms on his bent knees and stared out at the training yard. The practice dummies were a ghost regiment swinging almost in unison in the light night breeze. Crickets and night birds kept cadence for the make-believe army.

"It is not fair!" He brought a fist down in the dirt beside him. "I should go as well. You need someone to protect you."

"I will be fine. I would feel better knowing you were safe." She reached to smooth his hair but he shirked away.

"I am not a babe to be protected. I am the best ward in combat training and nearly as good as Rii with the saber and long bow." He realized he was whining, but he didn't care. Every fiber of his being longed to be a member of the Hya's party. But he had to remain behind.

"You are not yet a Sentinel. Josn said there will be many dangers, even perhaps before we reach the Keep."

"Yes, I know." Orrat glanced at his sister and then back at the yard, then said resignedly, "I am sure the Hya will protect you."

"I do not need the Hya's protection! Why does everyone think me so helpless?"

"From what I have seen, you would not mind it so much."

"You have seen nothing!" Elayna got to her feet. "I must be up before sunrise."

"Elayna," Orrat's voice stopped her. "Do you still hate the Hya? I do not think you do."

"You speak of things you know nothing about."

"As I said, I am not a babe."

Elayna turned to him as the true meaning of his words penetrated. She really looked at him then. His shoulders had broadened. He no longer had the swagger of a boy, but stood straight and confident, ready to let his skill prove his manhood. He was a handsome, dashing youth even in the paleness of the moonlight. His blond hair, as fine as silk, almost white in the pale glow that surrounded them, fell just past his shoulders. He was no longer the mischievous boy of Avoreed, for the discipline of his training had made him tough and so much older in spirit. No, He did not appear to her to be a boy any more.

"I fear I will not see you again," he said softly as he went to her. "And it worries me to see the look of hatred in your eyes when you speak of the Hya. You try so much to hate her."

"I cannot get Caly out of my mind," Elayna admitted.

Stroking her arm, he said, "The Hya did not kill Caly. It is time to make room for someone else in your heart, Elayna. I know it is lonely for you here, but only because you make it so." Orrat took his sister's hand and kissed her cheek. "Fair journey, Elayna."

"Take care until my return. And stay out of trouble!" She stroked his cheek with the back of her hand. She again tried to walk away, but Orrat held her hand and she looked at him questioningly.

"If she wishes to protect you, let her," he winked wickedly and released her. With a final wave, Elayna turned, and drawing her cloak around her, hurried back into the kitchen entrance of the palace.

☐ ☐ ☐ ☐ ☐

Valkyra sat on a log in the clearing, pulling her woolen cape around her shoulders. The night air was chilly and the small fire was barely keeping her warm. She rose as her mercenary band slowly trudged from the cave, disgruntled at having their gambling interrupted. A wise commander, Valkyra knew that her men were getting restless and weary of milling about their cave site. They had become so unruly on their frequent trips into Mauldar that Valkyra had ordered Pak to keep them all within his sight. And so they had been repairing harnesses, sharpening weapons and tending their mounts. But they were restless. Having already gambled their spoils away, they lusted for more.

The sight of their tall and striking leader always left the men in awe. Such beauty, cleverness and cunning were almost enough to earn her their undying loyalty. Almost.

Valkyra had begun making plans since hearing Zavia's report to the Hya. If she was going to secure the remaining finances needed to maintain her steadily increasing army, then she had to have more onas and lathium bars to buy supplies and sustain the camp during the coming winter. This could not be done as easily as before with the Hya and the Sentinel Guard roaming about in the woods between Windsom Keep and Mauldar. It would be that much more difficult to raid the remaining villages. She was well aware that her company consisted of thieves and cutthroats and adventurers, not highly trained and skilled warriors. They would be no match for a Sentinel patrol. There had to be another way.

Valkyra's breath smoked in the chilly night air as she began to speak, looking from one scarred, unshaven face to another.

"Pak has told me of your concerns," she began. "And I have no intentions of letting you starve through the winter." This last was met with a murmur of approval from the men. Valkyra held up a hand to silence them.

"Ginnach holds the richest tax house. Enough to see us through until spring, when we mount our first campaign against Mauldar."

"We have heard rumors of tribesmen coming down from the mountains!" someone yelled. "What if they take Ginnach before us?"

"That is not likely, as you will pack and begin marching tonight!" she announced.

This brought a murmur of disapproval.

"Silence!" Valkyra bellowed. The men settled down, shifting nervously. Pak dared to speak what the rest of the men were thinking.

"Captain Valkyra, the fastest route to Ginnach from here is through Wen Yor marsh. The marsh is deadly enough in the light of day. It would be foolish to pass through at night."

Valkyra turned stormy eyes on her lieutenant. She was not close enough to strike him again, but from the look on her face, he felt as though she had run him through with her saber.

Her words barely veiled her fury at Pak's outspokenness.

"Then why do you stand here debating the issue? Your pace will determine at what time of the day you arrive at Wen Yor. I shall be riding with the Hya's party, but I will slip away and lead the raid myself, if you do not feel..."

"I am your second. I will lead the raid."

Valkyra went to him and graced him with a cool smile.

"I was beginning to think I had made a poor choice, Lieutenant Pak. Do not make me doubt you again."

Briefly, Pak was lost in the scent of her. Her nearness. But he abruptly returned to his senses and with a curt bow, started to walk away.

"Lieutenant?" Pak stopped and slowly turned to face her. "If, by some mischance, the Hya's party happens to be in Ginnach at the time of the raid...."

"Yes, Captain?"

"I shall hold you personally responsible for making sure that the Hya and the Avoreedan witch traveling with her, do not escape alive." Valkyra turned on her heel and stalked into the cave as her lieutenant absorbed the chilling significance of her words.

Pak stood stunned, alone in the clearing, as the company of mercenaries noisily gathered their belongings to prepare for their long march.

6

RITDON WOOD

The Hya's mounted party, cloaked against the predawn chill, awaited her in the courtyard. They were shadows in the mist of their own breath as a fog swirled around them. The rhythm of the impatient clip clop of the horses' hooves on the cobblestones of the courtyard echoed their own eagerness to leave.

Valkyra positioned herself beside the Hya's mount, in the middle of the company, thinking this her rightful position. Fifty accompanying Sentinels were mounted two abreast. The last twenty soldiers in the rear would double back after two or three leagues to secure their backs and make sure they were not being followed. The Hya had selected the best of the Sentinel Guard and they sat proudly, each apprehensive and yet anxious for the journey to begin.

Their tack was polished to a glass sheen. On the Hya's orders, they did not wear their Sentinel uniforms or the Sentinel masks—black full-face helmets streaked with red up along the cheek bones, with slits for the eyes, nose and mouth. She did not want to broadcast who they were, thereby discouraging an attack. She was deliberately inviting danger, treachery from thieves and tribal scouts, for she wanted live prisoners to interrogate.

Their packs were rolled and filled with a full supply of rations that might or might not last until they reached Windsom Keep, perhaps not even through the Ritdon Woods. But they would hunt game along the way to keep themselves stocked. They wore leggings of deer hide, woolen tunics and heavy woolen cloaks to protect themselves from the morning chill and the early mountain winter. In short, they were an impressive company.

Elayna was positioned behind Valkyra and the Hya, though she would have preferred to ride in the rear. Any position was better than this one. Josn had seen to her provisions, providing her with leggings, like the others, and new boots which were beautiful, but tight. The old woman had assured her the tightness would disappear after a time, as the leather became more supple. She was glad for the warm clothes. The skirts she had been wearing around the palace were heavy and cumbersome and she wondered if these fine skins were hers to keep. She pulled her cloak up around her shoulders, praying that the sun would break through soon, and with a shiver, vigorously rubbed the neck of her beautiful bay gelding. Secretly, she was proud that her mount was as fine as the others.

The Sentinels behind her were chatting excitedly amongst themselves as they waited. Their camaraderie only reminded her of how alone she was. Now it seemed that even Orrat was building a life without her. Abruptly, she came out of her reverie to see Valkyra turned in her saddle, watching her. The expression on the Commander General's face was not pleasant.

"Be mindful of your place during the course of this journey, witch!" she hissed. "I have not forgotten my debt to you."

Elayna said nothing in response, but felt somewhat comforted knowing that someone had strapped a saber in with the rest of her gear.

Just then, Cydell strode briskly from the palace. She cut a striking figure in her black woolen tunic, belted at the waist with a sash, and the burnished leather belt of her scabbard. The black riding pants hugged her figure and the thigh-high boots clicked on the stones of the courtyard. She pulled on her black leather riding gloves as she gave last-minute instructions to Josn, who was trotting to keep up with her long strides. Elayna looked down at her hands and compared her riding gloves with Cydell's. They were of doeskin, lined with fur on the inside, but fine just the same. She wondered if the Hya herself had selected her gloves. A gift, perhaps. Like the saber.

"Mind my palace, old woman," Cydell teased as a tear began trailing down the old nurse's cheek.

"You mind yourself in your cockiness! What shall I say to the Council?"

Cydell swung into the saddle and rubbed her horse's neck with fervor.

"My scouts will see that each member of the Council knows that I will be...away...for a time," she said as she looked back in approval of her company. And then she smiled down at Josn, "And that I have every intention of returning."

Cydell's eyes rested on Elayna for a moment before she turned and raised her hand.

The company moved forward at a walk through the sleeping city, out of the gates and down the roadway that would lead them north to the Ritdon Woods and the dangers therein and beyond.

口 口 口 口 口

The eastern sky turned a brilliant orange as prelude to the rising of the sun, on that sixth day of the turn. Elayna heard the Sentinels talking and laughing behind her, enjoying the easy pace the Hya set. There would be enough to worry about once they reached the woods. As the morning sun burned off the chill in the air, the riders let their cloaks fall open to take in the warmth.

The roadway was crowded with travelers. A few sat in the shade of the trees lining the embankment on both sides of the road. Merchant caravans plodded along. Single family wagons and small bands of mercenaries, some mounted, some not, made their way to their own destinations, too involved in their own journeys to be curious about the mounted party passing by.

Their Hya was a mystery woman who they thought never strayed from Mauldar. Most had never had an opportunity to go to the palace. Those who were summoned often never returned home, having been found guilty of a crime and subsequently imprisoned or executed. So the company of Sentinels were met with nods, smiles, and oftentimes whistles of admiration, for among the men, there were an impressive number of strong, attractive women. They appeared to be the expansive entourage of an important diplomat en route to some affair of state.

They had traveled barely ten leagues when a rider in the distance halted his mount in the middle of the road and stopped to wait for the approaching party. As they drew closer, Elayna recognized the Hya's cousin and stifled a giggle. Kovi saluted them grandly in greeting. His broad smile split his features like a streak of lightning in the night.

The company came to a halt as Kovi sidled up to Cydell.

"It is about time you happened along. I was growing weary of waiting."

"This is no holiday, Kovi. We are on important business. You should be about defending your own lands," Cydell admonished him.

"Would that important business happen to involve Windsom Keep? Yours are not the only spies in Mauldar, Cousin," he replied smugly.

"Evidently," Cydell said dryly.

"I would like to join your company. I can be of service to you," Kovi offered, hoping against hope that she wouldn't deny him. The truth was, he was dreadfully bored and looking for any diversion he could find that would hold his interest for longer than a sun.

"I must think on the matter, Cousin," Cydell began. "None of us will have the time or the inclination to help you up and down from the back of that enormous creature you are riding."

The Sentinels laughed out loud. Elayna covered her mouth with her hand, for Kovi's mount was smaller than a standard pony, but it was just his size. Mount and rider were dwarfed by the rest of the company.

"Are you done with your sport?" Kovi asked smartly. Cydell was enjoying herself and he knew it. As much as he loved to joke at the expense of others, he was terribly thin-skinned when the tables were turned.

Finally, Cydell became serious, "I know not what perils await us, Kovi. But you are welcome to share them if you wish."

Kovi grinned and nodded in acceptance. "My most gracious thanks, Cousin. I will not be a hindrance. I swear."

"See that you are not. Fall in." They all waited while Kovi looked the company over, trying to decide where to position himself. Spying Elayna riding by herself, his eyes lit up.

"Ahh! No one should be alone in the company of others." He fell in beside Elayna, much to the relief of the Sentinels and the amusement of Valkyra.

□ □ □ □ □

Orrat and Rii crouched in darkness against the city walls, their eyes fastened on the guard tower as the sentry paced back and forth. The Hya's party had been gone for two suns. It had taken Orrat that long to plan his escape and only seconds to convince Rii to join him.

He had made up his mind the night he and Elayna said goodbye. He was convinced that the fighting skills he'd acquired since becoming an apprentice would be all he needed to keep himself safe. He had his saber. Rations would not be a problem as he was a good hunter of small game. What he didn't have was a horse. But that didn't worry him either. A good thief could always secure a good mount.

Rii nudged him so hard he almost lost his balance.

"Put your hood over your head," Rii whispered. "It will be your hair that betrays us!" Orrat did as he was told. "How do you propose we acquire horses?" Rii asked. He had gathered the length of his cloak around him so as not to entangle himself if they had to move quickly.

"First we get out of the city. Then we worry about horses." As he spoke, a wagon caravan loaded with miners stopped at the gate. Orrat was on his feet, pulling Rii to his.

"Hurry! This is our opportunity."

"A mining caravan?!" Rii's eyes were wide and bright in the darkness. "I will follow you, my fair friend, but not into a Mauldaran mine. I cherish my freedom too much!"

"We only take the wagon so far. Come before our chance is gone!"

In silence, they ran along the wall to the caravan, the darkness covering their movement. One of the drivers was having a loud difference of opinion with the sentry. Orrat indicated the last wagon, which was not occupied by miners but covered with a tarp. The boys hopped into the back of the wagon, slipped under the tarp and shimmied in among barrels of swill, used to feed the stock at the mining yards. They held their breath against the stench and covered themselves with their cloaks, barely allowing themselves a sigh of relief when the wagons began to rumble slowly out of the gates and down the roadway.

◻ ◻ ◻ ◻ ◻

Masses of angry tribesmen milled about the grounds of Windsom Keep. All of the northern tribes had left their permanent camping grounds, their hearth fires, their women, their duties, to answer the compelling summons of the Keep Master.

The shell of what had been Madras Sadiin stood out on the study balcony looking at the thousands of small campfires that lit up the night like so many fireflies. One would have expected noise and raucous laughter, swaggering drinking songs bellowed from tribesmen too full of ale to stand, much less fight. But there was only silence. An ominous, haunting silence. The Master kept a tight reign on them and allowed no distractions from his demonic goal. In a carefully orchestrated plan, each tribe awaited its turn to venture forth from the mountains to conquer Mauldar and wreak destruction on the villages in their path.

A slow, sinister smile marked Madras' features for a brief second. It was not Madras' smile. He had long since forgotten the joy of simple things. The former Madras would have marvelled at the huge wave of potential destruction gathered below him, awaiting his orders to strike. His minions had already destroyed three villages in the foothills. They had ravaged and burned and raped unchallenged. And then they had moved on. The initial tribal battalions had been very successful. There was no need to send these reserves. Yet. The Madras shell stood deep in thought, observing the scene below. Suddenly, it raised its left hand before its face to study the oozing wound there. The bandages would have to be replaced. Again. For the fourth time that sun.

□ □ □ □ □

When Orrat woke up it was dark and it took him a while to adjust his eyes to the black of night. He grimaced as he got a good whiff of himself and stretched his legs before he tried to stand.

The night was eerie. No birds calling. No small animals scurrying about in the brush. Too quiet. He ventured out of the small brush-covered cove where he'd been sleeping, and tripped, landing face down in the leaves. Rii's laughter echoed through the stillness.

"You are very clumsy for a mighty Sentinel," he teased. He was sitting back against a tree, watching Orrat recover himself.

They'd fallen asleep in the mining wagon, and having been discovered by the driver when the caravan had stopped along the road, were tossed none too gently into a bank of trees. Stinking, hungry and exhausted, they'd reached the Ritdon Wood on foot, found a heavy undergrowth of foliage and fallen asleep. They had sabers and short blades, but no food or water or horses.

Orrat settled himself beside his friend. This was not turning out as he had anticipated. His feet were sore from walking and he was starving. But he was not going to turn back.

"I hope you had a good nap," Rii said as he handed Orrat a handful of live beetles and some roots. Disgusted, Orrat swore and tossed the roots and insects out into the darkness.

"If that was supposed to be a joke, I am not laughing!"

"That was your dinner, idiot! And the only source of water I could find!" Rii argued.

"You expect me to eat beetles?!"

"What have *you* found for food? Were you hunting in your dreams, perhaps?"

Orrat jumped to his feet in anger.

"Does it make you the better warrior because you can hunt beetles in the dark?"

Rii stood as well. "I am the better warrior. It was I on watch while you slept. It was I who provided food you were too good to eat! What good will you be in combat if you are too weak to fight?"

"Who are you calling weak!?"

"You! Why, you can barely stay on your feet most of the time! You swallow more dust than a dungbeetle!"

Orrat dropped and clipped Rii at the ankles, sending him sprawling. Rii was on his feet in an instant, saber drawn.

"Will you never learn, ward? Never have you defeated me with the saber," Rii challenged.

"There is a first time for all things, Prince of the Barrach!" Orrat said between clenched teeth.

The two wards had to strain to see each other in the darkness, but they were determined to fight, so they did. They were not aware of the tribesmen until Orrat yelled for Rii to duck.

"You will not trick me with that old ruse!" Rii jeered.

Ignoring him, Orrat charged and knocked Rii to the ground with such force it took the breath from both of them. By then they were surrounded by three tribesmen who bore down on them. Their sabers were out of reach, lost somewhere in the darkness.

"If I am to die, I do not want to be on my back!" Orrat shouted as he kicked out at their attackers. The tribesmen were caught off guard long enough for the young men to get to their feet. They fought in complement to each other, doubling their strength in the face of death as they had been taught. But the tribesmen would not relent and the boys began to tire. Their blows were quickly losing their effectiveness, but their pride and fear would not allow them give up.

And then, out of nowhere, arrows streaked through the darkness. Tribesmen fell away and turned to face the deadly shadows. But the arrows came too quickly and found their marks one after the other, until in the end, five bodies lay still on the floor of the wood.

Rii and Orrat collapsed against each other, sinking to the ground, too exhausted to worry about who had saved them.

Four women stepped over the fallen tribesmen and approached the boys. They wore skin leggings and short cloaks, the hoods thrown back.

The leader of the archers stood over the boys threateningly while the others retrieved their arrows from the bodies of the dead.

"Identify yourselves," she ordered ominously.

"I am Orrat. This is my comrade, Rii."

Zavia suspiciously eyed the two for a moment. "What is to prevent me from slitting your throats? For all I know, you are in league with these tribesmen."

"We are not! We are Sentinels of the Hya Cydell Ra Sadiin."

Zavia cocked an eyebrow, "Sentinels? So poorly armed?"

"We are wards," Rii corrected, rolling his eyes. Orrat would get them killed yet.

"Ahh." Zavia seemed to relax. She offered her water skin to Orrat. He took a huge swallow and passed it to Rii. Zavia squatted before them, adjusting the straps of her quiver.

"What are you doing out here? Where are your mounts?" she rebuked them.

The two boys looked at each other. Orrat explained how they'd left the palace on their own and ended up in the woods.

"I am amazed you did not have the entire tribe here with that smell about you," Zavia teased as she crinkled her nose and fanned the air.

"Who are you?" Orrat finally asked.

"Scouts for the Hya. We are on our way to report to her now." Orrat was on his feet.

"Then you can take me to my sister! She is one of the Hya's company."

"Yes," Zavia rose. "I could do that. However, I would not be so anxious to meet up with the Hya, if I were you two. She does not deal well with disobedience."

That was a small detail Orrat had not considered. Cydell would be furious. And Valkyra? He looked at Rii, who must have been reading his mind.

"We should have let them kill us," Rii moaned.

They passed the night without incident, in the protective custody of Zavia and her scouts. But neither of the wards slept well. They were not looking forward to their impending confrontation with their Hya.

❏ ❏ ❏ ❏ ❏

Ritdon Wood cradled the Hya's company below its towering density of trees, limbs raised gracefully up towards the slow-moving clouds of the evening. Intermittent shafts of moonlight reassured the travelers in the eerie shadows, for the Hya had ordered that their camp be dark, no cook fires. The closer they came to the foothills, the more cautious they were. Sentinel guards kept watch on the perimeters of the camp. The faint smell of distant smoke wafted over their wary, silent camp and they all realized, with dreadful certainty, that another village had been sacked.

Valkyra and the Hya were restless. Cydell paced a few feet from the camp. Valkyra busied herself by checking the Sentinels on duty and the mounts which were tethered close by. Kovi sat across from Elayna in the clearing they'd chosen for their campsite. He regarded the beauty quizzically. The breeze of the night was not chilly, but rather comfortable. Too comfortable, he thought, for the young woman to sit swathed in her heavy cloak as she was.

Elayna's sense of foreboding intensified, for the heartstone had been burning since they had entered the wood. Fearing someone would notice, she kept it hidden beneath her cloak, no matter how unusually warm the night air had become. When she looked up, Kovi was standing over her. He had babbled incessantly since joining the party, and at some point during the journey, she had shut him out. He talked still, but she was lost in her own thoughts. Now he stood looking down at her with that impish smile on his lips. It seemed to Kovi that his cousin was purposely avoiding anything to do with the green-eyed beauty. In fact, they seemed to be avoiding each other. The trip could not be very enjoyable for either of them, especially with the Commander General along.

"Are you so chilled by this warm night air?" he asked inquisitively. Uninvited, he settled himself beside her. Elayna was not looking forward to more of the little man's chatter.

"I am unused to the night air," she replied, mentally willing him to go away. Kovi found himself consciously fighting a strong urge to retreat to his spot on the other side of the clearing.

"It seems there is much you are not used to, regarding Mauldar."

"I am learning." The stone was hot against her skin but she did not dare adjust it.

"This is such a morbid gathering. I was hoping for a bit of sport."

Impatiently, she said, "There is a great danger we face. This is no time for sport."

"You believe, then, this talk of the power of Windsom Keep?" he asked.

Elayna jumped. Kovi frowned.

"I did not mean to upset you," he apologized.

Elayna clutched the heartstone, and trying not to panic, searched the darkness as she rose to a crouch.

"Something is out there," she whispered.

"If you are hearing things, it is probably my cousin and her Commander General doing what they are best at," Kovi leered, dismissing Elayna's alarm. But she shushed him in a whisper. It was then they heard the battle cry and the clash of sabers in the distance.

Courageously, the little man drew his knife as he helped Elayna to her feet. She screamed as something like a human form jumped from the shadows and overtook Kovi. She shrank back against the tree, watching the Hya's cousin attempt to save them both. The attacker was a human, dressed in the loincloth, his chest painted with the symbols of his tribe. His hair was wild and his eyes glazed with battle lust. The tribesman stalked Kovi, sensing an easy victory, eyes wild and vacant, unseeing. But Kovi's size made him extremely agile, and when the tribesman lunged, Kovi rolled out of reach as Elayna had seen the Sentinels do in practice.

At that moment, Cydell rushed into the clearing, breathless, her saber drawn, dripping crimson. Two more creatures were on her heels and she turned in a crouch just in time to miss being beheaded by the stroke of the short-bladed broadsword. She fought both at once, kicking one in the chest while slashing the other across the midriff with a side stroke. Valkyra entered the clearing with her back to Elayna. She fought two more assailants. Skillfully, the Sentinel who had been on watch drew their attackers into the clearing, out from the cover of trees and brush. Valkyra downed her attackers and started on three more, who quickly replaced their fallen comrades.

Elayna stood round-eyed, feeling helpless. Kovi was tiring, having fought off the first flood of wild-eyed attackers. Nevertheless, he engaged one of the three new tribesmen who were closing in on Cydell. The clearing was littered with dead tribesmen. Elayna watched her companions fight the seemingly endless stream of tribesmen running into the clearing from all directions. One Sentinel fell from a stroke from behind. Cydell's shout brought Elayna out of her haze.

"See to the mounts!"

Elayna was riveted to the spot. Her feet would not respond. The tribesmen seemed to close in on her and there was nowhere to run.

"Elayna! The horses!" Cydell's voice was strained from the exertion of the fight. Elayna broke into a run in the direction of the horses when something grabbed her ankle, tripping her. A dying tribesman held her, pulling her toward him with his ebbing strength. She tried to pull away, to twist herself out of his grasp, but he held on. In her struggle, her cloak fell open.

Magically, the clearing was bathed in a brilliant blue-white light. The fighting stopped as the combatants shielded their eyes from the light and searing heat, from a blaze they instinctively knew was fatal. The tribesman holding Elayna suddenly released her, screaming in pain. She watched in horror as the scream froze on his contorted features. His body blazed from the searing ray of power that was emanating from the stone. Kovi's attackers stopped in their tracks and dropped their weapons, for the rays had stunned them. They covered their eyes, backing away, finally running from the clearing. But they were not saved. Their screams echoed through the tumult of the night, finally fading out into the darkness.

The company watched in amazement as one by one, the dead bodies lying about the clearing flashed, were engulfed in the white light, and then vanished. Only the fallen Sentinel remained after the destruction. In the eerie silence which followed, not even the stench of burned flesh lingered.

When Elayna could see again, the clearing was empty save for her companions. The Sentinels, Kovi, Valkyra and Cydell stood in stunned silence, watching her. No one offered a hand to help her to her feet. It was as though they had all stopped breathing, though their chests heaved and their bodies sagged with exhaustion. It seemed an eternity before Elayna rose, unsteadily. She tentatively touched the stone and tucked it inside her tunic. It was ice cold now. Still, no one spoke. She noticed the fallen Sentinel holding her side as blood seeped through her fingers. Elayna went to her, but as she knelt to tend her, the Sentinel cringed away, fearful of the wielder of such power. Trembling and confused, Elayna slowly rose and looked at them each in turn.

The others slowly turned their gaze on Cydell, wondering what her reaction to the witch's display of power would be. After a moment, the Hya shrugged with a wan smile. She wearily ran her fingers through her curls and squatted, balancing her weight on the balls of her feet.

"Indeed. It seems you are not so defenseless after all," she said quietly.

Elayna could endure their scrutiny no longer. She turned in the direction she had started in earlier, and without a word, disappeared into the night to be with the horses.

Murmurs of conversation carried on the night breeze to where Elayna sat by the horses. She had no desire to rejoin the company after securing the mounts. They'd all looked at her as though *she* were something evil, something to be feared.

Now she understood the things her mother had told her about the heartstone and the powers that were granted to the wearer. She had told Elayna that the stone would come to full power when the time was right. How could she have foreseen the evil that threatened them now, devouring Mauldar? Elayna held the stone in her hands. It pulsed orange now. Almost as though its heart were beating in cadence with her own. It was beautiful and dangerous in its calm. Sensing a presence, she looked up. Cydell stood a few paces away, watching her. The Hya went to her and offered a satchel of rations. Elayna's first thought was to refuse, for she hadn't realized she was hungry until this moment. She accepted the dried beef and bread. Cydell set the water skin down beside Elayna and turned to go back to the camp.

"You do not have to leave," Elayna said softly, surprising herself.

"I was leaving because I was not asked to stay."

Elayna made room so Cydell could join her. She winced as she gingerly sat, smiling to hide the pain when Elayna glanced at her. The Hya watched in silence as Elayna hungrily ate.

"Thank you," Elayna said at last as she wiped her mouth. She was a little embarrassed, for she was eating as though she were starving.

"We are the ones who owe you thanks. As skilled as we are, we had no defense against such numbers."

"I did nothing. In truth, I am surprised to see you here. Are you not afraid of me?"

"Granted, I do not wish to be roasted like a boar on a spit, but I am not afraid of you," Cydell smiled.

Elayna was relieved. She was at ease with the Hya and very glad for the company, however brief it might be.

"I do not claim to understand this power of yours," Cydell continued, "but I must say I have of late developed a great respect for it. I am curious. What more can you tell me of this heartstone of yours?"

Elayna was uneasy under the Hya's gentle scrutiny and did not meet her eyes as she spoke.

"It belonged to my mother's mother, who was much favored by the goddess. Before my mother died, she taught me the healing powers of the heartstone. But she warned me of its other powers as well. She said that at the proper time, those other powers would awaken and protect me against an unfathomable evil.

"I did not realize until now that this stone held the power of death." She looked into the Hya's eyes then. "I felt its fire first around the mysterious stranger in the training yard. And again this night. It seems to have a will of its own."

Cydell had been listening intently and finally, she sighed.

"Interesting, indeed. Perhaps it *is* the will of your goddess that you make this journey. Fortunately, your heartstone spared my Sentinels, where the tribesmen did not. There are many who have need of you." Cydell rose too quickly and grunted in pain.

"You are hurt!" Elayna jumped up.

"I am afraid I was much quicker twenty Passes ago. It will heal."

"Let me look at it."

She saw the Hya tense as she started toward her. Dejected, Elayna stepped back again.

"Your troops have need of me, but you do not?"

Cydell sighed, closed her eyes, and grudgingly lifted her soiled tunic. The wound was wrapped, but not well enough to stop the blood from seeping through.

"I see none of our company knows the healer's art," Elayna said as she unwrapped the bandage and tossed it aside.

"It is a scratch."

"A scratch that will become infected if not properly treated." Gently, she pressed the area around the wound.

"Must you do that?!"

"Be still!" Elayna barked back, and as an afterthought, addressed her sweetly and properly, "...Hya."

"There are no more bandages," Cydell murmured, trying to think of anything that would keep her mind off the pain.

"None are needed." Elayna stood up seconds later. "You may open your eyes now."

Cydell looked down. The wound was gone except for a thin scar. She looked at Elayna in amazement, but could think of nothing to say. She lowered her tunic and watched as the breeze brushed loose strands of silky blonde hair across Elayna's face. She couldn't move. Couldn't think. All the emotional weakness she had been taught to subdue came rushing to the surface. She saw something in the greenness, the pools that were Elayna's eyes, that frightened her, excited her, caressed her.

Suddenly, a familiar voice intruded, "I wondered where you had gotten to." Valkyra stood watching them, hands on her hips. The spell was broken.

"Elayna was tending my wound." Cydell stated matter-of-factly, and as she turned back to Elayna, "Thank you. It is best that you return to camp now. These woods are not safe. A Sentinel will watch the mounts." She indicated that Elayna go before her, and they walked past the glaring Commander General as though she were not there.

When they returned to the campsite, there were three more people than when they'd left. Zavia leaned with one foot against a tree, talking to Kovi. She looked up to see Cydell and followed the Hya's gaze to the center of the clearing, where Rii and Orrat sat on a log, hungrily devouring dried strips of beef and hunks of cheese. They looked up to see Cydell, and immediately dropped their food and sprang to attention.

The Hya stared in disbelief at the boys, entering the clearing slowly and walking around in the dimness until she faced them. There was a vacuum of silence, filled only by the call of nightbirds. Elayna, who had begun tending the injured Sentinels, knew there was nothing she could do to rescue her brother. Everyone in the company braced themselves for the storm.

The Hya's voice was steady, too steady, when she finally spoke. "What are you doing here, wards?"

Rii looked to Orrat as if to say, it was your idea. You explain it.

"I...we have followed to protect my sister, Hya," Orrat managed after swallowing the mouthful of cheese he'd been holding.

"Were you under orders to pursue your sister, ward?"

"No, Hya. But..."

"I assume, then, that you left the palace and Mauldar with your trainers wondering what has become of you. Perhaps they are scouring the city. Taking badly needed sentries away from their posts protecting thousands, to search vainly for two disobedient wards!"

"I did not think of that, Hya."

"You did not think!!" she roared.

Rii flinched when she turned her attention on him.

"And you! Is your foolish companion now your commander?!"

"No, Hya. I thought he should not go alone."

"I see. You are blood-bonded and thus together in all things." She walked around the table. "I can spare no one to escort you back to Mauldar. I will risk no more scouts or Sentinels in your behalf. As we may not turn back, I have no choice but to take you with us."

Orrat fought the urge to smile. He had accomplished his objective. But his heart sank with her next words.

"As it seems you both have such an aversion to following orders, you are hereby stripped of your ward status and will be assigned less demanding duties upon return to Mauldar, if indeed we do return. At your ease."

The boys and Elayna stood stunned. Zavia stopped in the midst of honing her blade. Cydell seemed to be the only body in motion as she gathered her cloak and stalked off into the woods.

Elayna and Orrat sat up long after the others had settled into their bedrolls for the night. Rii was in deep despair, unable to sleep. The Hya's voice announcing his fate played over and over again in his mind. He felt as though his very life had been taken away from him. Indeed, he felt that there was nothing of joy left for him now.

7

GINNACH

Pak dismounted from his weary gelding and stood on the rise, looking down on the village of Ginnach. It was dusk on the tenth day of the turn, four suns after breaking camp at the cave.

The forced march of the mercenary band had met with one disaster after another. They had wasted no time in breaking camp and beginning the trudge to Ginnach through Wen Yor marsh. But they had not traveled fast enough. Disgruntled men fought along the way. Whenever they made camp, there was a fight among the more avid gamblers of the company. Two men had been knifed to death. One was so superstitious about the marsh that he had deserted in a panic, slipping away during the night. They had had to fight off a small band of northern tribesmen along the way. The tribesmen had attacked the mercenary campsite at dawn on the second day of the journey. Fortunately, the mercenaries had been quick in recovering themselves after the initial surprise attack, and had fought off the bloodthirsty tribesmen with a vengeance. Pak had only lost six men in the skirmish.

Crossing the marsh had been a nightmare in itself. Pak had heard the rumors of the horrors of Wen Yor marsh since childhood, but had never ventured there in all his travels. Only the promise of lathium bars and a prestigious command in Valkyra's army held him to the task of getting one hundred and fifty men through the dreaded bogs.

They had reached Wen Yor marsh at dusk, after a sun and a half of constant marching. The men were fatigued, disgruntled and apprehensive, not knowing what dangers they would face after the sun went down. When they arrived, it was just dark enough for the eerie atmosphere of the marsh to settle around them. It crept into the bravest hearts, causing them all to remember every horrific tale they had ever heard. Even Pak had stopped at the edge of the marsh as they all dismounted to walk their skittish mounts through the mire.

The mercenaries traversed the gloom of the marsh slowly, two by two. They stepped warily and looked around them, their eyes wide in the darkness. Marsh mist hid their bodies from the waist down. Their footfalls met with the soft, wet mud that gave way with each step and made a sucking sound as they lifted their feet to take yet another step. Noises from creatures they had no desire to meet face to face echoed in the shadows all around them. Piercing screeches and howls; baying and growling, as though the animals who lived in the marsh were in a constant battle with unseen forces. The marsh was surrounded by tall, misshapen trees. Moss hung low, tendrils almost reaching down to touch the dense reeds and marsh grass. One of the mounts stumbled. Its wild splashing was a chaotic implosion in the haunting silence. The horse's owner slipped as well. A second after he did, they all heard the soft splash of amphibian bodies slithering into the water, drawn to the man's panicked wailing.

The quiet procession turned into an alarmed and terrified rout of men, horses, and creatures unknown. Pak did not dare stop. Someone had to come out on the other side and hopefully, he thought, the men would just keep moving. If they could just keep moving until they reached solid ground, there would be sanctuary on the other side of the marsh. Pak trudged on, stepping on things in the muck that were soft and slimy. Underwater creatures clutched at his boots, reluctant to let go. He cringed and turned a deaf ear to the shouts and disorder behind him. In the darkness, there was nothing he could do. No way he could save anyone, if he dared. The marsh had the chill of death around it. The sooner they were on the other side, the better.

Five men and three horses did not make it out of the marsh. The rest of the company pulled themselves, wet and muddy, onto solid ground on the other side, terrified, winded and weary. Pak let them sleep wherever they fell. Now Lieutenant Pak squatted in the dewy grass of the rise. Dark clouds loomed threateningly overhead. Already the wind had picked up, and the chill it brought made him blow on his hands and rub them vigorously together for warmth. His men were just beginning to stir. The aroma of marin heating on the small campfire wafted up to him where he stood on the rise, but he remained there a few moments longer. He watched the small village below wake to a new sun. The last sun they would ever see, if all went according to Valkyra's plan.

◻ ◻ ◻ ◻ ◻

The village of Ginnach boasted the finest weavers in the region. It was nestled in the heart of rolling pastureland, perfect for the many shepherds who grazed their sheep there. Wealthy merchants from surrounding provinces and distant countries journeyed to the village constantly in search of the perfection of a fine Ginnachan wall tapestry or rug. Ginnachan wools were dyed in a variety of colors, distinguishable at first glance to those with a discerning eye, and there were several shops in the village specializing in fine woolen cloaks or leggings or intricately woven blankets. Thus, the village coffers were always full, as trade was always brisk and plentiful.

The Smiling Ram was the largest and most notoriously popular inn in Ginnach. It catered to a varied, if at times questionable, clientele and its doors never closed. Occasionally, a rowdy patron was propelled out into the street by the burly owner, but there was always someone of interest in the hearthroom to keep the rest of the patrons happy and drinking until the sun rose. The inn was often frequented by wandering bards who belted out bawdy drinking songs or crooned heartrending ballads.

Soupel, the owner, kept a sharp eye on his kegs and on his patrons. His ale was never watered down and his wine was of the

best Mauldar had to offer. The Smiling Ram was his kingdom and
Soupel was lord. He was built like a bear and sported a full, bushy
red beard and long red wavy hair that he kept pulled back and tied
with a thong, so it could not be grabbed when he was forced to settle
a dispute in an ungentlemanly fashion, he oftentimes would explain.

Every evenfall he stood in the wide archway between the
taproom and the hearthroom, watching the comings and goings in his
establishment, with his hock-like arms folded across his massive chest.
He wore a nearly white apron over his linen shirt, leggings and heavy
black mountain boots. He was a threatening, bear of a man to those
who did not know him. Strangers were so awed by his size that they
often missed the mischievous twinkle in his deep brown eyes. Red
bushy brows sat like two friendly caterpillars over his eyes, and his
nose was wide and a little off center from having been broken so
many times.

Soupel ruled his kingdom with the finesse of a true states-
man. He knew his regulars personally, and strangers who ventured
into the Smiling Ram did not remain strangers for long. Soupel also
kept a fatherly eye over his comely serving girls and taught them
how to handle themselves around the ruffians and bullies amongst
his clientele. And if any of the young gentlemen got out of hand,
there was thick length of wood from the spoke of a wagon wheel that
was kept behind the bar to teach the young man manners.

Adventurers, travelers, warriors, and entertainers from all
over Mauldar eventually ventured into the Smiling Ram, its reputation having been spread, without exaggeration, throughout the country. There was a stable that would accommodate over fifty horses
and a company of stable hands to see to their care.

Soupel's rooms were always clean, linens changed, floors
polished and pallets newly stuffed with freshly mown straw and turned
religiously. The Smiling Ram offered eight large rooms on the front
upper floor, and a dozen smaller ones in the upper and lower rear.
Soupel's lover, a slender, dark-featured and clean-shaven ex-officer
in the Mauldaran regular army, was the master of the kitchen. This
evening, the aroma of roasted mutton, steamed potatoes and carrots,

freshly baked bread and pastries mingled with the smell of pipe smoke, leather and horses.

Even Soupel did not know what to make of the large party of rain-soaked travelers who strolled into his inn that evenfall: twenty-five nondescript riders, each wearing sabers, a blonde beauty, two young boys, and a dark, dwarfish man who appeared to be of some wealth, by his fine clothes. There was a tall, red-haired woman who carried herself like a warrior and never took her hand away from the hilt of her saber.

Soupel made his way to the bar to confront the striking, dark woman whom he took to be the leader. As he addressed her, he kept a wary eye on the riders, who filtered into the hearthroom, their dripping cloaks leaving trails and puddles on the wood floor, and scrutinized each of his guests as they sat eating their dinner or nursing a pitcher of ale. They stationed themselves in every corner of the large room and at the bottom of the stairwell. Four walked casually back behind the bar and into the kitchen area and never returned.

Valkyra cast discreet glances into the hearthroom. There were no men there whom she recognized, and she wondered if her mercenaries had survived their journey through the marsh. They better had, she thought. Time would reveal all on that score. Lieutenant Pak had his orders.

Orrat and Rii stood in the foyer with their mouths hanging open, awed at the prospect of spending the night in an inn. Mesmerized, they stepped aside, first in one direction and then the other to let the vivacious, smiling serving girls go past to attend their other customers. Kovi grinned slyly while nodding in approval of the comely local girls as he breathed in a deep lungful of kitchen smells.

Cydell noted the apprehension in the innkeeper's eyes as he watched her Sentinels going about their duties. Finally, he turned his attention to her. Soupel's first notion was to question her about her companions, but something in her eyes gave him pause. And something in her voice when she spoke made him glad he had not interrogated her.

"Are you the owner of this establishment?" she asked simply.

"At your service, Lady. Soupel Azor Uyan welcomes you and yours to the Smiling Ram," Soupel boomed and nodded his head.

That was as close as he would allow himself to a formal bow. He did not once take his eyes off of the lady before him. Something about her and the strange behavior of her companions led him to believe that all was not as it appeared to be.

"I would not normally impose on your graciousness this way..." she smiled and indicated the others, "...with so many unexpected guests...but we have a fair journey ahead and are already drenched to the bone. Personally, I have no desire to pass the night on the floor of a rain-soaked forest."

Soupel scratched his beard thoughtfully as he silently counted the members of the party.

"The upstairs chambers are all full. No traveler wants to be about on a night such as this. I can offer three small chambers in back and all the stable space you require, lady."

"Done," Cydell agreed. Brushing her wet cloak aside, she pulled out a leather pouch and placed six lathium coins on the bar with a chink. Soupel was so preoccupied with staring at the hilt of her saber that she had to clear her throat to get his attention. He met her eyes again with a new formality.

"This should be enough to cover hot meals for each of us, the chambers, stable space and the care of the mounts," she said softly. She looked up at the innkeeper, who was virtually speechless. He looked down at the lathium coins and then back at her.

"More than enough. I will have a girl show you to your chambers," Soupel bowed his head again, his heart suddenly fluttering. "If there is anything more that you require..." he grinned excitedly, "anything at all, please feel free to call on me and mine, Hya."

Cydell quickly put a finger to her lips to quiet him, but not without a smile and a nod of thanks.

Soupel hurried away to oversee the accommodations for his prestigious guests. Murmurs of speculation filtered through the low conversations of the other patrons as they watched the party suspiciously, wondering who they might be.

Cydell briefly issued orders to the Sentinel guards, who were to take shifts in the stables and standing watch, conspicuous though they would be, through the remainder of the night. Two were posted outside the Hya's chamber door, and one was assigned to keep a watchful eye on Orrat and Rii to make certain they returned to their chamber after their meal. Kovi was left to his own devices, with a pointed warning from his cousin not to overindulge himself with ale, as they would be on their way at first light. Valkyra angrily stalked out of the inn and out to the stables when it became clear that Elayna was to share quarters with Cydell. This pronouncement took Elayna by surprise, but she was too tired to argue. Wearily, she trudged through the maze of tables in the hearthroom behind Cydell and the Sentinels.

The chamber was small but clean. There were two thickly packed pallets on the floor with a small table between them. One of the Sentinels stepped forward and deftly lit the candle in the brass holder, bowed to Cydell with a glance at Elayna, and smartly turned and left the room, closing the door behind her.

Silently, and without a wasted movement, Cydell took off her sopping cloak and hung it on one of the pegs behind the door. She then went to the one pack she had brought in, and dug through it looking for a dry tunic. Not finding one, she swore and began laying out her damp clothes so they could dry, hopefully by morning. Elayna did not have much and decided to busy herself with her herb pouch. Much of her healing herbs would be of no use to her wet, so she set each packet out on the table. Cydell paused in what she was doing to watch as the Fair Witch checked each small vial, each packet of dried herbs. Elayna was so involved in what she was doing that Cydell's voice startled her when she spoke.

"You will be chilled through if you do not take off your cloak," she said, and crossed the small room before Elayna could object. Gently, the Hya lifted the rain-soaked cloak from Elayna's shoulders and put it on the remaining peg. Then she went to the small hearth at the other end of the room and knelt. There was kindling, but not very much. They needed a fire to take the chill out of their bones and she began to build a fire, a small one, for the tiny room would get very warm, very quickly.

Cydell glanced at Elayna, who had finished with her herb pack and was now going through her clothing to find something dry. Like Cydell, she began taking out her tunics one by one and spreading them out. When she looked up in the silence, her gaze met Cydell's. The Hya smiled wanly. Elayna could see that she was weary as well.

"I cannot decide which I would prefer to do first," Cydell said as she rolled her shoulders. "Fill my belly or sleep." Elayna smiled back at her, but said nothing. She walked a little closer to the small fire, wondering how Cydell had made it so quickly.

Elayna felt the Hya's closeness when she stood up and vigorously rubbed her hands together over the steadily increasing flames.

"Does it disturb you to share a chamber with me?" Cydell asked at last. "I thought you would prefer this to a hay bale in the stables."

"I am just glad to be out of the rain, Hya." Elayna answered, wondering why it was suddenly so difficult to talk.

"Fine. Shall we then go down to our meal?" She went to the door and opened it, letting Elayna pass before her.

Both women turned heads as they made their way to one of the few empty tables in the hearthroom. Orrat and Rii waved happily from the table they shared with Kovi. As they sat, Elayna noticed that Cydell still wore her saber. There were several men in the room who noticed as well. Cydell rolled her eyes as snatches of the conversations caught her ear. A group of rowdy travelers, adventurers by their dress, whistled and stomped as they called lewdly to Elayna in loud whispers. The Sentinels posted in each corner of the room watched Cydell for any sign that she wanted the men silenced but Cydell shook her head. Instead, Soupel stepped in quickly, warning his guests to mind their manners. The adventurers quieted, but did not stop staring.

Soupel himself served them, bringing in platter after platter of steaming roast lamb, vegetable pudding, and fresh hot bread. He repeatedly refilled their mugs with chilled honey cider until they both had to convince him that they had had enough.

The comely serving girl who came to clear the platters away brushed against Cydell as often as she could and made a great show of talking to her, smiling and giggling. She leaned in close so that her ample bosoms were almost loosed from her bodice. Cydell, who found the flirtation amusing, humored the girl and laughed with her. But Elayna felt the heat rising up along the back of her neck as she watched the shameless display.

Excusing herself, she got up to make her way back to the chamber. She had taken five steps when one of the adventurers rose from his table to block her path. Elayna looked at him in annoyance and tried to sidestep him several times, but he blocked her path, much to the amusement of his friends. By now, everyone else had noticed the confrontation and let their conversations lapse to give the scene their full attention. Orrat started to rise and go to his sister's aid, but Kovi and Rii on either side of him held him to his chair with firm hands on his shoulders.

"Let me pass," Elayna said calmly. It was an effort. All she wanted to do was go to her chamber. The young man swaggered before her, stumbling from too much ale. Apparently, his leather tunic and leggings had been fine at one time. Now they were dirty and tattered. His hair was long and stringy and his two front teeth had rotted down to black nubs. He smelled as if he had not bathed in a turn, and Elayna involuntarily took a step back to distance herself from the stench.

"Where art thou off to in such a hurry, my fair one? Why not share a pitcher of ale with me and my companions there? It has been many suns since we have had the company of one so lovely as thyself." He reached out to stroke her cheek but Elayna flinched away.

"And many more suns shall pass before I share your table. Let me pass," she repeated hotly. The young man's companions whistled and shouted and encouraged him, calling out his name, Terren.

"I must wonder if the rest of thee is as hot as thy tongue." Terren smiled lewdly and moved in closer. As he reached out to touch her, Elayna raised her hand, palm out, to block him. Terren yelped in surprise and pain and quickly stuck his singed finger in his mouth.

The expression on his face changed from bewilderment to fury as he glared at the green-eyed beauty. But as he raised his hand to strike her, he felt the prick of a saber tip under his chin.

The room grew quiet. No one had even seen Cydell leave her table, much less draw her saber. Everyone who had jumped to their feet to rally behind Terren now stood deathly still, a Sentinel's saber pointing directly at their bellies. Terren's companions had been snatched from their table by Soupel, a length of wood clenched threateningly in his massive fist.

"We will have none of this, boys. You know the rules here," Soupel growled. The other patrons cleared a path for him as he herded the companions to the door. After he threw them out into the torrential rain, he paused with a satisfied grin. What a pity the Hya and her Sentinel Guard could not remain in Ginnach forever.

The Hya's gaze was intent on Terren, but he did not dare back down.

"Thou requires so many at thy back in a fight?" he snarled.

"They are here only to balance the odds," Cydell replied coolly.

"Shall we stand then, warrior to warrior, and settle our differences thus?" Terren's gaze wandered to Elayna, but the saber tip jabbed, not too gently, up under his chin and he turned his attentions back to Cydell. She smiled without humor when she spoke.

"I have no quarrel with you, really. Other than the fact that you have the manners of a DeRuvian sow. And, in truth, you do rather smell like one." She frowned as she saw the young man tense at the insult. His anger and pride almost got the better of him. Was there no one who would come to his aid and challenge this woman?

"The lady would like to retire. Let her pass. And do not approach her again." Cydell slowly lowered the saber and gave Terren time to collect himself. With an angry glare at both women, he grudgingly moved aside and Elayna rushed by him. When she was gone, he stood, still facing Cydell, not knowing what to do and afraid to turn his back on her.

"Perhaps you should join your friends," she offered, as she inclined her head toward the door. Terren scowled and brushed by her. He stopped to collect his cloak from where his companions had left it at the table and started to leave, but he paused at the door and looked back into the hearthroom. The two women were gone and those guarding them had resumed their posts.

"Who do they think they are?" he grumbled aloud to the nearest ear, which happened to be Soupel's. "If I had had the chance to draw my saber, I would have..."

Soupel looked at the fool and slowly shook his head. "You would have died, boy," he said matter-of-factly. "You would have definitely died."

□ □ □ □ □

Elayna was furious. She and Cydell were barely back in their tiny, stifling room with the door closed when she turned on Cydell and almost said what was on her mind. Instead, she went to her bed and began to fold her tunics with a piqued briskness.

Cydell stood by the door with her hands folded across her chest, watching the display. Of course, the Sentinels could have handled the situation downstairs, but it hurt nothing to have a bit of sport with the ill-mannered boy. She was very certain it would not have gone any further than a bruised ego or two. But she did not speak her thoughts as she watched Elayna stuff her tunics into her pack with a vengeance.

Finally, Cydell sighed. "Free your tongue before you swallow it," she said as she opened her arms in a gesture of innocence. "I promise I will not retaliate."

Elayna whirled, unable to contain herself any longer. "That speaks well of you! Can you also promise to stay out of matters that do not concern you?!" she seethed.

"I suppose it would have been better had I sat and let that arrogant drunkard and his friends rape you where you stood?!" Cydell fired back. Elayna paced in her agitation.

"It would have been better if you had let me defend myself! How often must I tell you that I am not helpless and I do not need your protection!"

"Would you have brought every hired blade in Ginnach down upon us, flashing that heartstone of yours?" she asked Elayna hotly. "Can you determine with your powers who was a spy among all of those who were watching? I dare say we have enough to concern ourselves with, without you turning everyone who approaches you into a steaming pile of horse dung!" Elayna was silent as Cydell continued.

"It is difficult enough to travel discreetly with a Sentinel regiment, two wayward pups who fancy themselves Sentinels, and my lecherous, adventure-seeking cousin! Now I have to contend with a temperamental sorceress!"

Elayna left Cydell steaming in the middle of the room as she went to her bed, snatched up her pack and angrily flung it over her shoulder. But she realized after she had done so that Cydell was blocking the door. Cydell watched her for a moment and then spoke to her as though she were admonishing a naughty child.

"Put your pack away," she said with a wave of her hand. "There is nowhere for you to run to."

Elayna met the Hya's gaze squarely. She was determined that she would not pass the night with a woman she despised now more than ever.

"It *does* disturb me to share this chamber with you. I shall seek other...arrangements," she announced stubbornly.

"Oh?" Cydell walked slowly to the hearth, considering Elayna's words. It occurred to Elayna that her way to the door was now clear, but for some reason she did not step toward it.

Cydell spoke softly as she knelt and tried to stoke the dying embers. "Then go. I am certain Terren and his companions, or any of the other travelers downstairs, will be more than willing to share a chamber with you. And a bed."

Elayna could not stop the tears of anger and humiliation that welled in her eyes. She could not turn to face Cydell, knowing the Hya had been right to intervene. Elayna knew it was within her power to have blasted Terren, and anyone else who angered her, to cinders. She also knew that if she were going to be true to her grandmother's legacy, she would have to learn to control her own temper and the power of the heartstone.

"Speaking of bed," Cydell began, with an odd tone in her voice, "how are you sleeping of late?" She rose slowly while intently watching Elayna's reaction to her question. Crossing the short distance between them, Cydell said, "It seems, Fair Witch, that *you* cannot stay out of matters that do not concern *you*."

Elayna turned around to stare directly into Cydell's eyes, shaken at being caught off-guard about the erotic dreams.

"I did not intend..." she mumbled softly, lowering her eyes.

"Regardless of the intent, I believe you had the desired effect, did you not?" Cydell said accusingly as she stepped closer. Elayna fumbled for words.

Cydell continued. "Was it your intention to bewitch me? Haunt my dreams? Drive me to madness in my waking hours? Do you know the dreams I speak of?" Cydell barked in the silence.

"I know not how it happens," Elayna said simply.

"Do you not?" Cydell shouted, then quickly calmed herself. She took Elayna's arm and slowly pulled her closer. "Will I ever again make love to a woman without wishing it were you?" she whispered intensely. "Whatever the spell, Elayna, I demand that you release me."

Elayna looked up into Cydell's eyes. At that moment, she felt a true warmth and caring in her heart that threatened to rush to the surface. She had no defense against it. Even the power of the heartstone seemed to fail her and she was left to acknowledge that her intense hatred of this woman had somehow been replaced by a more tender feeling.

They stood that way for what seemed like an eternity before Elayna quietly said, "I cannot," and hung her head.

Gently, slowly, Cydell lifted Elayna's chin. Their lips were a breath apart.

"Then I shall have a taste of the reality," Cydell whispered, and kissed Elayna's lips with a soft, lingering kiss.

□ □ □ □ □

In the quiet, just after the last raindrop fell, the mercenary army swept down upon the sleeping village of Ginnach. The Sentinel Guard unit stationed in Ginnach was waiting for a Mauldaran detachment to arrive with additional numbers in case of an attack by the tribesmen. They had not anticipated the possibility of such an attack before their reinforcements arrived, but they were quick to organize a defense just inside the Ginnachan border as over a hundred mercenaries galloped over the rise, intent on an easy victory. Those mercenaries who first engaged the Sentinel Guard of Ginnach gravely underestimated the skill and fierceness of their female opponents and did not make it beyond that sentry point. But their sacrifice allowed their companions to slip by the Sentinels and proceed to wreak all manner of destruction on the unsuspecting village.

A Sentinel rider galloped through the streets, rallying the villagers out of their beds. Word spread quickly as enraged and frightened Ginnachans poured into the square, some from burning homes and shops that were set ablaze by torches thrown through windows. Black smoke billowed in the sky like low-hanging, flame-licked clouds. In the ensuing chaos, parents screamed frantically for their children and other loved ones, lost in the massive hysteria.

The Sentinel Guard burst in on Cydell and Elayna just in time to warn them of the attack. The raiders were already thundering through the inn and had just reached the back rooms where the Hya's party was quartered. There was no time to shout orders. No time to gather their belongings. Elayna dashed out of the room behind Cydell, who immediately engaged one of the raiders who was leading a small group of his comrades through the back of the inn. The Hya disposed of the man in two strokes and was immediately occupied with another.

Elayna was trying to inch her way down the corridor to get to Orrat and Rii when two raiders caught her by the arms and pinned her to the wall, both leering in anticipation of having her for themselves. Cydell and her guards were battling two raiders each. Kovi was almost invisible in the melee, until a raider screamed and went down, clutching his legs where the little man had sliced calves and knee caps. Elayna struggled with her captors as they repeatedly slammed her against the wall, trying to knock her unconscious.

The heartstone scalded her where it hung between her breasts. She felt its power, as hot as her own fury, and knew that it was building, mounting for release. The raiders roughly groped her with dirty, bloody, calloused hands.

"If you do not harm me, you may have the jewel around my neck!" Elayna managed to shout. The two men paused a second, looked at each other and laughed uproariously.

"We shall take everything of yours!" They grinned menacingly and moved in closer, smelling of blood and horses and sweat. As soon as they ripped her blouse open, they did not have the chance to even scream. White streaks of light shot from the heartstone and blasted both men so hard that they were lifted off the floor with the impact, slammed back against the opposite wall with a thud, heads lolling as they slid down into a sitting position. There was a small, neat smoking hole in the middle of each of their foreheads, and their eyes were still open in shock. Suddenly, Cydell was standing between Elayna and the raider who had hoped to replace his two fallen comrades. He did not have a chance to raise his hand to strike. Cydell finished him with a swift stroke across his belly that sent the raider howling in pain. He stood there in the midst of the fighting, stunned at the blood pouring from him.

"Cydell!" Elayna screamed. Cydell whipped around and crouched in time to see a blast of white heat streak from Elayna's outstretched palm and singe the scalp of the raider who was about to sweep Cydell's head from her shoulders. Wide-eyed and panting, she looked at Elayna, who was standing there, staring at her own hands.

"Come!" Cydell snatched Elayna out of her confusion and grabbed her wrist in an iron grip. "We have to get to the stables!" She charged through the jumble of twisted, wounded bodies and sabers and blood, pulling Elayna behind her, and engaging three more raiders before finally running out into the alleyway behind the kitchens.

Bodies were everywhere. The smoke was blinding and suffocating. There was a mass of people, some stumbling about with no idea how they had gotten where they were. The sound of clashing sabers was all around them as Cydell stood, trying to see through the haze to get her bearings. Elayna was slumped beside her, drained from the energy of the heartstone. Cydell tried to keep Elayna on her feet with an arm around her waist as she almost dragged her through the ankle-deep mud to the stables.

Someone ran up behind Cydell and she turned as quickly as she could to challenge them. She recognized the Sentinel mask with an audible sigh of relief.

"Hya! How do you fare?" the woman asked. She was bloodied and muddy, her saber dark with blood.

"Take her," Cydell wearily shifted Elayna into the Sentinel's arms. "Take her to the stables."

"There are no more stables, Hya. The people have gone to the cellar under the tax house for safety."

"Fine. Take her there..." Cydell was saying as they heard a great roar and a rumble of falling beams. Flames licked through the roof of the shop that was joined to the inn. "Dornea..." she whispered. "Rii and Orrat! Have you seen the them?!"

"I saw them last fighting in the inn, Hya....NO, DO NOT..!" The Sentinel's protest was lost in the chaos around her. She swore as she watched her Hya run back up the alley toward the inn. The Sentinel half-carried Elayna down the alley, determined to get the sorceress to safety and then return for the Hya.

Cydell half stumbled into the back entrance of the inn and paused in the kitchen, now a shambles, to draw a weary arm across her sweaty brow. Her linen tunic was stained and torn, barely hanging on her shoulders. Most of the bloodstains were from the raiders who had fallen by her saber, though she had her share of nicks and cuts with a more serious gash up her forearm. But there was no time now to take inventory.

She moved stealthily through the great kitchen, stepping over fallen raiders and one or two patrons she recognized from the hearthroom earlier in the evening. She was saddened and angered at the carnage. So many innocent people brought to such a wasteful end. She followed the sounds of sabers and men yelling, heavy footfalls and someone stumbling and falling over furniture. As she raced out to the tap room, she nearly fell over Soupel's body. He lay on his back, slumped down against the bar with his legs stretched out before him. He was drenched in blood, a clotting stream from the gash across his throat, ear to ear. There were slashes on his arms and legs and along his cheek. The hearty innkeeper had gone down fighting to the very last. The more wreckage Cydell saw, the angrier she became. Who were these raiders and why were they doing this?!

The fighting she heard had moved into what remained of the hearthroom. Slowly, quietly, she slipped in unnoticed and hid herself behind a portion of the archway that separated the tap room and the hearthroom. She peeked in to see Orrat and Rii trying to handle a giant of a man with a thick red beard. He had the two boys cornered and was moving in for the kill. Evidently, he had been toying with them up until this point, and had finally grown tired of the game.

The boys looked tired and desperate, swaying as they stood together, trying to distract their attacker while first one, and then the other, poked and swiped at him with their sabers. The giant raider growled and then disarmed them with a stroke of his broadsword. Rii fell back, clutching his arm as blood seeped through his fingers. Orrat's attention went back and forth from his wounded friend to the monster who was about to finish them.

Cydell stepped quietly out of the shadows and cleared her throat. The big man spun around, momentarily forgetting about the boys, and focussed his attention on this new threat. Orrat helped Rii to his feet and supported him with an arm around the young Barrach's waist. They headed in the direction of the kitchens, but the raider stopped them with the flat of his blade. He looked from the boys to the tall dark woman and back again with a sneer of triumph on his lips. The four people in the hearthroom were in a world within the world of death and misery outside. They still heard the screaming and the horses and the clashing sabers, but it seemed as though that battle were being fought far away, and they were standing on the fringes of some horrific nightmare.

"Let the boys go. You have no need of them," Cydell stated quietly, lowering her saber tip to trace lazy circles in the air.

Pak watched the movement, mesmerized by its deceptive grace, and somewhat impressed by the woman's nerve. There was something familiar about her. He stared. And then something clicked in the back of his mind. Valkyra's voice echoed there and he nodded to himself in response to it. All had been going according to plan, except for one minor detail, and here she was, boldly standing before him. Waiting.

"Agreed. My men shall recapture them quickly enough," he shrugged. Even after having been dismissed, the boys were too stunned to move.

Cydell frowned darkly. "*Your* men? So this is your doing? You are the devil who is spreading this death and destruction? Who are you?"

Pak bowed curtly and straightened. His eyes danced with anticipation as he took the hilt of his broadsword with both hands and ceremoniously held it out to take measure of the woman he was about to kill.

"This is only a small part of the greater plan," he explained arrogantly as he twirled the sword around first his left side and then his right, stopping with the blade pointing at Cydell.

"I am afraid, serpent of the abyss, that you will not live to carry out the greater plan." Cydell seethed as her fury flared. By sheer will, she kept it from overtaking her. She must focus all her passion on this fight.

The two warriors, the man and the woman, mentally surveyed the fighting space. There were too many obstacles; tables to back into, overturned chairs to trip over. They circled each other in what little space they had. Close combat. Almost too close for saber and broadsword.

Pak struck first. Cydell parried the blow. He moved in again quickly, not wanting to give her time to think. She parried the next three and let him come. The woman would not back down. Pak knew he would have to control the fight. She was already wounded. So was he. But he was stronger physically, and if he managed to land a blow, it would certainly disable her.

He fought like a brute, relying on his strength and the power of his blade. Cydell ducked sweeping strokes and parried the blows that followed. Steel against steel. She waited, looking for an opening, studying his style, reading his moves. There was no pattern to his attack and she was not certain if he intended to knock her out with the flat of his sword or run it through her. Pak slowed the pace a bit and then abruptly charged in. He forced Cydell back with a series of shattering blows. She stumbled in her retreat and fell back against an overturned table. Pak moved in, but Cydell staved him off with a foot to his belly. She shoved with a grunt of effort and jumped to her feet as Pak regained himself. She was stronger than he thought.

When he came at her again, Cydell saw an opening and struck so quickly that Pak looked down in amazement at the thin red line spreading across the front of his tunic. He took two swipes at her, which she easily avoided, and while he raised his sword for a third, she landed two swift kicks to his windpipe with her left foot and then whirled to land another in a back kick with her right. Pak stumbled back, gasping for breath. His recovery was slow. He was tiring. So was she, though he had expended more energy. Cydell's advantage was quickness and she made the most of it. She knew that he had the heavier weapon and that if he had the chance to land one of those crushing sweeps, she would never recover from it. He charged in again and met Cydell's stroke before he even leveled his blade.

Pak reeled from the pain across his knuckles but did not let go of the sword. The hilt was slippery with blood. He gripped it tighter and came at her again and again. In the beginning, he was certain he could outmaneuver her with his sword. But he had not counted on her deft feet and balance. Her kicks came out of nowhere. Before he recovered from one, she had landed another and another. His kidneys ached on both sides. Such pain. Valkyra had not warned him of the Hya's skill. One of the many things Valkyra had not told him.

Cydell's leg muscles burned. The big man was coming at her much more slowly now, but coming at her nonetheless. She was not sure she had the strength to duck and kick any more. *End it*, she ordered herself. *End it now.*

Pak came on yet again. This time, Cydell did not kick. She
let him come. Pak thought she was preparing to duck his attack. But
the Hya dropped to one knee instead, her saber pointed out in his
direction. Pak charged with all the momentum he had left. He saw
the tip of her saber just before he impaled himself on it. Cydell had to
hold her saber with one hand, bracing her other hand on the raider's
chest to keep from being crushed by the dead weight of him. He balanced above her, slowly sliding down to the hilt of her blade. Her
hands were covered, sticky red with his blood. Endless seconds later,
he finally fell over onto his side with a thud.

Cydell knelt beside him, winded and sick from the odor of
blood. The man's red beard was saturated and his breath gurgled in
his throat. She saw his sides heaving with the strain of breathing.

"On whose orders do you kill my people? Who are you, damn
you?" she panted.

Rii and Orrat saw the Hya lean over the dying man before he
shuddered and stilled. Cydell could not get back on her feet. Her
world spun around and around as the sounds from outside the inn
faded in and out and in again, and she became lost in a downward
spiral of darkness.

◘ ◘ ◘ ◘ ◘

Ginnach lay smoldering in the rose chill of sunrise. Desolate
villagers milled about like lost souls, searching despondently through
the charred ruins of shops and homes, looking for any of their possessions that might have been spared. Battle-weary Sentinels tended
the many and scattered funeral pyres as individuals and families
huddled in tattered blankets and cloaks taken from the dead. They
solemnly stood watching the flames, grieving for those lives lost.

Cydell sat alone on the stone steps in front of the ravaged
tax house, her arms wrapped around her aching body, a blanket draped
over her shoulders. She saw the devastation and still could not believe it. Pallets had been laid out in the cellar of the tax house. It was
a large open room, with thick wooden beams that reached from the
packed straw floor to the ceiling. Rows of very small windows high

up on the four walls let in shafts of light. It served as a storage place for bales of wool not yet shipped out to other provinces.

Every available healer in the area had been summoned or, after hearing of the raid, had come to Ginnach on their own to offer their services. In spite of the Hya's adamant but weak protests, Elayna had healed the gash on Cydell's arm and given her a potion to help her rest. Cydell had to admit that she felt better physically. But her heart sank as she took in the destruction and looked into the dirty, tear-streaked faces of a group of children who had lost their families.

Cydell ran her fingers through her hair with a heavy sigh. The company's packs were lost. Her tunic and riding pants were torn and stained, her boots streaked with mud. Shielding her eyes from the sun, she nodded in grave satisfaction as another unit of Sentinels galloped over the eastern rise and down into the village. She watched as the lead rider stopped and pointed south, and then at the tax house. The riders broke formation and the leader headed in Cydell's direction. Cydell's scabbard scraped against the steps as she rose, shrugging the blanket from her shoulders. Her moment of solitude was gone.

The Sentinel swung down from his mount and approached the Hya where she stood. He bowed and then sprang to attention.

"At your ease, Enaad. What news?" Cydell asked as she looked around to make certain that no one was lurking about the ruins of the buildings close by. "There is a small room off the cellar down below. We shall have more privacy there. Follow me." She turned and led the way into the tax house and down into the cellar.

The small pantry was just off the main cellar and was only large enough for a table and two chairs, which Enaad found and brought in, along with a fresh taper. The strapping Sentinel almost filled the small room as he stood before his Hya and made his report.

"We engaged several small bands of tribesmen on the way here, Hya. Minor skirmishes. Nothing serious. But they were heading southeast. Toward Mauldar."

Cydell listened intently, pacing like a caged animal in the tiny space. Enaad continued. "We met two units of the Rogelle guard, who were told of the attack here by a party of scouts."

"Good. That means Zavia has been informed and should be arriving here soon. I have need of her," Cydell added more to herself than to the Sentinel. "In the meantime, dispatch a rider to Mauldar without delay. I want Mauldaran and Sentinel regiments on full alert and battle-ready. Dispatch two regiments of each to Windsom Keep as quickly as possible. I will try to make it there in two suns' ride." Suddenly, she paused and with a tilt of her head, frowned a question at Enaad. "Did you see Commander General Valkyra as you rode past the sentry post?" she asked.

"No, Hya. Perhaps she is meeting with her troops regarding cleanup detail."

"Perhaps," Cydell said softly. Then she added, "Assist the Ginnach guard in every way you can. Help them to secure what is left of this place, take inventory of what is needed, and then send to Tyroda for supplies. Be sure the supply wagons are heavily guarded. Also, Enaad, I want four fresh mounts, provisioned and ready to leave here by mid-sun."

Enaad looked at her strangely for a moment before nodding, "Yes, Hya." He hesitated and shifted uncomfortably as he looked at the Hya. "Permission to speak freely, Hya."

"Speak."

"Travel is very dangerous, Hya. Especially with the tribesmen killing everything that moves. I assume you still plan to ride to Windsom Keep."

"You have assumed correctly."

"With all respect, Hya," Enaad swallowed hard but plunged forward, "I strongly urge you to return to Mauldar. To safety."

Cydell regarded him for a moment. Her travel plans must be causing quite a stir among the Sentinel ranks. It was their sworn duty to protect the Hya at all costs. Her two personal guards had given their lives for her during the mercenary attack in the inn. They had died with honor, defending her back against the onslaught of raiders in the narrow hallway. But they had not gone down without sending many mercenary souls to the abyss.

Now Enaad stood before her. She looked up at him. He was resplendent in black mail, black riding pants, leather leggings and black boots. The red harness across his chest, decorated with the single lathium eight-pointed star on the cross strap, identified Enaad as a captain in the Sentinel Guard.

His eyes were fixed on her, not knowing if she was going to reprimand him or acquiesce.

"Captain," Cydell began after what seemed to Enaad to be a Pass. "I appreciate your concern. But this is something that must be done. Before the tribesmen march on Mauldar. Before any more people die. All of Sylvan is in danger. I must do what I can." After a silence, Enaad nodded and snapped to attention with a Sentinel salute: right forearm up across his chest to his left shoulder, palm down. Cydell returned it.

"When Zavia arrives, send her to me at once. It is a matter of the utmost urgency."

"Yes, Hya." Enaad started to leave but her voice stopped him.

"Also...select twenty-five of the best guards we have here in Ginnach and have them ready to move out with me at mid-sun." She smiled somewhat as Enaad breathed an audible sigh of relief, bowed and then quickly left to carry out his Hya's orders.

Cydell sat at the little table with her fingers steepled under her chin, deep in thought. She was more determined than ever to get to Windsom Keep and destroy the evil menace that now threatened Mauldar.

"Cydell?"

The Hya looked up upon hearing her name. Elayna stood in the doorway and seemed a little tentative about entering before Cydell smiled and beckoned her in. Elayna entered and gingerly sat a steaming cup of something on the table in front of Cydell. Cydell leaned forward and peered skeptically into it. Her eyebrow shot up as she looked at Elayna.

"Something more to make me sleep?" she asked suspiciously. She didn't want to be drowsy. There was too much to be done.

"It is not a potion," Elayna reassured her. "Only an herbal brew to take away the chill. There is not a bean of marin to be found." She watched the Hya bring the cup to her lips. It must have tasted good, for the Hya closed her eyes as she swallowed and sniffed at the steam, savoring the aroma. As tired as Elayna was, she was glad she had risen early and gone out by the sentry posts at the village border. There among the brush, she had found some of the herbs she had lost with her pack and had somewhat replenished her supply.

"Thank you," Cydell whispered before taking another sip. She looked up at Elayna then. The riding pants Elayna wore were torn and stained with mud and dried blood. A linen tunic replaced the blouse the two raiders had virtually torn off of her the night before and it, too, was filthy. A tattered blanket draped her slightly slumped shoulders and the sparkle in her eye had been replaced with heavy-lidded fatigue. Her hair was pulled back from her face and tied with a strip of cloth. A few loose strands fell into her eyes and she brushed them away with the back of her hand. The raid had taken its toll on the Fair Witch, but to Cydell, she was more than beautiful.

Elayna had extended herself in the use of her powers, during and after the raid. The survivors of Ginnach had come to know and respect the Avoreedan sorceress, for she had saved many of them, even in her own physical weakness. Dornea, Cydell thought, they were all tired, and they were still many leagues from their destination. Cydell herself was anxious to be underway and would have ridden out at first sun, if not for the fatigue and waiting for the reports from her guard. Now she had to wait for Zavia. She had to. At least in the meantime, her company would have a chance to regain its strength before pressing on to Windsom Keep.

"It is rumored that we ride out at mid-sun," Elayna probed. Rii and Orrat had been helping the Sentinel cleanup detail while Kovi had been going around telling tales of his own heroics during the raid to anyone who would listen. The three of them had returned to the tax house excited at hearing some of the Sentinels talking amongst themselves about accompanying the Hya to Windsom Keep and Elayna had been elected to confront Cydell and ask if the rumors were indeed true.

"Yes. We have delayed overlong, though it was not our intention to do so. The Sentinels have things in order here. It is past time we move on." Cydell stood up and went to Elayna, "Elayna," she said as she took the sorceress's hands in her own and looked into her eyes. "Thank you for all you have done. We would have lost many more if not for you. We owe you much."

Elayna shook her head, "I cannot take credit for the grace of the goddess. It is she who guides my hand."

"And I grow more and more impressed with your goddess with each passing sun." Then she looked at Elayna and grinned, "Never again will I doubt your ability to defend yourself."

Elayna smiled mischievously, "You mean, I do not have to convince you further?"

Cydell threw up her hands in mock resignation and shook her head, "Oh no. I am quite convinced. You saved my life. I am in your debt. And I thank Dornea that your aim is true. Otherwise, I would have a third eye where I did not particularly desire one. I just have to remember to stay in your favor," the Hya smiled.

Elayna replied shyly, "That need not be a concern. You *are* in my favor." She looked up into Cydell's eyes and remembered the kiss of the night before. It had ended all too abruptly for her liking and she knew, at this moment, that Cydell's thoughts mirrored her own.

The Hya pulled her closer and just held her in a warm embrace. Elayna closed her eyes, lost in the Hya's closeness.

"It pleases me to hear that," Cydell whispered in Elayna's hair. "It pleases me very much. Were we back at the palace, I would be sorely tempted to...compromise your honor." She looked at Elayna and shrugged lightly. A smile played on her lips. "As it stands, all I can think about are clean clothes and a steaming hot bath. Well... those things are *almost* all I can think about," she teased as she drew Elayna to her. Elayna laced her arms around Cydell's neck just as Zavia Weyer bounded into the room. The scout stopped short. Whatever she was about to say was lost in her throat. She tried to stifle a grin as she quickly turned to leave.

"Stay!" Cydell held up a hand and waved Zavia in, with an apologetic shrug to Elayna.

"I have wounded to attend," Elayna announced and, embarrassed, hurriedly brushed past the grinning scout. Zavia entered the room, absently brushing twigs and dirt from her hair. Her face was mud-smudged, as were her dark brown, long-sleeved woolen tunic, hose and high black boots. Her long bow was across her shoulders with a full quiver of arrows slung over her back. Scouts always wore two daggers tucked away in their wide black belts, and anyone who had ever fought one of the Hya's chosen discovered that they had knives hidden in their boots as well.

Cydell flopped down into her chair and glared at Zavia.

"What took you so long?" she barked crossly.

"Tribesmen are crawling all over the mountains!" Zavia explained as she adjusted her quiver with a frown. "One cannot be too careful. And besides, Hya," she looked pointedly at Cydell and then out the door where Elayna had fled, "you seem to be passing the time well." Zavia had been in the Hya's service for eight Passes and they had developed an easy way between them. But she also knew when she could tease her sovereign and when she couldn't.

"Well, indeed. Fighting a renegade army of mercenaries." Cydell stood up, frowning. "We know now for certain that they were mercenaries. A few Sentinels recognized some of them from various taverns in Mauldar." She looked at Zavia. "Do you think it too late to pick up the trail of those who fled?"

Zavia replied confidently, "No, Hya. I spoke to the sentries as I came in. Apparently, the mercenaries approached the village from the west."

"Wen Yor marsh?" Cydell asked, surprised.

"Yes, Hya. We should have no difficulty picking up the trail. Several of my scouts are very familiar with the marshlands."

"Good. Leave at once. Take as many Sentinels as you need to accompany you, and report to me as soon you can. I will be leaving here at mid-sun."

Zavia calculated mentally, "You should be twenty leagues due west of Tyroda by then. I will find your camp." She bowed slightly and turned to leave.

"One more thing. Did you see Valkyra on your way in?" Cydell asked darkly, somehow dreading the answer.

Zavia thought for a second before she replied, "Yes, I did."
Suddenly, she looked at her Hya. "She was riding out. Due west."

Cydell walked purposefully through the ash-covered streets
of the village, past the debris strewn about the marketplace, until she
came to the temple. She had one more thing to attend to. Kovi's mes-
sage had been cryptic but urgent in his request for her to meet him
there. Down in the baths, of all places, Cydell thought.

She shielded her eyes as she glanced up to see the position of
the now brilliant sun. Soon it would be overhead. Mid-sun. Whatever Kovi wanted, she would have to hurry him along with it. Everything had been prepared for their departure, and she did not want to
be delayed from leaving for the Keep any longer than was absolutely
necessary.

All of the provincial and village temples had baths in their
lower depths. The temple cellars were separate buildings—some
served for the storage of foodstuffs; others contained vast pools of
warm water. The priestesses often scented them with precious oils,
and hired the best tilesetters to surround the pools with expensive
tiles, imported from the mines. Sometimes, the servants of Dornea
landscaped the bath areas with flourishing gardens— exotic flowers
and miniature trees— as the baths were designed to be places of peace
and meditation.

She strode through the deserted temple and headed down the
steps to the baths. As she traversed the main chambers and the corri-
dors, she noticed that most of the rich tapestries that used to be there
were gone. The priceless wall hangings had depicted stories of the
goddess and her great works, and those among her servants whom
she had favored with the ability to perform miracles and display great
healing power in her name. The raiders had taken everything they
had deemed to be of value, but at least, Cydell thought, they had not
burned the temple down. Cydell's footfalls echoed off the walls of
the great pool. She stood in the silence for a moment, looking at the
reflection of the water on the walls as bright rainbow rays of sunlight filtered in from the small windows high up on the walls. The

place was quiet and bright. The steaming water was inviting. Its soothing trickle was the only sound to be heard.

There was no sign of Kovi. Cydell dismissed her cousin's
absence with a shrug and hurriedly began to peel off her clothes. If
she was to die at Windsom Keep, she thought as she struggled with
one boot and then the other, then at least she would be clean.

Cydell sighed luxuriantly as she slid into the pool, submerged
to the neck. The steady trickling sound of water, coming from somewhere unseen, lulled her. Its warmth felt good to her aching muscles
and she lay there with her eyes closed, aware but relaxed.

Suddenly, she opened her eyes, sensing a presence. Looking
toward the entrance to the baths, she saw Elayna standing there with
a bundle of clothes in her arms, smiling. Cydell breathed a sigh of
relief. But mentally, she berated herself for leaving her saber with
her pile of dirty clothes on the other side of the pool. *Careless*, she
thought.

"Something amuses you?" she called across the pool to
Elayna. Her voice echoed in the stillness.

"Kovi said you would turn down a wagon full of lathium
bars for a hot bath. Your cousin knows you very well," Elayna teased
as she set the clothes on the tiled floor.

Cydell harumphed, "The little snit. He prides himself on how
much he *thinks* he knows." She eyed Elayna suspiciously. "So, he
did not wish to meet me here after all. And you knew of this?" Elayna
nodded, still smiling. Cydell relaxed again. "Well, he has done worse."

"Enaad found a change of clothes for you," Elayna said, and
added apologetically, "It is Sentinel garb. He said you would not
mind."

"I will wear anything that is not splattered with mud and
blood," Cydell mused, and then frowned, "with the exception of those
cumbersome long skirts." She looked at Elayna and flashed a smile.
"We all have our limits, do we not?"

"I suppose." Elayna replied. She stood there for a moment in
silence looking longingly at the water. Finally, she said, "I shall leave
you to your bath. I would like to gather more herbs before we leave."

She started away. Cydell noted Elayna's dirt-smudged face and hands. Wisps of limp hair hung in her face.

"You do not have to leave," Cydell offered as she watched her.

"I was leaving because I was not asked to stay, Hya," Elayna said over her shoulder. Cydell laughed as she recalled her own words from the woods. It was the first time Elayna had heard the Hya laugh out loud and the sound was very pleasing to her.

"My quick-witted sorceress," Cydell grinned. "Come. Share the bath with me. We have, after all, shared a chamber. To share a bath would not be so terrible." Elayna hesitated. The Hya's eyebrows shot up imploringly and she playfully cocked her head to one side. "The water is exquisite," she offered temptingly as she slowly moved a hand back and forth in the water, creating seductive ripples that flowed to the side of the pool where Elayna stood. "And we do not have much time."

Elayna shrugged, resigned, and began to slip out of her tunic. She paused and looked pointedly at Cydell, who had been watching her. Grudgingly, Cydell turned her back on the sorceress, shaking her head at Elayna's modesty. But she turned around as soon as she heard Elayna descend the steps leading into the pool and was awed by the golden woman's finely sculpted body. Elayna submerged herself and came up again, slowly rising out of the steam. Cydell was mesmerized. Unable to move. Unable to speak.

Elayna splashed water over her face, over her head, relishing its refreshing warmth as it streamed down her face and through her hair, over her shoulders and breasts. For a moment, the evil mysteries of Windsom Keep were far, far away; as though it was all a part of someone else's life. She wanted it to be that way just for a little while longer. For now, she only wanted to enjoy the baths and the sparkling sunlight on the water.

Elayna did not know when Cydell crossed the pool. When she looked up, she was there, taking Elayna in with her steady gaze. There was no trace of laughter in those eyes. Elayna dared to look into them. The Hya's eyes wove a spell of their own. They were as hypnotic as a candle's flame. They were like fingers reaching into her depths, drawing her closer to the tall, dark woman; strikingly beautiful, her rich skin aglow with the water's oils. Cydell's hair clung to her scalp with wetness. A small, jeweled saber, the emblem of Mauldar, hung from a fine, delicate lathium chain around her neck.

Cydell reached out and tenderly caressed the side of Elayna's face. Elayna planted small kisses in her palm and nuzzled it with her lips and cheek. She took Cydell's hand in her own and slowly, softly, kissed each fingertip. Beneath the surface of the water, Cydell's arm encircled Elayna's waist and drew her closer, so that their bodies met. Elayna placed Cydell's hand on her breast, moaning as Cydell cupped it and held it, kneading it softly. Their lips met as Cydell's thumb tweaked a nipple and she let her hand travel downward to feel the soft contours of Elayna's waist and hips. Her other hand roamed freely, slowly caressing the smoothness of Elayna's buttocks, gently squeezing and releasing, first one and then the other. Eyes closed, Cydell traced lingering kisses on Elayna's neck and nibbled at her ear lobe. She felt Elayna's leg encircle her and the soft tingle of their mounds meeting; a whisper of a touch under water. Cydell pulled Elayna closer and they both began to move in harmony with each other, feeling the warmth of the growing fire between them. Elayna brought both her arms out of the water and laced them around Cydell's neck, to get her balance. She felt Cydell's hand cup her mound and she gasped with surprise and pleasure as she felt two long fingers gently probing inside her.

Elayna covered Cydell's hand with her own where it teased her. She groaned as she quickened their rhythm, as she guided the Hya's ministerings with her own urgency and need, moving her hips in small, sensuous circles. Cydell stroked the bud of Elayna's womanhood, rolling it with her thumb, and felt Elayna's breathing grow more and more labored. She whispered sensuously in Elayna's ear. Elayna threw her head back, eyes closed, but with a smile and grimace of pained ecstasy on her flushed face. The final thrust of Cydell's fingers was met with a groan of passion as Elayna stiffened, pressing Cydell's hand against her for dear life, and holding it there as the tremors raged through her. Cydell held her tight as Elayna gasped again and again, moaning in the final throes of her passion; panting limply against Cydell's breasts, weak-kneed and trembling.

The Hya's company was mounted and waiting in front of the tax house as she and Elayna hurried from the temple toward them. A Sentinel held their mounts, a blank expression on her face as the two women quickly mounted. Someone had thoughtfully left a pile of clothes—riding pants, new leggings and boots, and a new woolen tunic and belt for Elayna beside the pile of clothes Elayna had brought for Cydell. They never knew anyone else had entered the baths. And now, Cydell was resplendent in the Sentinel uniform. She cut a striking figure in the black mail shirt, black riding pants, leather leggings, and boots.

Cydell acknowledged the Sentinel who held out a cloak for her with a nod, and taking the reins, proceeded to swing into the saddle. Elayna did the same, while feeling that she had been abruptly snatched out of a deep dream, still groggy from the lovemaking. Orrat and Rii grinned at each other as they watched the two women. Kovi rolled his eyes toward the skies and began to loudly whistle an obscure ditty, while casting knowing glances at his cousin.

The Commander General watched the Hya and the witch with hooded lids, a great ire rising from deep within her. She looked from one woman to the other. Elayna did not meet her hard glare. But Cydell did. Valkyra did not attempt to mask her fury as she said hotly to Cydell, "Pleased you were able to join us, Hya."

Cydell turned cold and knowing eyes on her Commander General, daring her to say more.

"Likewise, Commander," Cydell replied pointedly, and then raised a gloved hand to move her party forward.

8

WINDSOM KEEP

The Hya set a hard and swift pace, traveling steadily through the remainder of the day and on until dusk. Enaad had secured four fine mounts and enough dry rations to supply the company through the journey to the Keep. Ten of the Sentinel Guard rode in a protective circle around the company. Another ten paired off to scout ahead and double back. Every so often, a shrill whistle rang out around the company, to be answered a beat later by a more melodic trilling from another direction. Cydell was thus assured that Zavia had dispatched some of her scouts as escorts to the Keep.

The company rode in silence. There was not much countryside to see. The roadway they followed just outside Ginnach was surrounded by meadowland, and for leagues in any direction, all one could see were sheep grazing. Orrat and Rii talked and teased each other in loud whispers. They had already seen more fighting than they could have hoped for as wards and they chatted excitedly back and forth about the Hya's prowess in combat; this move and that kick.

Valkyra frequently broke away from the company, when she could stand the silence no longer, to join the Sentinel Guard on their patrols, only to return to find the company as silent as before. Often, she would pause by the roadside, her mount prancing impatiently. As the company rode by, she glared at Elayna, looking as though she wanted to challenge the Fair Witch right then and there. Elayna never met the Commander General's gaze and Valkyra never said a word.

As the company started up the rise that would lead them into the dense woods at the very foot of the Mauldaran Mountains, Valkyra rode off again. Kovi seized the opportunity and, urging his little mount forward at a trot, rode up beside his cousin.

He grinned pleasantly up at her. Cydell cut an eye at him and then focussed her attentions on the trail ahead. Kovi clicked his tongue derisively as he bounced along to his mount's uneven gait. He had not been able to salvage any of the lordly finery he had been wearing when he'd begun the journey, but had coerced a Ginnachan citizen into finding a woolen tunic, riding pants and a worn, tattered cloak.

"I trust you enjoyed the bath?" Kovi eyed his cousin. His eyebrows rose and fell conspiratorially. Unamused, Cydell cut an eye at him.

"And when did you bring the clothes for Elayna?" she asked wryly.

"Have no worries, Cousin. I was quick about it and did not linger. After all, women are all the same. Different only from the neck up." At this, Cydell looked down at him and slowly shook her head and said dryly, "Now I know why you have no mate."

"But *you* do! So I cannot understand why you are in such a poor humor! Not even a 'Thank you, Kovi, for your consideration.' Not a single 'My gratitude to you, dear Cousin, for such sweet privacy.'" He hung his head, feigning hurt.

Cydell turned on him in annoyance. "Stop your babbling," she commanded. "She is not my mate!" she protested in a loud whisper. Turning a little in her saddle, Cydell saw that Elayna had dropped back and was riding beside Orrat. She and her brother and Rii were having an animated conversation. Cydell faced forward again. She could not stop thinking about Elayna—the feel of her; the softness of Elayna's breathy whispers in her ear. They had dressed so hurriedly that there had been no time for sweet words and lingering caresses. All Cydell knew was that she never wanted to be apart from her. She had never felt that way about anyone before, and the intensity of the feeling frightened her. It worried her that one woman could manage to pull so much from her, so much of what Cydell did not even realize she had the capacity to feel.

"Cousin?" Kovi reached over and tapped his cousin's booted leg. He had been talking to her all this time and she had not responded. Cydell usually silenced him before he had the opportunity to fully explain himself. The sorceress must indeed be in her thoughts, no matter how much his cousin would deny it.

"Were you speaking?" Cydell finally looked at him, a frown creasing her brow.

"I was offering you my advice, based on many Passes of experience, on the trials of love and how one should proceed..."

Cydell turned on him, "I do not need your advice!" she snapped. "And I am *not* in love! Now be gone, before I decide to have you bound, gagged, and tied to a post for wolf bait!"

Sputtering, Kovi reined in his mount so abruptly that the rest of the company had to ride around him to prevent a collision.

"As you wish!" he yelled to Cydell's back. "And something more! We have been in the saddle for leagues. At this pace, we shall all be dead of exhaustion before we reach that Dornea-forsaken Keep of yours!"

Cydell halted her company at the fork in the trail that would lead them up through the eastern sector of the Ritdon Woods and north to the Keep. They made camp a quarter of a league off the well-traveled trail, in a clearing at the base of a dense stand of towering trees and underbrush. Valkyra gave orders to the Sentinels, assigning the patrols and the watch. Everyone was travel-weary and did not have much to say in the way of conversation. They wasted no time making camp.

Elayna was already busy sweeping the clearing with a bunch of fallen tree limbs she had gathered. She looked across the clearing as she knelt to build a fire. Cydell stood by a small stand of trees with Orrat, checking her horses' hooves. As she handed over the reins, she turned and looked directly into Elayna's eyes. Elayna smiled, and as she did, she touched her index finger to her lips. Instantly, a wisp of glowing light appeared. The sorceress softly blew it in Cydell's direction, and the tender spark floated gently across the clearing to alight on the Hya's lips. Then, in the next instant, it magically faded into the air. Cydell beamed her delight at the charmed surprise, and with a nod of appreciation to Elayna, moved on to inspect the next horse.

Valkyra halted as she stepped into the clearing. She could barely contain her rage at the intimate display she had just happened to witness. Steeling herself, she strode purposefully toward the sorceress. Elayna looked up and saw the Commander General approaching. She read Valkyra's intent from the scowl on her face and quickly rose to meet her.

The Commander General stopped two lengths away from Elayna, glaring, her hand on the hilt of her saber. The Sentinels who were in camp and attending to their gear stopped in the midst of their tasks to watch the confrontation between the two women.

"We have unsettled business between us," Valkyra seethed between clinched teeth. "Perhaps the Hya will like you less once your face bears the mark of my blade!"

Calmly, Elayna replied, "Leave our quarrel in the past, Valkyra. I have no desire to harm you."

"You? Harm *me*?!" Valkyra laughed wickedly.

"She could, you know. And very badly," Cydell said as she stepped into the clearing. "We have greater things to contend with than you and your temper, Valkyra. Leave off."

"Greater things, indeed!"

No one had been aware of the scouts' approach. Zavia walked up to Valkyra, daring the Commander General to move. Her deerskin tunic was caked with mud, as were her boots and leggings. Her eyes showed the depth of her displeasure and her mouth was set in a stern line. She inclined her head to Cydell and then leveled her gaze at Valkyra.

"Hya, I have much to report," she announced, "most of which involves your Commander General."

"Proceed," Cydell ordered. Zavia walked slowly toward Valkyra as she began. At her signal, two of her scouts walked out of the brush, struggling with the weight of a large strongbox that they carried between them. Valkyra watched, her face deceptively impassive, as they brought the box forward and set it down in the middle of the clearing and then retreated the way they had come. Zavia shrugged her cloak back over her shoulder so that her dagger hilt was visible. As if to warn Valkyra against any sudden moves.

"We picked up the trail of the mercenaries who attacked Ginnach and followed it across Wen Yor marsh, back to a cave in the foothills. We hid ourselves in the trees surrounding their camp and listened as they licked their wounds and bragged about the lives they had taken in the raid, the women they had raped and then murdered. Since their lieutenant, one they called Pak, had not returned, they made plans to divide the taxes and the rest of the booty among themselves, and then to break camp before their captain returned to claim it all. They spoke of the boasts of this Pak. That he claimed his captain had promised him twenty lathium bars if the Hya did not escape the raid alive."

A murmur passed among those gathered in the clearing. Cydell raised her hand for silence and indicated with a nod that Zavia continue.

"We took them by surprise and rounded them up to take them back to Mauldar, where the Hya may do with them as she sees fit."

"And their captain," Cydell prodded urgently. "Did they name their captain?"

Zavia stood directly in front of the Commander General and faced her squarely. Valkyra's hand still rested on the hilt of her saber and Zavia saw her tense, but the Commander General's not-so-subtle warning did not deter Zavia from her duty.

"Commander General Valkyra," she stated formally, "it is my duty, in the name of the monarch of the country of Sylvan, the Hya Cydell Ra Sadiin of Mauldar, to place you under arrest for the offense of high treason and conspiracy to assassinate the Hya."

Before Valkyra could move, ten scouts stepped out of the trees, arrows notched, and aimed at the Commander General's heart. Valkyra looked from face to face in the silence. Her Sentinels watched her, disgust in their eyes. And one by one, as she met their gaze, they turned their backs to her, the ultimate dishonor for a Sentinel.

The Hya stepped forward to face her ex-Commander. Whatever affections she'd felt for the women she thought she knew were gone. Cydell had known Valkyra to be capable of many things, of many acts. But she had always thought, always hoped, that there were some redeeming elements, something of the better part of human nature that still remained in Valkyra. Their lovemaking had been voracious, but never tender. They had shared the pleasures of the body, but never the warmth and intimacy of true lovers. They had never confided tender secrets in the night; never felt the warmth of true love. Now, as Cydell looked into Valkyra's eyes, she thought she saw the fleeting shadow of something, an instant of tenderness. But it was gone in the next heartbeat. The green eyes were steel and filled with anger once again.

Cydell reached out and removed the Commander's three-pronged star from Valkyra's Sentinel sash. When the Hya spoke, she could barely be heard above the crackle of the fire and the haunting, desolate calls of the nightbirds.

"Why?" she asked softly. "So much destroyed. So many innocent lives taken. For what, Valkyra? Lathium bars and onas? A few coins in the pocket?"

Valkyra threw back her head defiantly and then leveled her gaze at Cydell as she answered.

"I would have raised the greatest army in Sylvan. An army to rival even the Sentinels!" She looked around the clearing, "All of you...would have bowed at my feet." Then she looked at Cydell with just a hint of tenderness in her eyes and reached out to touch Cydell's cheek, but the Hya shied away from her hand. "You were my heart, and never knew it. I would have shared it all with you." Then abruptly, she sneered, "But I would not share you with *her*. I shall not lose you to her! Never!"

Valkyra's dagger flashed in the firelight as she lunged for Cydell.

"NO!" Elayna screamed and dropped to one knee as she fired a sizzling bolt from her fingertips. The impact from the blast exploded in Valkyra's chest before Valkyra could deliver her blow. Everyone in the clearing backed away, shielding their eyes from the blinding, shimmering white light. When they could see again, the Sentinels and the scouts converged on the spot where Valkyra had stood. They stopped and stared mutely at the singed ring on the ground. The place where Valkyra's body should have been.

◻ ◻ ◻ ◻ ◻

The grounds around Windsom Keep were deserted. There was no sign of the tribal armies. The thousands of raving warriors, in their mad obedience, had been dispatched to Mauldar, there to head off the Sentinel and Mauldaran forces in the mountains, and then to march on the great city. Madras/Isom's minions could take care of themselves for the time being, at least until they actually reached the city walls. But his tribal army could not think as a unit. They could not plan for battle. They could only rush in, without a strategy or plan. Surprisingly, they had been successful in spite of this lack of order in the raids on the smaller villages. Sheer numbers and the element of surprise had brought Madras/Isom's legions to victory in those battles. But to take a city as well defended as Mauldar, his army would require a leader. A warrior, skilled in strategy, who could devise a battle plan that would bring the great city to its knees.

Madras/Isom, clad in his hooded, long black priest's robe, glided slowly back and forth, hovering just above the carpeted floors of the great study. The light from a dozen candles flickered and danced and created shadows of flame on the walls. There was a fire roaring in the hearth, a fire that had not been built from wood or flint. It burned cold in its silence and did not spark or spit embers.

Tomes of spellbooks were scattered about the long, polished table in the middle of the room. Mentally, Madras/Isom devoured them all. The yellowed pages of the great volumes turned themselves as they fed their mysterious and deadly secrets to the evil mage. He had felt the ripple of the heartstone's power several times in the past five suns. Most recently, just after dusk that evenfall. Such tremendous and all-consuming power. He had to be prepared to face that power, to battle it and win. The final phase of his plan was beginning to unfold.

The shell that was Madras stood in the middle of the study and, closing his eyes in concentration, suddenly, gracefully, hurled a ball of fire into the chill fire in the hearth. Almost immediately the cold flames there were replaced by a vision of a clearing in the woods. Good, he thought. The heartstone was a sun's ride away from the Keep. In silence, he watched the scene being played out before him. It was wise to know one's victims before actually facing them. To learn of their weaknesses before a meeting. Frowning, he leaned closer. The tall red-haired woman in black intrigued him. He followed the course of the confrontation between her and the tall, dark woman facing her. He knew her to be the Hya. All of a sudden he noticed the hilt of the Hya's saber. Something in him tensed. Some thread of what remained of Isom's memories coursed through Madras and for a brief second, he felt a keen sense of dread. There was something vaguely familiar about the hilt of that saber. It stirred a memory of Passes ago. Of a night when he was supposed to have died.

Madras/Isom shook the dread memory away and focussed on the scene unfolding in the hearth, just as a powerful ray of energy shot from the other side of the clearing, aimed at the redhead. Reacting quickly, he mumbled a spell and traced a symbol in the air. There was a brilliant flash inside the hearth. A bolt of hot blue lightning laced an invisible path around the study, as a sudden and cold wind blew through him and around him, teasing the dancing candle flames. Abruptly, the wind died. Madras/Isom's robe settled about his emaciated body in a swirl of black wool. In the silence that followed, the mage glided to the other side of the table and hovered there as he looked down with a nod of satisfaction on the body of the red-haired woman.

Madras/Isom looked down at the still figure of the red-haired warrior lying face down on the rich CoDachan rug. He studied her for a moment, tilting his head this way and that. She did not appear to be injured from the ray that surely would have killed her if he had delayed for one heartbeat longer. He glared down at the Sentinel uniform she wore, a uniform he had come to despise of late. It did not seem so befitting of her now.

He passed his hands slowly above the length of Valkyra's body and watched, nodding in approval of his own power, as the black mail shirt and leggings transformed into a deep, burning red. The red mail of the shirt glimmered in the candlelight. The red riding pants hugged the woman's curvaceous legs and hips. Her red leather Sentinel chest harness was replaced with one of shining black leather. The black leather boots were now emblazoned with detailed lathium serpents up the sides. The hilt of her saber was now an intricately crafted serpent with ruby eyes, the body becoming the grip of the hilt.

Valkyra slowly stirred, attempting to raise herself on her hands as tendrils of long red hair brushed the carpet. Dazed, she rolled over onto her back and propped herself up on her elbows, shaking her head to clear it. The last thing she remembered was raising her dagger to kill Cydell. And then a blast. With some effort, she sat up and looked at her hands. The dagger was gone and there was no blood on her hands. Did Cydell still live?

It was then she noticed her change of uniform and the black-robed figure hovering a length away from her. Startled, she managed to rise to a defensive crouch and then, swaying, brought herself fully to her feet. She drew the saber and then looked at it in surprise when she realized that it did not have the feel of her own blade. She surveyed her surroundings at a glance. Nothing was familiar. And who was this man?

Valkyra stared at him, trying to focus her eyes in the dimness. He was dressed like a priest, but somehow, she knew he was not. His hands were hidden in the vast cowl-like sleeves of his robe. Wisps of white hair barely covered his high forehead. His face was dark and gaunt, hollow-cheeked, with deep, dark circles under the eyes. Those eyes were fixed on her. There was something deep within the steel-blue pools that made Valkyra want to run, shrieking in fear; to cover herself and hide her soul to keep it safe.

Not knowing what else to do, Valkyra raised the saber. But the man waved his hand and the weapon flew out of her grasp and hovered over the table in the middle of the room, where it floated down slowly, as if not to scratch the surface of the table or damage itself. Valkyra stared at it. She instinctively reached for the knife she always hid in her boot, but there was none. Confused, she looked down at herself and then up at her captor, who had not moved.

"Do you know where you are?" he asked at last. His voice filled every corner of the great study and reverberated in the recesses of Valkyra's mind. At the sound of his voice, the inanimate objects in the study came to life for that brief second; as though this man's breath itself was their own lifeblood. Pages of the great books still turned as though by some invisible hand. Quills rose from the table, tips down, and danced a spiral dance before settling down again. The tall candelabra swayed to a silent rhythm, as if they were being blown by a wind only they could feel.

"When I ask a question, I expect an answer!" he boomed. The intensity of his displeasure forced Valkyra back a step. All she could do was look at him, stunned for a moment, before answering.

"So this must be Windsom Keep," Valkyra thought aloud. It was clear that this creature could destroy her at will. If he was so powerful as to have transported her to the Keep from the wood, what couldn't he do? She also realized that if he wanted to kill her, he would have done so by now, or he would have let her be killed by that damned Avoreedan witch's blast. Valkyra turned her focus back on the mage. Her own angry thoughts of Elayna seemed to give him that much more power, for his eyes widened wickedly as he stared back at her.

"Anger. Good. It seems we have a common enemy." His voice chilled her and crept up and down her spine. *Yes*, Valkyra thought as her sense of dread eased somewhat. *I must be of some value to this being. Perhaps my position here is better than I at first thought.*

"Who are you? Why have you brought me here?" she demanded boldly. She still kept her eyes on the mage and the saber on the table.

"In answer to your first question, that information will be revealed to you at my convenience. As for the second, I have brought you here to serve me." This last, Madras/Isom stated intently as he looked into Valkyra's eyes.

"Why would I want to serve you?" Valkyra tossed her head and folded her arms across her chest, standing with her legs apart.

"Several reasons," Madras/Isom said as he glided around the table. Valkyra watched and tried not to let her amazement show on her face. With a sweep of his bony hand, the mage's tomes disappeared from the table. But he left the saber lying there. Valkyra looked at it. It was a magnificent weapon.

"Not the least of all these reasons is that I snatched you from your death. I feel something along the lines of gratitude is in order for that little feat. And then there are your various indiscretions regarding your Hya. You have been dishonored by the Sentinels and will probably lose your head, should you ever return to Mauldar."

The mage was in front of her again before Valkyra realized he had moved.

"I can offer you the power you seek. I require a warrior, such as yourself, to lead my tribal forces against Mauldar. You, Valkyra, shall command the greatest army in Sylvan and after our victory, you shall rule Sylvan as my second."

Valkyra almost smiled, for this sounded like the offer she had made to Pak. She regarded the mage defiantly as she asked, "Why do you not simply use your own powers to take Mauldar, to take all of Sylvan?"

"To rule, one must have subjects. What is the gratification in ruling a desolate land, devoid of souls to do your bidding?" He glided away from her to stare into the cold blaze in the hearth. "Besides, at present, I need every ounce of my strength for...other purposes. My tribal army requires your skills. Now."

"And if I refuse?" Valkyra asked insolently. Madras/Isom did not look up from the hearth as he addressed her.

"You and I both know that you have no intention of refusing." Valkyra was listening, but she was also thinking about the saber in the middle of the table. "You may try for it, if you wish," Madras/Isom said coolly. "I realize it is the nature of a warrior to take risks."

Valkyra hesitated for a heartbeat longer before lunging for the saber and then charging fiercely at the mage. Again, the saber flipped out of her grasp, but this time, the tip of the blade shoved itself up under her chin, forcing her to back away to keep from having her throat cut. She was forced back against a section of the wall. The saber was so close under her chin that she could feel her own blood trickling down her neck where the tip of the blade nicked her. Finally, the pressure of the saber tip eased. Valkyra gathered herself and glared hatefully at the mage as she wiped the blood from her neck. The creature stared at her coldly.

"I must have a Second whom I can trust," he snarled as his mouth curled into a sneer. "You will never make such an attempt again."

Before Valkyra could respond, Madras/Isom's right hand shot out in her direction. A pinpoint of flame was propelled from his index finger. It landed high on Valkyra's left cheek with such searing pain that the warrior screamed in agony. The brilliant ember trailed a thin line of scorched flesh from just under her eye, down along her cheekbone. Valkyra slowly sank to her knees, sobbing in anger and from the intensity of the unbearable pain.

"Rise!" the mage commanded. Valkyra felt herself being pulled to her feet by an invisible force. She stood, sagging against the wall. The deep scar on her cheek burned. It was raw and oozing. She could not bring herself to touch it, nor could she bring herself to meet the mage's eyes. She felt his eyes boring into her. "Kneel before me!" Trembling in anguish and rage, she gradually sank down to one knee.

Madras/Isom looked down on the whimpering warrior-woman. His hands were once again hidden in the sleeves of his robe.

"You will serve me," he stated coolly.

Valkyra did not hesitate when she answered in a whisper, "Yes, lord."

"Master will suffice." He glided closer and reached out to the kneeling woman. Valkyra shrank away, steeling herself for more torture. Madras/Isom touched her cheek and traced the scar. When he took his hand away, Valkyra's pain was gone. She warily rose and gingerly touched her face. The wound was healed, but she could feel the bold scar along the length of her cheek.

Her eyes met Isom's. She did not look away this time, but held his gaze with a contemptuous sneer on her lips. A new feeling began to burn in her, a feeling which overpowered the fear. She would destroy this beast if it killed her. She promised herself in that moment that after she had led the tribal armies to victory in Mauldar, she would find a way, some way, to exact her revenge on this evil.

No one of the Hya's company was at peace that evenfall. The Sentinels who were not on watch sat in huddled groups, whispering among themselves about the ex-Commander General and her disappearance. They cast occasional, wary glances at Elayna, who sat quietly alone, wrapped in her cloak, on the other side of the clearing, her eyes closed in meditation. She did not see them, but their barely hidden trepidations invaded her silent entreaties to her goddess. Elayna had to visualize herself away and alone on a far mountain peak, not to let their fears affect her prayers.

Everyone felt the tension of the coming battle. Whatever immense power that now inhabited Windsom Keep, it was something to be feared. Elayna had told them there was no other explanation for Valkyra's disappearance, for it had not been her doing. And they believed her. The only good to come out of it was that the Hya was still alive. Elayna's blast had caught the ex-Commander General in midstrike and then, nothing. Not even a shred of her clothing had been left of the former Sentinel.

The woods closed in around them in the deep darkness of midnight. Towering treetops were silhouetted against the glow of the two blue moons. There was a stillness to the night that crept like smoke into the camp and surrounded every member of the company. Kovi, Rii and Orrat sat on their bedrolls, silent, unable to sleep. The Sentinels who were not on patrol or preparing for their watch forced themselves to sleep, knowing that their shift would come much too soon.

The Hya had ordered their campfires extinguished, fearing that tribesmen would be roaming the woods to intercept the company and prevent their arrival at the Keep. Thus, Elayna had cast a spell that would allow those in the company to see each other as though they were surrounded by moonlight. But for the Sentinels and scouts, the magical illumination was awkward and disconcerting. They were grudgingly grateful for her help, but they stayed as far away from the sorceress as possible.

Cydell, Zavia and Jana, the captain of the accompanying Sentinel Guard, sat in a circle in the middle of the campsite. The steady low murmur of their voices was reassuring to the rest of the company. Elayna had warned them all that her spell would not last the night. So the three women conferred while they could still see each other in the pale yellow glow that surrounded each of them.

"My scouts and I will break camp at first light," Zavia said wearily. She turned to Jana and asked, "Do we have enough Sentinels on watch to secure the area? My scouts need rest after trekking through Wen Yor marsh and then covering the distance here. I at least owe them a good night's sleep after all of that."

Jana nodded. "More than enough. In truth, Zavia, there are those among the ranks who much prefer the uncertainty of the tribesmen to returning to this camp. They have all heard of what happened to Commander General Valkyra. They are leery of witches and magick." The captain's gaze wandered across the campsite to where Elayna still sat with her eyes closed. Captain Jana was a Rogellen beauty with smooth, ebony skin and piercing black eyes. She was darker than Cydell and her hair, though much coarser, cascaded down her back in a long braid. She wore lathium bracelets on both wrists and was infamous for her skill with the dagger. She appeared to be a shadow, lost within the blackness of her Sentinel uniform, the red crossed harness across her chest and the brightness of her eyes and teeth being the only distinguishable features about her in the dim light.

Cydell looked across at her and frowned. "The witch may be our only salvation against the powers of the Keep," she reprimanded the captain softly. "Thank Dornea she is with us and not against us."

"Yes, Hya," Jana whispered contritely.

Zavia frowned as she questioned Cydell, "Are you certain it was the power within the Keep that took Valkyra?"

Cydell shrugged, "That is what Elayna tells me, and I believe her. The goddess appears to speak to her directly."

"Then how can we fight what we cannot see?" Zavia countered. "How may we even approach the fortress, if this power knows we are here?"

"We have no strategies to battle sorcery, Hya," Jana said, with a hint of frustration in her voice. Cydell listened patiently to her warriors' concerns, staring out beyond them, into the darkness. After a while, she rose and kicked the cramps out of her calves. Jana and Zavia exchanged glances and rose as well. Waiting.

In her mind, Cydell replayed the conversation she had had with the priestess just before embarking on their journey to the Keep. The priestess had emphasized the importance of Elayna's involvement and had insisted that the Fair Witch accompany the Hya's party. She remembered the whispered warning of the dark stranger who had died in Elayna's arms. Looking across the clearing, she saw Elayna sitting on her bedroll, watching the threesome with a puzzled expression on her lovely features.

Zavia and Jana shifted impatiently. Finally, Cydell seemed to come to a decision. She looked at both of her captains in turn.

"Perhaps we will not need to attack the Keep. We do not even know what it is we are fighting. I think this...power...should reveal itself." Again, she glanced over at Elayna. "We have something it wants. Let it come to us and get it. Maintain the watch and the patrols. Jana, when are the reinforcements due to arrive?"

"If they have fared well against the tribesmen, Hya, they should be here before mid-sun on the morrow," Jana replied confidently.

"Good. I hope that is soon enough. I have the feeling we will end up at the Keep, regardless. After your scouts have rested, Zavia, I need them as close to the Keep as they may get."

"Yes, Hya," Zavia replied crisply.

"And this evenfall," Cydell said with a curious smile on her lips, "I shall learn all I can of Elayna's powers."

Jana snapped a salute and strode off into the darkness. Zavia lingered and Cydell raised a questioning brow at her.

"I think, Hya," Zavia began with a mischievous smile, "that you have learned quite enough about Elayna's powers already."

"If your arrows are as poorly aimed as your wit, Scout Captain Zavia, this will be a long battle indeed, will it not?" Cydell shot back. Zavia cleared her throat as her smile faded and with a hurried salute, she disappeared into the brush.

Elayna and Cydell sat talking on their bedrolls long after the rest of the camp had fallen off to sleep. As weary as they were, Cydell insisted on finding out everything she could about the heartstone and its powers. Elayna fought to stay awake. Though her meditation had helped her to relax, she nonetheless found herself uneasy over the prospect of facing whatever awaited them at the Keep. As they talked, she wondered how Cydell could sit with her in the darkness, calmly asking questions. If the Hya was apprehensive about confronting the power of the Keep, it did not show in her voice. And though the Hya sounded impassive, Elayna felt there was so much more Cydell was not saying. At this moment, Cydell was the ruler, not the sweet and tender lover Elayna had known only a sun before. There was no indication from Cydell that they had even touched, much less made love. And she treated Elayna as though she were one of her own captains, planning a war strategy, as she and Zavia and Captain Jana had done earlier that night.

Elayna felt her heart grow heavier with each question Cydell asked. It was clear that the enemy they were about to face had awesome powers. Was she a match for him? And Elayna had questions of her own; things she wanted to say to Cydell, but felt this was neither the time nor the place to do so. She wanted to tell her how glad she was that Valkyra's blade had not found its mark. She wanted Cydell to know how much she felt for her, how much she yearned to feel Cydell's gentle caress again.

Cydell continued to bombard Elayna with questions about her powers until Elayna thought her head would explode. She told

Cydell everything she had discovered about the heartstone's power
during their journey, and all that she remembered of her mother's
teachings.

When finally Cydell seemed satisfied, she wrapped herself
in her cloak and abruptly stretched out, exhausted, on her bedroll.
Elayna lay back in her own bedroll after a moment, frustrated and
confused, almost to the point of tears. She listened to the Hya's even
breathing beside her for a while and thought Cydell was asleep, until
she heard the Hya's soft whisper in her ear.

"Elayna," Cydell whispered in a tired voice. "You know that
the wielder of this...power...will come for you."

"Yes, I know," Elayna replied softly.

"In a way, I feel I am sending a mere child to do battle alone
in the depths of the abyss. Yet, I know very well that you are not a
child."

"I am not afraid, Hya." Elayna tried to reassure Cydell and
herself. Then, in the darkness, Elayna felt Cydell sit up and look
down on her.

"While I am not a god and I have no magick, no power besides the skilled stroke of my blade, know that I will do my best to
stay by your side. You shall not face him alone." Cydell leaned over,
gently kissed Elayna's cheek, and before turning over and settling
down to sleep, she whispered, "And, Elayna, I have not forgotten."

Elayna smiled, relieved and content, and closed her eyes to
sleep away the brief moments before dawn.

□ □ □ □ □

A sudden sense of foreboding startled Cydell awake. She sat
upright in her bedroll and knew that Elayna was gone before she
even looked down at the empty place beside her. Cydell was on her
feet before she was fully awake, saber drawn. Before she could arouse
anyone else, there was a distant blare from a Sentinel horn. Two short
blasts and one long one. They were under attack.

The Sentinels in camp were on their feet in an instant. The
distant clanging sabers and longswords echoed through the trees and

over the surrounding mountain peaks. And the sound was drawing closer. Twenty-eight Sentinels guarded the perimeter of the campsite with the Hya enclosed within. They broke to let Kovi, Orrat and Rii through the protective circle. Orrat was leading the Hya's stallion. Briefly, Cydell looked into the boy's eyes and knew that he was aware that Elayna was not with them. He was fighting the panic he felt as he handed his Hya the reins of her mount.

Before she could speak, he said, "You cannot keep me here! I ride with you!" His defiant voice rose over the encroaching melee.

"There is no time to argue!" Cydell yelled back as she swung into the saddle and spun the stallion around. The black warhorse reared up in anticipation of the charge, already smelling the blood of his enemies on the chill morning air. Jana bounded out of the brush and caught Cydell's stirrup just before the Hya rode off. The Sentinel captain gasped for breath as she looked up at her Hya, her bloody blade still gripped tightly in her hand. Jana's uniform was streaked with blood and gore, but Cydell didn't see any signs that the Sentinel captain was injured. What she did see was the bright battle-lust in Jana's eyes as she hurriedly gave her report.

"We can hold them here and give you the time you need to reach the Keep. We will be at your back!" Jana reported breathlessly. Cydell nodded her approval as she and her captain gripped each other's wrists.

"Farewell," Cydell said grimly, and charged her stallion up the trail toward Windsom Keep, with Orrat, Rii and Kovi close behind.

Isom had grown tired of waiting. The Hya's company did not seem to be in any particular hurry to reach the Keep. Therefore, the mage had taken matters into his own hands and had seized the witch from the campsite as he had done with the Commander. The girl lay where she had materialized, in a corner of the great study. He had cleared away all the clutter: the table, the candelabra and spellbooks, the various wall hangings. All that remained was the cold fire in the hearth.

From his constant vigil and spying in the fires of the hearth, he knew that the Sentinels had engaged his tribal regiment in the mountains and were fighting their way to the Keep. Whatever he did, he had to do it quickly, before the Keep was overrun. He had kept a sharp eye on his new Commander. She was doing very well during the forced march to Mauldar, outmaneuvering the Mauldaran army that had been sent out from the city to ward off a possible siege. Of course, if he found he had need of her, he could always bring her back to defend him as well.

Thus assured, Isom turned his attention to the unconscious girl lying on the floor across the room. She was a beauty indeed. There was something painfully familiar about her face that stirred in him a spark of memory of Passes long ago; of something he had once felt that had been destroyed and lost to him forever.

The air in the great study hummed with the awesome power that Isom had absorbed. That power was the only source of illumination there, and it pulsed with the evil mage's every heartbeat. Isom had never felt so alive, so omnipotent. His bony fingers tingled; his mind and body surged with energy, ready for release, to be directed at his will.

He glided closer to the prone girl, his long black robe swirling around him. He was drawn, as though hypnotized, to the glowing heat of the heartstone, where it had fallen out of the girl's tunic and now lay on the floor, still attached to the thick black leather thong around her neck. As Isom drew closer, he felt the energy from the stone as it pulsed a counter-rhythm to his own surging powers. It was difficult for him to determine which was the stronger, which would engulf the other in the final battle. For now, he could only stare at it with the intoxicating realization that the heartstone was nearly within his grasp.

The closer Isom moved to the girl, the brighter the heartstone pulsed. Within its depths, Isom saw a fiery swirl of magenta and blue and brilliant orange. He was just close enough to reach out and touch the heartstone when the girl suddenly stirred. Isom quickly withdrew, drawing back to watch as she groggily sat up and took in her surroundings.

Elayna gasped, startled, as she suddenly realized she was no longer in the woods. She looked into the intense gaze of Isom Hawk and knew immediately whom it was she faced. The heartstone was fiery hot against her as she slowly and cautiously rose to her feet. She pushed herself up along the wall until she could steady herself. Her dirty linen shirt was untucked from her riding pants and her hair fell in strands across her face. She swept the hair out of her eyes, and looking quickly around the empty, massive room, saw that there were two huge doors to her far right. They slammed shut as she looked at them. There was a window at the far end of the room, just behind where the mage stood in front of her.

A chill, unnatural wind blew through the enormous chamber as Isom began to speak. Elayna did not feel it for the heat and power radiating through her body from the heartstone. But she did hear him and knew that whatever the outcome of their battle, she would never forget his voice as he intoned menacingly, "There is no escape, Fair Witch. Welcome to your doom."

□ □ □ □ □

The two wielders of magick inside Windsom Keep were not aware of the battle raging just outside its protective walls. The tribal force in the mountains had been forced back up to the very grounds of the Keep by the crush of Sentinel regiments that had fiercely engaged the tribesmen at first sun. Zavia's scouts loosed barrage after barrage of deadly arrows from the treetops, where they were posted around the perimeter of the Keep.

Isom's power fueled the savage attack of the tribesmen and kept them fighting ferociously. The grounds around the Keep were littered with screaming horses, masked Sentinel warriors and tribesmen covered in furs and skins and hide leggings. What the tribesmen lacked in skill, they made up for in tenacity. Their broadswords and daggers sometimes barely pierced the black mail of the Sentinel uniforms. And to their surprise, they found that the Hya's forces were more deadly unhorsed than they were in the saddle. One Sentinel could engage four tribesmen at a time, and still stand to take on four more.

Cydell halted her stallion just on the edge of the woods and looked out at the chaotic battle scene that separated her from the entrance of the Keep. Her mount danced in place, snorting mist in the chill morning air, anxious to join the fray. The Hya was not distinguishable from any other Sentinel in her black mail shirt and black leather leggings. She was sweat-soaked from the hard riding. Her black and gray curls clung to her head as she turned slightly in her saddle and looked to her rear. She saw that the two boys and her cousin were behind her, watching and waiting for her command, their sabers at the ready. Her Sentinel Guard had fanned out around her to form a protective 'V' as she made her way to the entrance of the Keep. She knew it would be pointless to try to send the boys to safety when she saw the hard determination in their young faces.

"I need you at my back!" she yelled to them above the roar of the ensuing battle. Both boys brought their sabers up as one in a Sentinel salute. With a grin of satisfaction, Cydell returned it, and with a powerful Sentinel battle-cry, charged forward.

The Hya's company charged forward bravely in their protective formation. The Sentinel troops in front of Cydell struck down the tribesmen who surged toward them with sweeping sabers. Other Sentinels were drawn in their direction, and they fought to get through to support the defensive wave. They cleared a bloody and body-strewn path for her, and Cydell moved steadily forward.

Numerous tribal warriors managed to slip through the Sentinel barriers. They struck at the regal-looking dark woman on the black stallion, figuring her to be someone of great importance to warrant such protection. But they did not count on her as a great warrior. Cydell fought to keep her path clear as tribesmen attacked her from all sides. She fiercely slashed at groping, bloody hands as they reached up at her in an attempt to pull her from her mount. Her stallion reared up wildly, the whites of his eyes glaring as he came down to trample the menacing tribal warriors who were unfortunate enough to stumble under his thundering, pounding hooves. At one point, Cydell had just disposed of a particularly worrisome tribesman, when she felt another one jump up behind her in the saddle. The attacker raised his short dagger with a mad whoop, and then suddenly, with a grimace of pain and shock, fell forward, his full weight against Cydell's back. With a grunt of effort and a look of disgust, she shoved the dead warrior out of the saddle. Looking down, she recognized the hilt of Kovi's own dagger protruding out of the tribesman's back. She glanced up briefly to meet her cousin's pleased grin. Then they both turned back to face new attackers.

To Cydell, it seemed to take forever to reach the entrance of the Keep, but finally, she did. She jumped from the stallion and raced past her Sentinel troops to the massive oaken doors. The mage was overconfident and had not deemed it necessary to bolt the mighty portals from the inside. Two Sentinels kicked the doors open and then engaged the tribesmen who seemed to rain down on them all at once, now that the invaders were breaching their stronghold.

The Hya paused only briefly in the imposing entrance hall, and then bounded up the winding stairway that spiraled high into the uppermost reaches of the fortress.

□ □ □ □ □

Elayna felt trapped in the vacuum of silence that surrounded her in the great study. Isom Hawk bore down on her, his steel blue eyes hooded and dark with evil intent. All of his power was focussed on the witch and the heartstone, both almost within his grasp.

"Give me the heartstone!" he commanded evenly. Elayna faced him squarely, even though every ounce of her being trembled. The power of the heartstone warmed her and reassured her. And somewhere deep within her being, she felt the strength and fury of the goddess. When she spoke, her voice was not her own, although she felt it was a part of her; something of the goddess that had coalesced with Elayna's purer self.

"Why do you not take it?" she challenged. Elayna did not miss the brief flinch on the mage's face as she spoke. Something within him knew the voice as well. But the heartstone beckoned to him, and its call was very seductive.

"If I must destroy you to possess it, then so be it," he threatened menacingly.

"Have done, then," she said quietly. But her calm defiance did not deter Isom. With a grand, all-encompassing gesture, he mumbled a spell, summoning the very essence of his power to his core. As it coursed through him, threadlike fingers of lightning streaked furiously through the great study. It danced through the air and formed a funneling spiral which spun around and around the body of the evil mage.

Isom's hands suddenly shot out from where they had been hidden in his massive sleeves. His lips still moved as he sent two searing blasts of white spellfire at Elayna. Instantly, Elayna raised her hands, palms out toward Isom. Blinding blue bolts of power shot forth, diverting Isom's attack, splaying his powerful rays out, at an angle away from Elayna, to explode against the walls on either side of them. In the midst of the smoke and the rain of debris, the sorcerer seemed to accept the deflection of his power calmly. In answer to his attack, Elayna dropped to one knee and held out the heartstone so that its brilliant and deadly fire was aimed directly at Isom's face.

The mage could not react in time, and in a flash, scorching blue rays encircled him like bands of white hot steel. Isom stood rigid, unable to move. It felt as though thousands of daggers were piercing his body, draining his strength and his power.

In the throes of agony, Isom mumbled another spell. Elayna watched mesmerized as the body of the mage shimmered and shifted. His body stretched thin as it grew taller, extending up toward the ceiling, beyond her bands of power. Isom's robes coiled around him as he rose, gradually transforming himself into the thick, long reptilian body of a serpent.

The great head of the monster towered above Elayna, swaying back and forth. Drool oozed from its fanged mouth, dripping in long thin rivulets to the floor. Its shiny black body undulated slowly as it uncoiled to give itself more length. The tip of its tail was raised.

Elayna stared terrified at the two-pronged barb that waved threateningly back and forth, a heart's-breath away from her face.

Abruptly, her attention was drawn to the creature's head, just as it reared back to strike. She stared, mesmerized, directly into the serpent's mist-blue eyes as it charged down at her with the speed of the wind. Elayna gasped from the shock of the impact, her breath jolted out of her lungs as the head of the serpent met the heartstone's radiant orange shield. The serpent reared back and let out a roaring hiss of pain and rage and bewilderment. Elayna slowly sank to her knees, drained from the force and power of the magick.

Isom could no longer maintain the phantasmagoric shape. The serpent's form shimmered and dissolved once again into the mage's true self. He stood swaying on his feet. The spell had sapped much of his power but still, he was not beaten. Elayna's head throbbed as she wearily pushed herself up. And then she squinted up at the sudden, familiar image that now glided closer and closer to her.

"Cydell?" she whispered. The familiar faced beamed and held out a hand to her. The power of the heartstone seemed to wane as Elayna herself weakened. She knew the tall, dark woman in the Sentinel uniform. A voice in the back of her mind demanded insistently that she relinquish the heartstone. It told her that all was well, and that the heartstone would be safe in her hands. The Hya's face, with its charming, lopsided grin, drew closer. Dazed, Elayna slowly slipped the leather thong that held the heartstone over her head and held it out. It was in that instant that she groggily recognized the evil blue eyes. Her own eyes widened in panic, and before she could snatch it back, a strong bony hand grabbed the length of the thong and yanked it out of Elayna's grasp.

Isom shimmered into his own image again. In his jubilation, he had to restrain himself from looking directly at, or touching, the heartstone itself. He held it away from his body and turned his attention back to Elayna's huddled figure on the floor in front of him. He towered over her, piercing her with his wicked glare. Elayna watched as he slowly lifted his other hand to reveal a saber. Isom paused as he held the weapon up high, ready to strike the fatal blow.

"I will take great pleasure in killing you in a more conventional fashion," he chortled.

Suddenly, the ornately carved wooden doors of the great study burst open. Startled, Isom looked up in amazement to see the Hya running toward him, saber at the ready. In that instant of the mage's inattention, Elayna focussed the remainder of her will on the dangling heartstone. It revolved slowly until its swirling brilliance faced the mage. Isom felt the movement, and without thinking, turned to look at the hand that held the thong. His piercing scream rang out through the mountains, high up through the treetops, and out across the hills and meadows of the grounds surrounding Windsom Keep. He was mesmerized by the glowing blue-orange heartstone as rivulets of power surged from its center, out into Isom's eyes. The mage's body quaked and trembled as the growl of rolling thunder shook the Keep to its depths.

Cydell stood, saber raised, as powerful gusts of wind swirled around the chamber. With a grunt of effort, she brought her grandfather's saber out and across her body. The lightning stroke sent Isom Hawk's head flying into the air. Still screaming, it finally landed in the cold fires of the hearth. The heartstone sailed across the chamber and plummeted to the floor, spinning furiously.

The powerful rays of the heartstone increased in their intensity. Tendrils of energy laced around the great study, creating an unnatural wind of their own. Cydell was thrown hard against the wall, where she sank down, unconscious.

Then the wild ribbons of energy slowed and converged around the body of the Fair Witch. Elayna lay trembling and convulsing as her body absorbed the raw power of the heartstone. Finally, with a cry of anguish, she gave herself fully to the darkness that closed in around her.

❑ ❑ ❑ ❑ ❑

Suddenly, the battle on the grounds of the Keep came to a grinding halt. The Sentinel warriors realized that the tribesmen had ceased to attack. Some of the tribal warriors stopped in mid-stroke and slowly lowered their weapons, staring at their Sentinel opponents with bewildered expressions. The Sentinels were the first to recover from the sudden and puzzling surrender of the tribesmen. They immediately began to herd the bedazzled tribal warriors out of the surrounding woods. Now they sat dazed and complacent, and heavily guarded, in huddled masses on the grounds of the Keep.

The Mauldaran army had charged out to meet the swarming tribal army before the great stone walls of Mauldar. The two opposing armies faced each other across a quarter of a league of battlefield, waiting for the signal to charge.

Valkyra rode up and down her front lines shouting instructions for the upcoming battle. She presented an awesome spectacle on her white steed, resplendent in her red mail and leggings, a black cape flowing behind her as she rode. She was fury and rancor personified as she galloped back and forth, her mane of red hair flaring out behind her. The front line of the Mauldaran army wondered, frowning across the distance, who the woman-warrior was who led the teeming masses of tribesmen against them.

Satisfied that her troops were ready, Valkyra got into position and with a raised hand, signalled her army forward. No one moved. She had started forward, her horse at full charge, when she reined in hard and spun her mount around. Her army was milling around as though lost. Some were sitting. Some held their weapons in their hands and looked at them as though puzzling over why they were even in this place.

The Mauldaran army sat stunned as they watched the tribal army disintegrating right before their eyes. They watched as the striking figure on the white horse shouted something inaudible, waved a fist at the sky, and rearing on the magnificent steed, thundered off across the plains.

A mighty cheer rose up from the ranks of the Mauldaran army and from those Mauldaran citizens who were prepared to watch the great battle from high atop the city walls.

9

CALM

Dusk wrapped Windsom Keep in a cloak of gray mist. Birds called across the rolling hills and slumbering valleys of the mountains. The deep silence was broken by the chunk and whisper of soil being shoveled for the burial of the dead, Sentinels and tribesmen to lie, at last, side by side. Finally at peace.

The Sentinel army had secured the Keep and restored the main hall as command center, while a detail worked on cleaning up the great hall. The Keep would be under the Hya's jurisdiction until another Keep Master could be elected by the Tribal Council.

Jana Qui AkDaan was appointed acting Commander of the Sentinel army after the mysterious disappearance of former Commander General Valkyra Haan J'teehl. It was Jana who organized and appointed the Sentinels to see to the burial details and the care of the Keep. She supervised the dispatch of Sentinels to all of the villages and mountain tribal camps to make them aware that the fighting had ceased. The dazed tribesmen now awaited the will of the Hya in fear, for the peace treaty had been violated.

It was Jana who sent relief supplies and food to the villages hit hardest, while Dassett assigned a continuous watch around the Hya's chamber within the Keep. No one was allowed to enter, with the exception of the healers. Dassett sent word back to Mauldar that the Hya and her party were safe and would return to the city when they were able to ride. She was certain the report would ease the collective minds of the High Provincial Council and of old Josn, who had worried herself to a frazzle since the Hya's departure.

On the evening of the third sun after the Keep had been secured, the Hya was out of bed and sitting at the desk in the anteroom of her chamber. The gash in her thigh was healing without infection, and she favored her aching side only a little. She gingerly ran her hand along the thin scar there and knew that Elayna had been responsible for healing her thigh. Her other wounds, not quite as serious, were mending nicely by themselves. The army's healers still tended her and brought her endless cups of hot broth and herbs. They objected adamantly when she insisted on meeting with Jana, but she had gotten unbearably bored lying in bed, and was also too worried about Elayna to rest.

Cydell remembered killing Isom, but then all had gone black. When she next awakened, she was wrapped in blankets, weak and in pain. Now her muscles ached and objected whenever she decided to stir too quickly. Her first questions had been about Elayna and the welfare of the rest of her company. She was told that Rii and Orrat had been wounded, but neither seriously. Kovi had taken the worst of it and was still unconscious. Cydell demanded constant reports on his condition. Elayna, she was told, was resting peacefully and was not to be disturbed. Thus assured that all was under control, she had summoned Jana.

The Sentinel entered the chamber and stood at attention before the Hya. Cydell waved her to her ease and leaned back heavily in the high-backed armchair. Jana settled herself in the chair across from the Hya and began her report.

She wore a fresh Sentinel uniform of black mail, saber and dagger strapped to her belt. Her high black boots shone in the glimmer of the candlelight. There was a soft hue to her nut brown skin. Her sparkling black eyes revealed just a hint of weariness, but there was no sign of weakness in the firm set of her angular jaw and the stern line of her full lips. Both of her arms were bandaged in various places, in addition to the fresh bandage wrapped around her head. Her long hair was in its traditional braid, and it lay over the tall warrior's left shoulder like a luxuriant black stream.

Cydell regarded her acting Commander and could not help thinking of Valkyra and her ultimate betrayal and disappearance. As the Hya listened to this competent young woman she thought, *Jana is not as seasoned as Valkyra, but is just as thorough in carrying out her assignments; just as fierce in battle.* Cydell found that she was very pleased with the acting Commander's apparent intelligence and initiative.

"Proceed with your report, Commander," she said quietly.

"Zavia and her scouts are aiding in the transport of supplies for the rebuilding. We lost many in the fighting, Hya. In addition to entire villages."

Cydell winced. "What is the status of the tribes?"

"They cannot believe they have perpetrated these horrors. It is as though they were asleep and merely dreaming. They mourn their loved ones and tribemates.

"Children wonder when their fathers will return. Mothers have no answers for them. They do not know what they have done."

Cydell rose, biting her lip against the pain and stiffness. "And the loss of Sentinels?" she queried with a frown.

"Minimal, in comparison to the number of dead tribespeople. However, our ranks will need to be replenished. Most have been sent on supply detail to those villages hardest hit in the attacks."

"How many wards are ready for their trials?"

"Enough for a fledgling unit, Hya. There is some question about two. Orrat of Avoreed and Rii of Barrach. They have been suspended by the trainers for leaving the compound in defiance of curfew."

"Yes," Cydell acknowledged solemnly. "I am aware of their infractions."

"They are the top two wards and were almost ready for their trial, but for this offense," she said regretfully.

Cydell thought for a moment and then pronounced, "Advise the trainers upon our return that all penalties against those two will be dismissed. I dare say they have proven themselves. But the wards are not to be told of my decision until I speak with them personally. I shall determine when they will be tested."

Jana started to speak but Cydell held up a hand. "That will be all for the present. Those cursed healers will be fluttering in soon, fussing like wet plains hens."

Jana smiled, "It is good to have you on the mend, Hya."

"Thank you. Though I must admit, I have felt better in my life. We shall speak again after evenmeal, Commander General."

Jana rose and started for the door before the impact of the Hya's salutation hit her. She turned with an expression of disbelief and looked questioningly into the Hya's smiling face.

"Your service in the aftermath of this disaster has been exemplary and should not go unrewarded. Congratulations! We shall have the formal ceremony upon our return to Mauldar. Pending my full recovery, the Challenge must still be performed. But between you and me, it will only be for show, in this instance. I am aware of your skill and prowess in combat."

Jana could not stop the tears of excitement and pride. She bowed low and snapped up into a formal salute.

"And I am well aware of yours. Thank you, Hya! I am deeply honored." Cydell inclined her head. Jana spun on her heel and left the chamber.

Cydell's urgent craving for a cup of marin would not go away. Though she was under strict orders from the healers not to stay on her feet for prolonged periods of time, she nevertheless felt the need to walk. It wasn't just for the exercise. She knew what she really craved. To be back in her palace. She wanted to return to Mauldar where she belonged. The Tribal Council was in the process of selecting another Keep Master. When that was done, Cydell would withdraw her army and return to Mauldar. *Until then*, she thought as she limped to the door of the chamber, *I am stuck in this stone prison.*

She started down the corridor to the stairwell that led to the back entrance of the kitchens. Passing Elayna's door, she paused. If she was awake, by some chance, she reasoned, she would probably want only to rest. Perhaps Elayna would not wish to see her at all.

But as she started to limp away, the doors of Elayna's chamber slowly swung open.

Cydell entered, not knowing whether to trust the silent invitation or not. She walked into the inner chamber to find Elayna seated on the side of the gauze-draped bed, wearing a robe. Sunlight streamed in from both small windows and her golden figure was the vortex of the brilliant rays. This vision of radiance and beauty took Cydell's breath away. She could only stare, mesmerized.

The chamber door closed slowly behind her of its own accord. Cydell didn't notice, so enraptured was she by the woman on the bed. She went to her and stood in silence. Lovely green eyes turned up to her and saw through to her soul. It was then she realized that the one comfort in all the long suns of recovering her strength was her feelings for Elayna. But the memories of holding her and loving her now only seemed part of a tender dream, interrupted by the brutal reality of the fighting and evil and death. During the past few suns, the growing realization of her love for this incredible woman had caused a different kind of ache, almost a sadness, a weakness caused by so much love. She had never experienced this feeling of tenderness and caring for another person. She was almost afraid to embrace that weakness, for it was a contradiction of everything she had been taught to feel. She had fought these feelings all her life. And now, as she stood gazing at Elayna, she took in the woman before her and realized she loved her more than life. Why, then, were the words so hard to speak?

"You would walk by and not stop to see me?" Elayna asked softly.

"The healers would have my head if they knew I was here, even now. They assured me you were well, but it is always best to find out these things for one's self," Cydell shrugged, embarrassed. Elayna rose and went into Cydell's welcoming arms. They embraced in a rush of emotion.

"To have lost you, Elayna," Cydell whispered, "would have made my life worthless." Cydell held her a moment longer, "Perhaps I should leave you to your rest now. You need to recover fully."

But Elayna would not let her go. Her breath was sweet and warm in Cydell's ear as she linked her arms around her lover's neck.

"My only need at this time," she whispered, as she pressed her body into Cydell's, "is you."

Cydell ran her hands along the contours of Elayna's body and drew her in. Their kiss was fervently magical, and Cydell forgot all about her desire for marin as they loved well into the evening.

Later, they entered the main banquet hall, hand in hand, radiant from lovemaking, and famished. Orrat and Rii were having a boisterous discussion about who had sustained the most wounds. Commander General Jana and three Sentinels sat with Zavia and two of her scouts. All heads turned and the room grew quiet when they entered. The Sentinels and scouts rose to attention. Orrat dropped a half-eaten drumstick as he and Rii jumped up simultaneously.

With respect and admiration in her eyes, Jana took her goblet in hand and held it up to the Hya. The others did the same in silent salute. Cydell smiled her acknowledgment and appreciation of the gesture, and gave Elayna's hand a firm squeeze as they took their places at the head of the table.

10

RETURN

Mauldarans turned out en masse to welcome their Hya and their army home, shouting and cheering their love and admiration. The company, escorted by a platoon of Sentinels, was spotted by the watch at mid-sun. A full two turns had elapsed since the battle at Windsom Keep, and the soldiers were as eager to be home as their anxious mounts straining at the bit. Everyone, from merchants to thieves, lined the top of the walls surrounding the city, waving colorful banners and flags. Those who found no room on the walls filled the marketplace and lined the roadway leading to the palace.

In triumph, the tired company rode through the city gates toward the palace at last. Crowds followed, walking along beside them and cheering. They tied large fragrant white blooms in the manes of the horses and gave gifts of fruit to the soldiers. Kovi blew kisses and grinned as his small horse almost lost itself in the midst of the excitement and revelry. Rii and Orrat waved to the crowd, but harbored a deep sadness in their hearts. The knowledge that they had lost their status as wards weighed on their shoulders like an iron yoke. The Hya had been friendly enough toward them at the Keep, but when they left, it was as though she was glad to be rid of them. Almost as though she was not aware of their pain.

Elayna took in the joyous scene around her. She saw the adoration in the people's faces and felt the love and esteem they had for their Hya. Although she loved seeing this, it struck her that she would miss the privacy they had shared at the Keep. She had been a little disappointed when the Tribal Council had finally elected a new Keep Master, for while the company had waited for that decision, she had gotten closer to Cydell. Not only in loving her physically, but in knowing her—the dreams she had for her people, her fears, her childhood, and the loneliness she had endured as successor to a powerful dynasty of rulers.

During those glorious days together, Cydell had taken to early morning rides, with Elayna accompanying her. They had followed the mountain trails and taken refreshing dunks in the icy streams. Wrapped in new woolen cloaks to protect them against the encroaching mountain winter, they would race their mounts across the open dales, laughing and shouting like children at play. When the business of the day was done, they would have light dueling practice sessions in the courtyard. Orrat and Rii would join them, sometimes forgetting that it was their sovereign they battled, as they enthusiastically included her in their games and teasing and mock challenges. She was free enough with them, for there were no pressing demands of state to worry her. The boys' playful spirit was contagious, and Cydell found herself laughing with them, and periodically, good-naturedly scolding them to improve this stroke or that maneuver.

Often Elayna would step out of the practice simply to watch. She marveled at the suppleness of Cydell's body, the body she now knew as well as she knew her own. There was no question that she loved the Hya. At last, there were no more rapturous dreams. No more fantasies. The reality was so much sweeter, so much more enchanting.

And now, returning to Mauldar, Elayna wondered if she would lose her love to the demands of ruling or to other indulgences that the Hya was infamous for. Would she have to live her love in dreams once again? She knew Cydell cared for her. It was evident in each kiss, each caress. But she had yet to hear the words from the Hya's lips, and she had begun to think Valkyra had been right. So many times, when they were alone, Elayna wanted to declare verbally how much she loved Cydell, but she had held her tongue. Perhaps those words would drive Cydell away from her forever. Thus, she had kept the truth of her own feelings silent. Only Orrat knew how deeply she loved and wanted to be loved by the Hya.

口 口 口 口 口

"Perhaps you will think twice about traipsing off into the woods next time!" Josn scolded, "Look at you! You can barely walk! Oh, yes, you put on a show for them!" She gestured to the window and the crowd still cheering and chanting below. "But you were astride a horse when they saw you. I am the one who must see how broken you are now and put you back together again!"

"Such a fuss!" Cydell smiled in spite of the scolding. She had missed the old nurse terribly while she was away, but she would never tell her so. Elayna stood by the window of the study, hearing but not hearing.

"Yes! I am making a fuss! The High Provincial Council has been in a dither since you left. They have been meeting almost daily. Discussing, Dornea knows what. And they request your presence on the morrow!"

Cydell answered Josn, but her attention was focussed on Elayna's silence.

"That is an audience I am not looking forward to." Then as an afterthought, she added, "Perhaps I shall take a holiday on the morrow."

Josn paused on her way out, her tray of lygen cups almost slipping from her grasp.

"Holiday?! Why, you have been on holiday for nearly two turns!"

"And I if choose, I shall have another," was Cydell's quick retort. From their constant bickering, one would never have guessed that only two suns ago, the Hya and her nurse had been wrapped in each other's arms in a tearful and tender reunion. Now, the old woman left the study shaking her head and muttering under her breath.

"What occupies your thoughts so heavily?" Cydell asked softly. Elayna had not heard Cydell come up behind her, but she welcomed the gentle arms around her waist. Cydell nestled in the nape of Elayna's neck, relishing the scent of her.

"What will you do on your holiday?" Elayna turned to face her and they embraced. Cydell released her much too soon and went back to her desk.

"In truth, that was a lie to stir a fire under the old woman. I can fairly guess what the Council has been clucking about. But I do not want to concern myself with them any sooner than I must." Cydell watched Elayna, who still stood by the window, looking pensively down on the courtyard. Together, they had walked the beautiful and expansive palace gardens before morningmeal. Elayna was radiant in the sunlight streaming in from the window. She wore the blue silk robe and slippers that Cydell had given her upon their return, and her hair was swept back and held in place by a pearl and onyx comb, also a gift. It was an effort for Cydell to fix her mind on the work piled before her.

Cydell thought she heard Elayna sigh as she went to the door of the chamber and looked back at her.

"Something more, my heart?" Cydell asked.

"It is just that I..." Elayna began slowly, and then quickly said, "Josn has promised to instruct me in weaving. I best not be late."

"Very well then," Cydell frowned, sensing that Elayna was hiding something. Elayna smiled awkwardly and quickly slipped from the chamber to leave Cydell to her work.

Noises from the wards at practice in the training yard filtered in through the huge open doors of the kitchen. Glumly, Orrat and Rii sat in high-backed wooden chairs with a large barrel of potatoes between them. Their individual basins were not even half full and they had been peeling potatoes since before sunrise. Their kitchen detail had begun at the same hour they used to rise for ward duty, which seemed to them a very long time ago.

Their short-bladed knives were limp in their hands as they gazed longingly toward the yard, squinting in the brightness of the morning sun.

"If I had known this is what the Hya meant when she said 'other duties,' I would have given myself up to the tribesmen," Rii complained as he held up a potato he'd been peeling. It was half its original size, as he had peeled off most of the meat with the skin. He tossed the small worthless ball out into the yard and reached for another.

Orrat concurred in a sulk. "Yes. After the welcome, this is quite a disappointment. Two of the finest wards in Mauldar, peeling potatoes in the palace kitchens."

"Former wards," Rii corrected.

"But you must admit," Orrat leaned back in his chair so that it balanced on two legs, " it was quite an adventure."

"Yes. A great adventure if you enjoy smelling like a pig, starving to death, being attacked by vicious madmen and listening to you and the Hya's cousin whine incessantly about everything!"

Orrat grinned broadly and slapped his thigh. "One good thing about it being over is that I no longer have to deal with that bragging little nuisance again."

"Anything is better than this, my friend," Rii said in disgust, throwing out another potato that was smaller than the previous one. "And I do not even like potatoes!"

Orrat wiped his hands on his apron and continued to look out beyond the kitchen doors to the training yard.

"We are warriors, not kitchen whelps. When my time here is served and I return to rebuild my village, they all will see that."

"Will Elayna join you, oh Prince of Avoreed?" Rii grinned. Orrat shrugged.

"There was a time when I was certain that she would. Now?" He paused as he looked at his friend. "She cares very much for the Hya. I think when I return to Avoreed, I will return alone."

Rii offered a hand and said, "Not alone, my friend. I have decided to return to Avoreed and assist you in rebuilding your village. After all, we are comrades. And who knows, perhaps someone in the new village will have need of a potato peeler."

Orrat accepted Rii's hand with a nod and a very wide grin.

A giggling serving girl timidly approached the boys and thrust a note into Orrat's hand. When he took it, he winked at her and she scurried away to huddle in a corner with her friends, who all looked back at the former wards and giggled louder.

"Love letter?" Rii asked, anxious for Orrat to read the note. But when he did, he did not like the puzzled expression on his friend's face.

"We are to report to the Hya at once," Orrat announced.

"Are we not peeling these potatoes fast enough?" Rii quipped. "Perhaps she requires more ground beans for her marin?"

Orrat shrugged at Rii's questions, but he was already standing and untying his apron strings. "Whatever it is, it must be better than this," Orrat exclaimed hurriedly. "Come!"

Cydell looked up at the timid rapping on the study door. She leaned heavily back in her chair and dropped her quill on her desk with a weary sigh.

"What is it?!" she bellowed irritably. Her frown dissipated as Orrat and Rii entered and stood stiffly at attention just inside the door.

"You wished to see us, Hya," Orrat answered, his eyes staring straight ahead.

"At your ease, Orrat. Rii." Cydell waved them in and indicated that Rii close the study door behind them. She rose and stepped from behind her desk. With her hands clasped behind her back, and frowning, she began pacing in front of the boys. Orrat's mind raced. *So the kitchens are not to be our fate after all. She has something worse in mind.* He shifted nervously and tried not to look his Hya in the eye.

Cydell paused and openly scrutinized the two young boys. They were so opposite in appearance; one fair, one dark. They were both nearly sixteen Passes in age, but their eyes revealed the wisdom of experienced warriors. And, Cydell thought, indeed they were.

"The cook reports that your performance in the kitchens has been less than satisfactory," she began as she eyed first Orrat, then Rii. Rii cringed and Cydell tried, with great difficulty, to hide a smile. She cleared her throat and continued, "I am at a loss as to what to do with you now. You both clearly have no regard for the discipline and obedience your trainers tried to instill in you as wards." Cydell shrugged and opened her arms in a gesture of hopelessness. "So, what must I do? Send you to the mines?"

"No, Hya!" The boys blurted out simultaneously. Then, Orrat swallowed and stepped forward.

"Hya, no matter where you send us or what you decide to do with us," he lifted his chin defiantly, "we are warriors! And will always be warriors." Then he hung his head in shame and said quietly, "Even though we have dishonored ourselves as wards and no longer deserve that distinction."

"I feel the same, Hya," Rii agreed softly. "And if it is the will of the Hya that I serve in those Dornea-forsaken mines, then I will serve in the mines."

Cydell paused briefly and regarded the boys, moved by their stoic loyalty.

"I have no intention of sending you to the mines," Cydell reassured them and finally allowed herself a smile. "I acknowledge your foolhardiness and indiscretion, but not dishonor. You both have proven yourselves in the face of battle and carried yourselves as true Sentinels, with courage and skill and loyalty. For these reasons, I am allowing you to proceed with your Sentinel trials."

She left the two boys standing in the middle of the study, speechless, while she went behind her desk, and withdrew two long articles wrapped in red velvet. Cydell ceremoniously unwrapped one and presented Orrat with his own saber, the saber of his father. Then she unwrapped the other and presented Rii with a magnificent saber of his own, one that she had had personally crafted for the young warrior. Rii's eyes shone with pride as he took the saber into his hand, testing the grip and silently admiring the craftsmanship. There was a wolf's head at the top of the lathium hilt, set with two brilliant rubies in the eyes.

"Thank you, Hya!" Rii whispered in awe. His eyes brimmed with tears at the cherished gift. Never in his young life had he ever dreamed of owning so fine a weapon. Orrat stood beaming with happiness, for his friend and for their good fortune. Cydell went back behind her desk, returning to her more formal self.

"Your trials are in three suns. I strongly urge you to spend all of your waking hours in the training yard."

"Yes, Hya," the boys promised excitedly.

"You are dismissed," Cydell said absently as she settled in her chair and picked up her quill. When she looked up, the boys held their sabers in front of their faces in the Sentinel salute. Cydell stood up and nodded her acknowledgment. Then Orrat and Rii saluted each other. And then, they both pivoted and strode from the chamber.

❏ ❏ ❏ ❏ ❏

Flickering candlelight, from dozens of candles in gold-branched candelabra, reflected on the walls of Cydell's chamber. She sat on the side of the bed smoothing oils onto Elayna's bare back. Elayna moaned as Cydell's gentle and experienced fingers kneaded her aching muscles. She turned over as Cydell set the ointment jar on the bedside table and leaned over with her supporting arm across Elayna's body. Cydell gazed lovingly into the sleepy green eyes. Golden hair fanned out across the pillow, a gold as warm as sunlight. Cydell's white satin robe fell open and Elayna traced one delicate finger from Cydell's lips, to her chin, and down her throat to the valley of her breasts.

"I thought you were asleep," Cydell whispered.

"Almost. Cydell?"

"Yes?"

"Thank you for reinstating Orrat and Rii," Elayna smiled. "They have talked of nothing else since their audience with you."

"It was their own bravery that won their reprieve. I was very proud to have them at my back in battle. I have always believed they would make excellent Sentinels. And," she smiled as she admitted, "you know I have always favored them both."

Elayna wrapped a loose curl around one slender finger and said, "I have not known Orrat to desire anything so much as he desires his Sentinel's sash."

Cydell leaned down and kissed her lips. "And is there anything else you desire?"

"I have all I want. And more," Elayna sighed.

"Are you certain?" Cydell whispered, frowning.

"Are you not?" Elayna countered. She sat up on one elbow. "Cydell, look at me. I have never been so happy," she said as she looked into her eyes. "Your heart is kind. Your touch excites me. But do I dare speak to you of these things? These deeper feelings? If I told you of my heart, would you cast me away as just one more indulgence?" She gently stroked Cydell's cheek. "Is it wise to share my feelings so, when I do not know yours?"

"How can you not know, sweet? I would give you anything."

Elayna sat up, disappointment clouding her features as she slowly reached for her robe of flowing pink satin. Another gift from Cydell. The fabric was cool against the warmth of her skin. Cydell stood up, looking confused, as Elayna left the bed abruptly.

"Where are you going?"

"To another chamber. My old one will do nicely."

"But why? You have had no need of that cramped closet since our return from the Keep. You would leave me now?"

The tone of Cydell's voice, her apparent desire, was almost enough to propel Elayna back into her arms. But she stood her ground, forcing down her own passions.

"I will not squander my affections to satisfy your whims."

"Whims?! What more must I do to prove how much I care for you?" Cydell asked, an edge of desperation in her tone.

"I require more than your care. Are the words so difficult to speak, Cydell?" Elayna waited as the question hung like a thick cloud between them. Finally, Cydell held out her arms to her.

"This is a child's game, Elayna. Foolishness. Come to me."

"It is not foolishness! You said you would give me anything, but it seems what I ask of you is too much. When you find the words, I will return to your bed, and not before."

"You are not dismissed!" Cydell's voice thundered with fury and frustration. Elayna turned her back, adamant in her resolve.

"I have dismissed myself!"

Cydell stood speechless after Elayna left the chamber. There was some part of her, deep inside her, that wanted to go after the beautiful witch and tell her how much she loved her. That she loved her more than life. But the pride of a ruler held her in place, and she convinced herself that Elayna's strange mood would pass, and soon things would be as they once were between them.

The Hya awoke the next morning sullen and angry. Morning meal was a disaster, as the serving girls could do nothing right for her. She chided them so badly that Josn sent them all back to the kitchen and served Cydell herself. It was a while before Cydell looked up from her brooding silence to see her old nurse.

"Why are you serving?!" she barked. "Are there not other duties you should be attending to?"

"The others are seeing to the needs of the council. They are already in the meeting hall awaiting your presence."

"Let them wait! I am not anxious to endure their endless self-righteous nagging. And again I ask you, why are *you* serving?"

"By Dornea, you have frightened the girls so badly, no one wishes to be near you!"

"Oh?! Well perhaps they would prefer the work of the mines to serving me!" She hit the table so hard that the marin cups trembled in their saucers. Josn simply looked at her with her hands on her hips. Unperturbed.

"To send them to the mines will not return Elayna to your bed."

"This has nothing to do with her!"

"It has everything to do with her, Sparrow," Josn answered softly, using the nickname she had given Cydell when the Hya was but an infant. Cydell's demeanor softened at once and she regarded her old nurse with a crushing sadness in her eyes. Josn always knew how to calm her. "I have never seen you this way over a woman. She has had a deep effect on you, no?"

Cydell leaned wearily back in her chair as she sighed, "It is as though she has bound my heart, my soul, and I cannot break free. She has found some part of me that I thought I did not possess."

"It is not such a weakness to love someone, Cydell. Your father and mother were lost in each other. Did you never see that?"

"I saw it, yes. But Josn, I never learned to feel what they felt. In all this time I have given willingly and easily of my body, never of my heart."

"And now?" Josn prodded.

"I have only known her for half a Pass, yet I feel the love I have for her with every waking breath." There was a silence as Cydell went to the window. "She has the choice to return to Avoreed for the rebuilding. She must know that she is free to go... but...." She turned to Josn, "Do you not understand that I cannot risk her leaving, now, when I am so...when I...need her...so much?"

Josn rushed to her, "Tell her what is in your heart. You must tell her. Let her know. Not by gift or deed. The words mean everything."

"I cannot...I will not give in."

"Oh, Cydell...."

"Leave me now."

Josn started for the door, but paused before she left the chamber. Cydell stood confused and frustrated, angry at having yielded to her own emotions and revealing such weakness of character.

"You are defying your fate," Josn began softly. "It is clear that the goddess has willed the joining of your hearts. Do not drive her away, Cydell. She loves you. She needs only to know that you love her, as well. You speak of weakness. Your father's greatest strength was his love for your mother. If you let Elayna leave, you will lose so much more than you think."

"I said leave me!"

Josn slipped from the chamber without another word.

□ □ □ □ □

Elayna awoke to a soft tapping on her chamber door. She stirred, still groggy from a deep sleep. Her head seemed to spin as she sat up, and she squinted at the rays of the morning sun streaming in from the small window.

"Come in."

Quietly, Josn entered and closed the door behind her. She invited herself to sit on the side of Elayna's bed.

"I have not come to scold you," she said. "Your weaving lessons can wait."

"I will sleep the day away if I do not rise now," Elayna grumbled, as she pushed the bedding back and swung her feet to the floor. A sudden wave of nausea swept over her and she sat with her eyes closed until it subsided.

"Are you well, child?" Josn offered a steadying hand.

"It is merely something I ate that did not settle well. It will pass." She rose slowly and stepped to the basin where she splashed cool water on her face. To Josn, Elayna still did not look well.

"The Hya is in a very dark humor this morning," Josn offered as she closely scrutinized Elayna.

"Is she?" Elayna frowned briefly. She was not in the mood to gossip with Josn. There were more pressing matters on her mind.

"It happens at times," Josn tried to shrug off her worry. "When she is forced to sleep alone."

"Perhaps it is time she grew accustomed to the idea." Elayna, tiring of the idle chatter, looked at Josn. "We quarreled. Is that what you have come to learn?"

"No. By now, the entire city probably knows you and the Hya have quarreled." The old nurse watched in silence as Elayna dressed and then said suddenly, "When are you going to tell her?"

Elayna stopped what she was doing and looked at Josn. "What are you talking about?"

Josn cocked her head and smiled knowingly at the sorceress. When the old nurse beckoned to Elayna, Elayna hesitated only briefly before going to join Josn on the bed. The kindly old woman patted

Elayna's cheek and Elayna made herself look into the sparkling, gray eyes.

"Do you think," Josn began softly, "that I have attended the women of this palace for so many generations, and would not know when one of them is with child?" Josn clicked her tongue as she watched a tear trail down Elayna's cheek. "Tears? Why, you carry the next Hya. This should be a time of great celebration," she admonished gently, "not of tears." Then, she took Elayna's hands in her own.

"I know one would think there would be a never-ending line of dark and tousle-haired children, lined up at the palace gates, claiming to be the product of one of Cydell's couplings over the Passes. All claiming the right of succession. But there have been none." Josn could hardly contain her excitement as she gave Elayna's hands a fervent squeeze. "This child is blessed by the goddess. But more than that, this child is the fruit of the love you and Cydell have for each other. You must tell her at once, for the news should come from none but you."

Elayna rose and slowly walked away from Josn. Sighing, she said, "I wish Cydell to love me for the sake of love. Not because of the child. And she does not."

"I do not believe that, and neither do you," Josn protested.

"She has yet to tell me otherwise," Elayna countered. "It is rumored that Cydell is dispatching a detail to begin rebuilding Avoreed. Is this true?"

"Yes," Josn answered slowly, dreading Elayna's next words.

"I will return with them."

Josn stood up. "What?!"

"There is no reason for me to remain in Mauldar. The workers, I am certain, will require a healer among them."

"You would truly leave her?" Josn asked sadly. Elayna could not answer for the lump in her throat. Josn wearily turned toward the door, hesitating for a brief moment before she spoke.

"The High Provincial Council has bitterly hounded Cydell, Pass after Pass, to produce an heir. And now, you would let her face them once again without knowing that she has truly fulfilled *all* of her responsibilities as Hya?"

Elayna looked up and started to reply just as the old nurse quietly slipped from the chamber, gently closing the door behind her.

□ □ □ □ □

Cydell sat at the head of the long meeting table surrounded by the High Provincial Council. The Council was comprised of representatives from every province, village and city in the Mauldaran region. She supposed the Council had its uses. If she should ever become senile, the Council would meet to scrutinize her actions, and thereby judge her unfit to rule. They were the voice of the people, and their protectors.

She looked at them now. Each face. Every color and complexion imaginable. Each with their own agenda and their own priorities. Some pompous. Some arrogant. Very few were wise. But they did enjoy the time they spent at the palace, for Cydell saw to their every desire.

The regular business finally done, Cordon of Deall sat down. The Deallan representative always reminded Cydell of a tree squirrel, with his nervous demeanor and small, wary eyes. She disliked him for his indecisiveness. Marla of Dane stood now and demanded the attention of the assembly. Marla filled the meeting chamber with her powerful presence. Her full mane of snow white hair framed her face like a cloud and softened her hawklike features. Cydell smiled to herself. Marla was the bird of prey. The strongest of the assembled representatives.

The Council members shifted impatiently in their seats. They would not return to the palace for another quarter Pass and there were many things they had yet to do, many pleasures and vices yet to be enjoyed. Cydell's mind was also elsewhere. There was a gnawing ache in the pit of her stomach that had begun when Elayna left her chamber. She did not like this feeling, this urgent desperate need for the woman. At the same time, she realized how worthless she felt without her.

"The country of Sylvan must never again be left without a leader," Marla was saying. "There *must* be an heir to maintain the Ra Sadiin line of succession. Hya, this issue has once again given us, the High Provincial Council, tremendous cause for concern." There was a general murmur of agreement from the other delegates. Marla held up a hand for order as she continued.

"We realize that as a representative body, we are powerless to dictate to you with whom you should mate."

"I am pleased that you acknowledge that," Cydell retorted dryly. Marla, however, maintained her calm demeanor. "But, by the same token, we do expect you to rectify this situation in some manner that meets with this Council's approval."

Cydell's mind raged. Though she could see the validity of the Council's concerns, she was not prepared to mate in order to reproduce herself under their ever-watchful eyes.

"Everything in its time, Marla. I cannot very well go ravaging through the city like a madwoman, mating with every eligible woman I happen to encounter!"

"Is this not what you have been doing all these many Passes?" Batees of Gensa was on his feet, his catlike green eyes blazing. "There is not a shepherd for leagues who does not know of the Hya's lascivious tendencies. There should already *be* an heir!" They all nodded in general agreement. Then the Rolman delegate rose to join his compatriot.

"And now there is this Avoreedan witch! What are your plans for her? How long will she warm your bed?"

Cydell jumped up in anger. This had gone far enough.

"That, Domar, is not your concern!"

"It is the concern of all Mauldar!" he shot back. "Granted, the witch is lovely. No one can blame you in that. But we grow weary of your never-ceasing dalliances. I say send the witch on her way and concern yourself with the responsibility of producing an heir!"

Cydell's eyes narrowed. Her tone was even though she seethed with anger.

"Do not mock me, Domar. It was the witch who saved Mauldar from an evil that would have destroyed us all!"

"And we are grateful. Grateful indeed," Marla said calmly. "But do you not see our concern, Cydell? You must admit that you do. You have ruled well. We all prosper and worry no longer of war in this Pass. You have fulfilled all of your duties admirably, save one." Marla was always the diplomat. But Kamas of Rapian was not so kind.

"I say you should turn the whore back out into the streets to practice her arts there. As far away from the palace as possible. If rumor serves, she is very powerful. And true, she was with us during the recent threat. But what would happen if ever she were to turn her power against us?"

"Mind your tongue, Kamas. Or lose it!" Cydell gripped the table in her fury. "She would not betray Mauldar. She would not betray me. I love her! And I will not turn her out simply to ease your foolish fears!" She eyed each member of the Council in turn, unflinching. Cydell's own words echoed in her ears, and it was then that she realized what she had said.

"So you love her!" Kamas snorted derisively. "Can she then simply pull an heir from the heavens? Is her magick that powerful?"

"If I may speak?" Everyone in the Council chamber whirled at this new and unexpected voice. Elayna stood meekly inside the chamber doors, which all within knew to be guarded and barred from the outside. Elayna's hair settled around her shoulders as though it had been brushed by the fingers of a soft breeze. She was dressed simply in an embroidered white linen blouse and a full, flowing, deep green woolen skirt that whispered with each footfall as she walked across the chamber. Finally, she stood next to the table where the Council, some angry, some fearful, watched her approach.

Marla of Dane was the only one who did not seem surprised by Elayna's sudden appearance. And a trace of a smile played on her lips as she watched the Hya watch the beautiful sorceress.

Domar, blustering, jumped to his feet. "This is a closed session, young woman. You may *not* speak!"

Marla placed a hand heavily on Domar's shoulder, forcing him to sit down.

"It will be refreshing to hear a voice other than yours, Domar," Marla smiled and nodded at Elayna. "Since Elayna is the subject of this discussion, she should be heard." Having said that, Marla sat down with a glare at the others that dared them to protest further.

Elayna addressed the entire Council, but her eyes were riveted on Cydell.

"Please forgive this intrusion, most esteemed Council," she began, "but I have something to say that might put the Council's concerns at rest." Elayna saw Cydell frown briefly, but still the Hya was silent as Elayna looked into her eyes and said, "This was not how I meant to tell you, Cydell, but I hereby claim the right of succession for our child, the next ruler of Sylvan, Hya of the region of Mauldar."

All of the Council members began jabbering excitedly among themselves. Marla immediately rushed to Elayna's side, as did Kamas and Cordon, and several others. Elayna was overwhelmed by their enthusiasm, but when she looked through the crowd for Cydell, the Hya's place at the head of the Council table was empty.

◻ ◻ ◻ ◻ ◻

Cydell's anger and confusion subsided into a dull irritation as she streaked across the fields on the back of her black stallion. The powerful surging of muscle beneath her had a calming effect, as did the unrelenting wind in her face.

She slowed the horse to a trot as she neared the grove and the pond her father used to bring her to when she was a child just learning to ride. She learned when she was older that it was the very place where her father had asked for her mother's hand. It was the one place she could come to be alone with herself. To vent anger. To cry.

She jumped down from the saddle and dropped the reins, knowing the young stallion would not wander far. It was then she realized she had come away without a cloak. She shivered, for the mild evening breeze held the chill touch of winter. Quail chattered in the distance and moved in the brush. Her presence did not disturb the squirrels who raced along the banks. One stood on its hind legs, forepaws folded almost as though in prayer. Cydell stood just at the water's edge and looked out through the trees to the other side. The landscape clouded over as tears streamed freely down her cheeks.

Silently, she admonished herself. This was insane. The leader of hundreds of thousands of people, a born ruler, crying amongst the trees like a babe. Sitting down, she leaned heavily back against a tree. *Take hold of your wits!* her mind screamed. She had always loathed the desperation of love in others. Laughed at it. Scoffed at it. Teased Kovi when he had come to her forlorn over a lost love. Thank Dornea her cousin could not see her now.

Suddenly, a voice broke into her reverie, "I brought your cloak."

Cydell sprang up at the sound of Elayna's voice, embarrassed at not having heard her approach.

"Leave me. I do not need a cloak. I need to be left alone."

"Have no worries. I intend to leave you alone. I am going with the army to rebuild Avoreed. I have no intention of thrusting myself or this child upon you, when it is clear we are not wanted," Elayna said quietly. "Now, take your cloak before you freeze." She pulled her own cloak around her shoulders while still holding Cydell's.

"I am not chilled," Cydell stubbornly refused and wrapped her arms around herself.

"No?" Elayna cocked an eyebrow. Cydell turned away and walked down the bank, shivering. Elayna followed and stood some distance from her.

Cydell looked at Elayna. Silken hair flowing in the breeze. Sadness in the eyes.

"Why did you follow me? Why did you not just leave?" She walked toward Elayna. "Why did you not set me free when I asked it of you?!" Cydell paced in her frustration. "As Hya, I could order you not to return to Avoreed. But I do not wish to force you to stay when it is not what you really want."

Elayna went to her, exasperated. "How do you know it is not what I want? How can you say this? It is I who does not know what *you* want. How can I know my place in your heart, Cydell, if you do not tell me? You have only to ask it of me, and I will stay. I love you. I have no wish to be apart from you. Ever."

Elayna waited in the silence, and after a long while, she turned and started up the embankment, tears streaming down her cheeks. She heard Cydell's voice, a forceful, halfhearted command.

"You will *not* have our child in Avoreed!" she yelled at Elayna's back. Elayna kept walking. "Elayna! I forbid you to go!" Elayna walked on.

And then, after a brief silence, Cydell's soft, urgent plea caught on the evening breeze and swirled in the sweet air around Elayna, making her pause. "I love you, Elayna. Please do not leave me. Please." Cydell strode toward her, "Please. Please...my love."

They moved together as one, and held each other tight as Cydell whispered in Elayna's ear, pleading with her to stay, trembling from the emotion...and the chill. They parted long enough for Elayna to drape the cloak around Cydell's shoulders. And there they stood, locked in each other's arms, as the last rays of an orange sunset faded behind the distant Mauldaran Mountains.

▢ ▢ ▢ ▢ ▢

The fragrance of rosewater wafted from Cydell's chamber when she opened the door. She closed and locked it behind them and followed Elayna into the inner chamber. She shed her cloak, then her tunic, and leaning against the wall for support, she pulled off her boots and tossed them over her shoulder. Sliding out of the riding pants quickly, she left them in a dark cloud at her feet. Elayna was already undressed and lying on the bed, looking so inviting amidst the pillows. She leaned on one elbow and watched Cydell with the glow of love on her face.

The elegant dark woman walked slowly to the bed. Candlelight shone on the delicate gold chain around her waist and added a velvet sheen to the even brown tones of her smooth skin. A smile played on her lips. Elayna drank her in with her eyes. How could this woman be so worried about growing old? She would never age, for she had the stature of an immortal. Strong, well-muscled and firm, the Hya was a goddess queen, the incarnation of the warrior queen of so many Mauldaran legends. Elayna could not wait to be in her arms, enfolded in the sweet, sweet strength that passed from one woman to another when they loved.

She stretched, her arms reaching back high above her head, teasing, giving Cydell full view of what was hers for the taking. The invitation had the desired effect. Cydell stood mesmerized. She feasted her eyes on the lithe golden body being offered to her as one who is starving eyes a banquet table. One long leg bent at the knee, and Cydell was upon her, nuzzling and kissing the length of Elayna's body. Their bodies began to move in a rhythm only the two of them could hear and feel. In a heartbeat, they were lost in each other's pleasure.

At first, Cydell thought the steady tapping on the door was her pulse racing through her veins.

"Go away!" she responded in a threateningly deep mono-tone, not once taking her eyes off Elayna.

It was Josn's voice that answered. "The Sididoran delegation has arrived. They demand an immediate audience."

"It will not happen this evenfall," Cydell said sweetly and did not budge.

"They have traveled all day, Hya. It is a matter of the utmost urgency!"

"Are they dying?"

"No, Hya."

"Is Sididor under attack?"

"No, Hya. But..."

"Josn, would you live to see the sun rise?" Cydell smiled wickedly as she heard the nurse's footfalls retreating down the corridor. "She is more the witch than you. Checking to be sure things are right between us."

"Are they?" Elayna asked in a whisper. Cydell lay beside her and they melded into one as legs and arms entwined. Breasts to breasts. Mounds to mounds. Lips to lips. Her hands caressed every inch of Elayna's body. Touch was a prelude to the hungry, teasing lips, the searching tongue and fingers. Elayna pulled Cydell up along her body so that they were face to face, so she could cherish and bask in the heat of her lover's body. She moved against Cydell's hand between her thighs and covered that hand with her own and closed her legs to imprison them there.

A soft moan escaped Elayna's lips as Cydell tongued and gently bit a taut nipple and then kissed her neck and the sensitive spot just behind her ear. She moved faster against the hand between her thighs. Her breath caught in a passionate sob as two fingers found their way inside her.

"Yes," she moaned. "Love me there...."

Cydell buried her face in Elayna's neck. She moved her fingers slowly and Elayna met every thrust, as they created their own rhythm. Faster. Elayna's cries of passion urged Cydell on. She caressed her more urgently, until Elayna's senses reeled. Finally, she exploded with pleasure, stiffening and writhing in ecstasy, her chest heaving from such sweet exertion. Their lips met in a long, long kiss and Cydell rubbed Elayna's abdomen as the tremors subsided.

Elayna lay in Cydell's arms, nestled at her breast and feeling the strong, steady beating of her dear heart. When she looked up, she saw Cydell frowning, as though she were miles away.

"Is something wrong?"

Cydell grunted and shook her head. "Nothing," she answered but the frown did not go away.

"Tell me," Elayna insisted, snuggling closer. She traced lazy circles with a single finger around Cydell's navel.

"I am curious," Cydell answered, but the frown did not go away and she had to fight with herself not to become distracted by Elayna's lustful purring.

"About what?"

"About what it must be like to carry a child. I think creating one is much more pleasing than carrying one. Or raising one, for that matter." Cydell mused.

"You would think that." Elayna teased. "But you will have plenty of time to consider such things." She snuggled closer, moving her body enticingly against Cydell's. Cydell looked down into her lover's hooded eyes and smiled as her own desires stirred once more.

"And once that screeching, red-faced, ill-mannered little blessing from the goddess arrives, do you think we will still be able to enjoy each other this way, as often as we please?" Cydell asked.

Elayna did not hesitate as she replied, "No, probably not." And pulled Cydell's head down to kiss her lips.

◻ ◻ ◻ ◻ ◻

Five suns later, supply wagons lined the circumference of the courtyard. Mounted Sentinels and workers from the city formed the remainder of the caravan. Entire families had their meager belongings piled in wagons, strapped on mules; Avoreedans preparing to return home to rebuild their village.

A mild winter wind whipped Orrat's cloak around him in the dawn mist as he faced his sister with tears in his eyes. Elayna stepped back to take a good look at him, sporting his Sentinel finery. She was sad at his leaving, but very proud of the fine young Sentinel before her.

"This is the first we have been apart," he said, trying to blink back the tears.

"We will not be so far away from each other," she said comfortingly. "Only two suns' ride. And when the rebuilding is complete, perhaps you will be assigned here with Cydell's special unit. I do have a bit of influence, you know," she smiled.

"But to leave you...." They embraced and Elayna held him tight.

"Do not be sad, Orrat. You wished me to be happy here and I am. Now remember, you must return soon to celebrate the birth of your niece. She will be one as this world has never seen, but she will still need her uncle to teach her."

Orrat smiled, "Yes, I can hardly wait. I must be notified at once and I will ride the wind to be with you."

"I promise."

Cydell joined them after seeing to the final travel preparations. She tossed a pouch at Orrat and he caught it. It was heavy with onas.

"It will take more than sweat to rebuild the village. Build it well. And stand to defend it, Sentinel."

He bowed to his Hya and smiled with the memory of that first ride on her stallion. It seemed an eternity ago.

"Yes, Hya. And you will see to the care of my sister?"

"I have been true to my promise since that first day, have I not?" she asked with a smile.

"Yes, Hya."

Cydell embraced him warmly. "Safe journey, Orrat. Return at your will. You are always welcome here."

Rii rode up from the back of the caravan. He also cut a fine figure in his new Sentinel uniform as he halted his mount, jumped down and hugged Elayna goodbye. His smile was brilliantly white against the darkness of his skin as he saluted his Hya. Cydell did not return the salute, but drew the young Barrach to her in a warm embrace that took everyone, especially Rii, by surprise. With deep respect, he looked into her eyes as she wished him well, and after an awkward moment, swung up onto the back of his mount.

"All is ready," he said to Orrat. "Shall we ride?"

With one more look at his sister and his Hya, Orrat mounted his gelding and secured his father's saber at his side. He looked back at the company, and satisfied, raised a gloved hand as the caravan started for the city gates.

Cydell and Elayna walked hand in hand back into the palace by way of the garden. Cydell plucked a fragrant winter bloom and handed it to Elayna with a flourish. Elayna smiled and kissed her cheek in return.

"So, do you think I am too old now to raise a child?" she asked Elayna, looking a bit worried.

"Not at all," Elayna smiled. Cydell was so intrigued by the pregnancy that she constantly bombarded Elayna with questions.

"But I have no experience in such things."

"No one does until they have a child."

Cydell thought about that for a moment before she asked, "This child of ours...will she inherit your powers?"

"Such a believer in magick you have become! Would it bother you if she were like her mother and her grandmother? One with the ability to speak with her mind? Would you love her any less?"

Cydell shrugged.

"I think not. But then, I do not expect we will have that problem. My child shall not grow up to be a sorceress! Her mother is quite enough for me."

"Very well," Elayna hid a smile and said with exaggerated meekness, "for you are the mistress of this palace and your will is law."

"It pleases me that you have finally come to understand that," Cydell teased. "Have we come closer to deciding on a name, sweet?" she asked, giving Elayna's hand a squeeze.

"I think so. Sorryn suits her." Elayna watched Cydell as she silently tried the name.

Finally, she said, "Yes. I like it. It is a good, strong name for her. How did you come by it?"

Elayna looked at Cydell, her love, the delight of her heart, and smiled.

"The Hya Sorryn Ra Sadiin has commanded it thus."

ABOUT THE AUTHOR

Jacqui Singleton is a playwright, singer/songwriter and sometimes theatrical director. Her plays have been produced Off-Off Broadway, at the New Freedom Theater in Philadelphia and the University of Connecticut. As a performer, she has opened for Spyra Gyra, Eric Anderson and the late Memphis. She has also performed as headliner at the Speakeasy in Greenwich Village.

Jacqui lives in Richmond, Virginia with two cats and some of the characters from **Heartstone and Saber**. Elayna and Cydell are constantly whispering in her ear, urging her to write their next adventure. Look for the sequel!

She enjoys horses, the ocean, unusual toys, and riding motorcycles. In addition to writing, she is running her own Moonwitch Music Publishing company. She has recently produced her debut album of women's music entitled "Careful."

IF YOU LIKED THIS BOOK...

Authors seldom get to hear what readers like about their work. If you enjoyed reading this novel, why not let the author know? Simply write the author:

Jacqui Singleton
c/o Rising Tide Press
5 Kivy Street
Huntington Station, NY 11746

MORE EXCITING FICTION FROM
RISING TIDE PRESS

RETURN TO ISIS
Jean Stewart
The year is 2093. In this fantasy zone where sword and superstition meet sci-fi adventure, two women make a daring escape to freedom. Whit, a bold warrior from an Amazon nation, rescues Amelia from a dismal world where females are either breeders or drones. Together, they journey over grueling terrain, to the shining world of Artemis, and in their struggle to survive, find themselves unexpectedly drawn to each other. But it is in the safety of Artemis, Whit's home colony, that danger truly lurks. And it is in the ruins of Isis that the secret of how it was mysteriously destroyed waits to be uncovered. Here's adventure, mystery and romance all rolled into one.
Nominated for a 1993 Lambda Literary Award
ISBN 0-9628938-6-2; 192 Pages; $9.99

ISIS RISING
Jean Stewart
The eagerly awaited sequel to the immensely popular *Return to Isis* is here at last! In this stirring romantic fantasy, Jean Stewart continues the adventures of Whit (every woman's heart-throb), her beloved Kali, and a cast of colorful characters, as they rebuild Isis from the ashes. But all does not go smoothly in this brave new world, and Whit, with the help of her friends, must battle the forces that threaten. A rousing futuristic adventure and an endearing love story all rolled into one. Destined to capture your heart. Look for the sequel.
ISBN 0-9628938-8-9; 192 Pages; $9.95.

WARRIORS OF ISIS
Jean Stewart
Fans of *Return to Isis* and *Isis Rising* will relish this third book in the series . Whit, Kali, Lilith and company return in another lusty tale of high adventure and passionate romance among the Freeland Warriors. The evil sorceress, Arinna Sojourner, has evaded capture and now threatens the very survival of the new colony of Isis. As Whit and Kali prepare to do battle with a seemingly unbeatable foe, Danu makes her own plans to avenge a beloved friend's death at Arinna's hands. Eventually, high in the Cascade Mountains, they will face Arinna's terrifying magical powers.

Once again, Stewart weaves a rich tapestry of an all-women's society in the twenty-first century, bursting with life— lovers, villains, heroines, and a peril so great it forges a bond between all the diverse women of this unforgettable place called Isis. ISBN 1-883061-03-2; 224 Pages; $10.99

FACES OF LOVE
Sharon Gilligan

A wise and sensitive novel which takes us into the lives of Maggie, Karen, Cory, and their community of friends. Maggie Halloran, a prominent women's rights advocate, and Karen Weston, a brilliant attorney, have been together for 10 years in a relationship which is full of love, but is also often stormy. When Maggie's heart is captured by the young and beautiful Cory, she must take stock of her life and make some decisions.

Set against the backdrop of Madison, Wisconsin, and its dynamic women's community, the characters in this engaging novel are bright, involved, '90s women dealing with universal issues of love, commitment and friendship. A wonderful read! $8.95

LOVE SPELL
Karen Williams

A deliciously erotic and humorous love story with a magical twist. When Kate Gallagher, a reluctantly single veterinarian, meets the mysterious and alluring Allegra one enchanted evening, it is instant fireworks. But as Kate gradually discovers, they live in two very different worlds, and Allegra's life is shrouded in mystery which Kate longs to penetrate. A masterful blend of fantasy and reality, this whimsical story will delight your imagination and warm your heart. Here is a writer of style as well as substance. $9.95

ROMANCING THE DREAM
Heidi Johanna

This romantic tale begins when Jacqui St. John cruises into the seemingly ordinary town of Kulshan, on the Oregon coast, which reminds her of the recurring dream that has been tantalizing her for months—a dream of a house full of women, radiating warmth, and of one special woman, dressed in silk and leather.... Jacqui soon learns that something quite wonderful is happening in this place—the women plan to take over the town and make it a lesbian haven. A captivating and erotic love story with an unusual plot. It will charm you with its gentle humor and fine writing. $8.95

WE HAVE TO TALK: A Guide to Bouncing Back From a Breakup
Jacki Moss

Being left by your lover is devastating. Suddenly, your world has been turned into something almost unrecognizable and barely manageable. Here's the first interactive guide specifically designed for lesbians who have been left by their lovers. With humor and keen insight, it will help you survive the pain so you can rebuild your life. $9.99

YOU LIGHT THE FIRE
Kristen Garrett
Here's a grown-up *Rubyfruit Jungle*—sexy, spicy, and side-splittingly funny. Garrett, a fresh new voice in lesbian fiction, has created two memorable characters in Mindy Brinson and Cheerio Monroe. Can a gorgeous, sexy, high school math teacher and a raunchy, commitment-shy ex-singer, make it last, in mainstream USA? With a little help from their friends, they can. This humorous, erotic and unpredictable love story will keep you laughing, and marveling at the variety of lesbian love. $9.95

DANGER IN HIGH PLACES: An Alix Nicholson Mystery
Sharon Gilligan
Free-lance photographer Alix Nicholson was expecting some great photos of the AIDS Quilt—what she got was a corpse with a story to tell! Set against the backdrop of Washington, DC, the bestselling author of *Faces of Love* delivers a riveting mystery. When Alix accidentally stumbles on a deadly scheme surrounding AIDS funding, she is catapulted into the seamy underbelly of Washington politics. With the help of Mac, lesbian congressional aide, Alix gradually untangles the plot, has a romantic interlude, and learns of the dangers in high places. $9.95

DANGER! Cross Currents: An Alix Nicholson Mystery
Sharon Gilligan
In this exciting sequel to *Danger in High Places*, freelance photographer Alix Nicholson is teaching photography at Pacific Arts, a college idyllically located on California's North Coast.
When her landlady, a real estate developer, turns up dead, and the police arrest Leah Claire, the woman's much younger lover, Alix is rapidly drawn into a complex web of intrigue and murder.
As she frantically searches for a way to free Leah, Alix unexpectedly finds herself at the dawn of a new romance...and on the brink of her own destruction. A satisfying, well-crafted mystery. $9.99

EDGE OF PASSION
Shelley Smith
From the moment Angela saw Micki sitting at the end of the smoky bar, she was consumed with desire for this cool and sophisticated woman, and determined to have her...at any cost. This sizzling novel, set against the backdrop of Provincetown, will draw you into the all-consuming love affair between an older and a younger woman. A gripping love story, which is both fierce and tender, it will keep you breathless until the last page. $8.95

CORNERS OF THE HEART
Leslie Grey

This captivating novel of love and suspense introduces two unforgettable characters whose diverse paths have finally led them to each other. It is Spring, season of promise, when beautiful, French-born Chris Benet wanders into Katya Michaels' life. But their budding love is shadowed by a baffling mystery which they must solve. You will read with bated breath as they work together to outwit the menace that threatens Deer Falls; your heart will pound as the story races to its heart-stopping climax. Vivid, sensitive writing and an intriguing plot are the hallmarks of this exciting new writer. $9.95

SHADOWS AFTER DARK
Ouida Crozier

Wings of death are spreading over the world of Kornagy and Kyril's mission on Earth is to find the cause. Here, she meets the beautiful but lonely Kathryn, who has been yearning for a deep and enduring love with just such a woman as Kyril. But to her horror, Kathryn learns that her darkly exotic new lover has been sent to Earth with a purpose—to save her own dying vampire world. A tender and richly poetic novel. $9.95

DEADLY RENDEZVOUS: A Toni Underwood Mystery
Diane Davidson

Lieutenant Toni Underwood is the classic soft-hearted cop with the hard-boiled attitude, and she is baffled and horrified by her newest case—a string of brutal murders, in the middle of the desert, bodies dumped on the Interstate. As Toni and her partner Sally search for clues, they unravel a sinister network of corruption, drugs and murder.

Set in picturesque Palm Springs, California, this chilling, fast-paced mystery takes many unexpected twists and turns and finally reveals the dark side of the human mind, as well as the enduring love between two women. A suspenseful, explosive, action-packed whodunit. $9.99

How To Order:

Rising Tide Press books are available from you local women's bookstore or directly from Rising Tide Press. Send check, money order, or Visa/MC account number, with expiration date and signature to: Rising Tide Press, 5 Kivy St., Huntington Sta., New York 11746. Credit card orders must be over $25. Remember to include shipping and handling charges: $4.95 for the first book plus $1.00 for each additional book. Credit Card Orders Call our Toll Free # 1-800-648-5333. For UPS delivery, provide street address.

Our Publishing Philosophy

Rising Tide Press is a lesbian-owned and operated publishing company committed to publishing books by, for, and about lesbians and their lives. We are not only committed to readers, but also to lesbian writers who need nurturing and support, whether or not their manuscripts are accepted for publication. We encourage submissions by new writers, and work intensively with them. Through quality writing, the press aims to entertain, educate, and empower readers, whether they are women-loving-women or heterosexual. It is our intention to promote lesbian culture, community, and civil rights, nationwide, through the printed word.

In addition, RTP will seek to provide readers with images of lesbians aspiring to be more than their prescribed roles dictate. The novels selected for publication will aim to portray women from all walks of life, (regardless of class, ethnicity, religion or race), women who are strong, not just victims, women who can and do aspire to be more, and not just settle, women who will fight injustice with courage. Hopefully, our novels will provide new ideas for creating change in a heterosexist and homophobic society. Finally, we hope our books will encourage lesbians to respect and love themselves more, and at the same time, convey this love and respect of self to the society at large. It is our belief that this philosophy can best be actualized through fine writing that entertains, as well as educates the reader. We firmly believe that books can be fun, as well as liberating.